Pra S Y

"Once again Ms
that is filled with
tension in relatio
firefighters and
lives."

—*Book Binge* on *Fully Ignited*

"*Hot Response* made a perfect weekend read for me: there was a comfortable mix of angst, action and banter and I loved reading about the interactions between the whole fire crew."

—Dísir of *Unstuck Pages*

"My new favorite Shannon Stacey book. I loved Rick. Loved, loved, loved. Loved. The last firefighting scene had me shivering, and the last scene sighing for more."

—MJ Fredrick on *Controlled Burn*

"Humor and genuinely affectionate family relationships ground Stacey's third book in the Boston Fire series, allowing it to be sexy and fun, even as it deals with fraught subjects such as workplace sexism, parental loss and high-risk careers. The chemistry and incendiary attraction between the leads are palpable, as is their gradual change of heart about the viability of a long-term relationship."

—*RT Book Reviews* on *Fully Ignited*, 4 stars

"*Heat Exchange* is a stimulating and fiery hot romance that I couldn't get enough of. Shannon Stacey writes remarkable contemporary romance and I was definitely hooked on *Heat Exchange*. It had a vibrant feel, a truly emotional read with great sensuality and in depth characters!"

—*Addicted to Romance*

"Finally, I am out of my reading slump. I've read too many books of late that have had unnecessary drama and weak storylines and it was refreshing to pick up and read a low-drama, low-angst, romantic story with a couple who were completely endearing. I love me a fireman and Rick Gullotti was just what I needed."

—*Goodreads* user Nicola on *Controlled Burn*

UNDER CONTROL

SHANNON STACEY

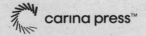

carina press™

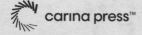

carina press™

Recycling programs for this product may not exist in your area.

ISBN-13: 978-1-335-96454-0

Under Control

Copyright © 2018 by Shannon Stacey

www.CarinaPress.com

Printed in U.S.A.

Life can be hard, and this book is dedicated to everybody who takes the time to help a person who's struggling. Whether saving somebody from a fire, offering tips to make the nightly homework battle a little easier or simply listening, extending a helping hand makes the world a better place for all of us.

UNDER CONTROL

Chapter One

Nothing made a guy feel conspicuous like walking down the hall of an office building in full turnout gear.

Or he would if anybody actually noticed him, Derek Gilman thought as he shifted to the right to avoid running into a woman looking down at her phone. How people navigated the hallways with their eyes glued to their screens was beyond him.

One guy actually looked up from his phone as he brushed by, and then did a startled double take. "Should I be evacuating?"

"You can evacuate if you want," Derek said, "but there's no reason to. We're just doing some high-rise training."

Which was a fact everybody in the building was supposed to have been made aware of before they arrived. They didn't have much in the way of glass skyscrapers in their neighborhood, so the crews of Engine 59 and Ladder 37 had schlepped across Boston on what should have been a day off to hone their skills.

Remembering to bring everything they needed from the apparatus was apparently *not* one of their skills, however. Though he was over a decade past being a rookie, Derek was new to this Ladder 37 crew, so he'd been sent to retrieve the paperwork Rick Gullotti—their lieutenant and the guy in charge of paperwork—had forgotten.

A woman stepped out of an office ahead and turned, walking ahead of him in the same direction. She was notable for two reasons. One, she wasn't looking at a cell phone. That in itself was enough to make her stand out in this crowd.

But it was her looks that captured Derek's attention. He only got a glimpse of her profile before she turned, but she had delicate features and dark blond hair drawn up off her neck in a loose bun. Her navy suit looked as if it had been tailored specifically for her body, and the coat flared slightly, accenting the curve of her hips. Her legs were long, and his gaze lingered on her calves before sliding up to the soft spots behind her knees that were playing peekaboo with the hem of her skirt.

And he'd never realized how sexy the click of high heels on a marble tile floor could be. When he was a kid, he'd hated the sound because the high heels usually belonged to an angry teacher he was following down the hallway to the principal's office. But following *this* woman as she walked down the hallway with long, confident strides was a hell of a lot more enjoyable.

Of course, she reached the elevator just as the door opened and a man stepped out. Because he'd slowed to leave enough space to appreciate the view, Derek knew there was a good chance the door would close before he reached it and there was no way in hell he was taking the stairs if he didn't have to.

"Hold the door, please," he called as the woman stepped in and pushed a button on the panel.

She looked up at him and he saw the hesitation in her

body language. She didn't want to, but he watched the
fact he was a firefighter register, plus it would be rude
to pretend she hadn't heard him after making eye contact. He smiled as she hit the button to hold the doors.

"Thank you." The button for the lobby was already
lit, so he stepped back as the doors slid closed.

She only nodded and pulled her phone out of the back
pocket of the leather journal she was holding, which
was stuffed with notebooks and paper from the looks
of it. But Derek could see her reflection in the highly
polished metal door and she was looking at him. And
not a quick glance to make sure the stranger was staying on his own side, but a lingering look.

He should say something, but he wasn't sure *what*
to say, since women wearing power suits in the Back
Bay were way out of his league. The floors were ticking past like seconds on the clock, though, and he was
running out of time.

She was taking a step forward, probably in anticipation of reaching the lobby level soon, when there was a
grinding sound and the elevator lurched to a stop. Off-
balance, she stumbled and—thanks to good reflexes and
maybe some good luck—he ended up with an armful
of beautiful woman.

Apparently he was getting an extension.

She tilted her face up to him, and he saw the distress
in her pretty greenish-blue eyes. "What's happening?"

"We stopped," he said, hoping she'd find the obvious answer funny. In his experience, humor relaxed
people. She didn't even crack a smile, and he cleared
his throat before continuing. "There are a few reasons
it could happen, but the system probably has a prob-

lem or a malfunction somewhere and it shut the elevator down to be safe."

"This is not safe." She wasn't in a full-blown panic, but her anxiety practically crackled around her, and she was clutching his arm so tightly he could feel her grip through the heavy bunker coat. "And what do you mean by a malfunction? So something could be *more* wrong than the fact we're not moving anymore?"

"Everything's fine." He had to let his arms fall away from her as she backed away, wincing a little. "Are you hurt?"

"No." He wasn't reassured by the quick way she said it, as if it was a reflex and maybe not the truth.

He pulled out his phone to send a quick group text to Danny Walsh—Engine 59's LT—and Rick Gullotti. Elevator's stuck. Why? Then he peeled off the heavy coat and tossed it on the floor, dropping the helmet on top of it while she sent a text message of her own to somebody. "We're okay in here. Just try to stay calm and we'll be out in no time."

"Stay calm," she muttered as her phone vibrated and she sent another text. "That's easy for you to say. Being brave in the face of death is part of your job."

That was a little dramatic, but she wasn't *totally* wrong. About his job, anyway. "You're not facing death. I promise."

His phone vibrated with a response from Walsh. Working on it. Stand by.

The woman's face was slightly flushed. "Shouldn't you… I don't know. Go up through the ceiling hatch and climb up the cable or something?"

Derek managed—barely—not to laugh outright at

her, but he couldn't hold back a short chuckle. "I'm a firefighter, not John McClane."

"Who's John McClane?"

Oh, she did *not* just ask that. "The greatest action hero of all time? The guy from *Die Hard*?"

"I've heard of those movies, but I've never seen any of them."

If he'd needed any more of a definitive sign this woman wasn't his type, that was it. There were six movies, so she had to *work* at not seeing any of them. "You're missing out. So, what's your name?"

"Olivia."

"Pretty name." Classic and elegant, and it suited her. "I'm Derek."

"Can you pry open the doors?" she asked, clearly not in a place to be distracted by small talk.

"With my bare hands?" He held them up, showing off his lack of tools. "I work out a little, but not that much."

Her gaze flicked over his body, and he stood up straighter and sucked in his gut. Not that there was much to suck in, but he wasn't in his twenties anymore. Hell, he was barely still in his thirties. "You work out more than a little."

Her tone of voice made it sound like just an observation, but he didn't miss her gaze lingering for a second on his chest or the way her eyebrow lifted as her mouth curved into a hint of a smile. She wasn't flirting, but she liked what she saw and he'd take the win. He'd need all the ego boosting he could get once the other guys started giving him shit for having to rescue him from an elevator.

Then she shifted her weight and, when she winced again, Derek gave her a stern look. "You're hurt."

"No, I'm not. I twisted my ankle a little when the elevator stopped."

"You need to get those shoes off and let me look at it."

She laughed and shook her head. "I don't care how nice this elevator is, I am *not* touching the floor with my bare feet."

Derek picked up his coat, letting the helmet roll free, and—with a flourish—spread it over the floor in front of her. "Your carpet, milady."

Olivia McGovern didn't have time to be stuck in an elevator today. Her schedule was so tight the Lyft driver who was hopefully still waiting outside for her after her text would determine the fate of her punctuality streak, and she hadn't been late to a meeting in the three years since she'd officially hung out her McGovern Consulting shingle.

But none of that seemed to matter when she looked into the warm blue eyes of the firefighter smiling at her right now. It had been the smile he gave her as he stepped onto the elevator that first caught her attention. That smile that was just a little friendlier than a polite thank-you and radiated warmth had been sexy, she had to admit. His helmet coming off to reveal tousled dark, dirty blond hair, along with the Boston Fire T-shirt showing off a very nicely built upper body, hadn't hurt, either.

But it was the boyish grin he gave her as he spread his coat out like a gentleman in a story that really kicked her heartbeat into high gear.

As did putting her hand on his arm to steady herself as she stepped out of the heels. The first time she'd clutched his arm—when she'd been thrown into his arms—he'd been wearing the coat she was standing on. But now she could feel the firm muscle and the warmth of his skin through the blue cotton.

"Thank you," she said in a slightly choked voice. Her ankle really wasn't that bad, but being out of the shoes for a few minutes would definitely help.

Then he dropped to his knees in front of her and she sucked in a sharp breath. His hands closed around her ankle and she pressed her lips together so she wouldn't make any sort of a sound when he ran his hands up over her calf muscle and back to her ankle. He pressed gently with his thumbs, and maybe it was her imagination, but it sounded like the deep breath *he* took shuddered just a little.

"No swelling," he said, pushing back to his feet. "It doesn't look bad, but you should elevate it while we're waiting. You can sit on the coat."

Getting into a sitting position on the coat while wearing a skirt was a challenge, but Derek had turned away to retrieve his helmet so she did it as quickly and with as much modesty as she could. She assumed he was going to use the helmet to prop her ankle up, but he simply set it right side up and then sat down at her feet.

An unexpected rush of heat flooded her when he lifted her foot and shifted so he could rest it on his thigh, and she hoped it didn't show on her face.

"It really should be elevated more, but we don't have a lot of options," he said. "Is this okay?"

His hand was massaging her ankle and she didn't trust herself to speak, so she nodded. He had calluses and his hands weren't abrasive, but just rough enough so a shiver went through her.

"Are you cold?" he asked, his thumb brushing over her ankle bone.

"I'm fine," she forced herself to say, but she was struggling with the awareness that for the first time in her life, she was very tempted to make out with a total stranger in an elevator.

"So, Olivia," he said in a low voice that turned her on almost as much as his hands on her ankle. "You know I'm a firefighter. What do you do for work? That's quite a book you've got there."

She looked down at the leather cover protecting a variety of notebooks and papers, then back at him. "I'm a productivity systems consultant."

"Oh. Cool." He obviously had no idea what that meant.

"I shadow a company's employees and talk to them for several hours, trying to get a feel for their business flow. Then I present several productivity suites I think would help them work more efficiently—whether digital, paper or a combination. I help them set it up and train them on how to use it."

"Huh." He gave her a look she'd seen many times, as if he still wasn't sure what she did. She was used to that.

Before she could say anything else, though, his phone chimed and he checked the message before sending back a brief reply. "They're going to pry the door."

It was utterly ridiculous that disappointment would be her first reaction to imminent rescue, but it was. Followed fairly quickly by the awareness of how much time had passed since she sent an update to her Lyft driver and her assistant, Kelsey Harris.

"Does that take long?"

"Shouldn't. They've probably already cut the power to make sure it doesn't start moving again at a bad time, so it won't take long to bypass the door restrictors and get the doors open. How's the ankle feeling?"

"Better, thanks." The ankle was better, but now the rest of her body was a little hot and achy. "I think I can get up."

He helped her, of course, taking her hands and pulling as she pulled her legs under so she was on her knees and then got to her feet. And he didn't let them go once she was standing. They were close—so close she had to tilt her head back slightly to see his face—and for a few crazy seconds, she thought he was going to kiss her.

And she wanted him to.

"Can you put weight on it?"

This time she knew the blush was visible because she could feel it on her face. He was holding her hands because of her ankle. "It's fine. It really wasn't that bad and sitting for a few minutes helped."

As did his hand massaging her ankle, though she didn't say so. And she managed to stifle the sigh of regret when he released her hands. Then she heard sounds on the other side of the metal doors and realized they wouldn't be in the elevator much longer.

She sent a quick text message to her Lyft driver. They're getting ready to open the doors. It shouldn't take long.

I can wait a few more minutes.

Olivia told herself she should be happy when the doors finally opened and another very attractive firefighter looked down at her from the opening. They could do a calendar, she thought, and was very thankful she hadn't said it out loud.

"Hi there," he said. "I'm Aidan Hunt, with Engine 59. We're going to get you out now."

"Took you guys long enough," Derek told him, even as Olivia silently wished it could have taken just a little longer. Then he turned to her. "You ready to get out of here?"

She nodded, but didn't move to the front. "I…they can't line up the doors with the floor?"

"The elevator's still stuck, so that would be a no. This is as good as it gets, but I'll give you a boost up."

A *boost*? Olivia wasn't sure what that meant, but it implied him picking her up, and maybe having to hand her up to Aidan, which might involve Derek's hands on her butt. Not that she'd mind that very much, but she was in a skirt.

"That doesn't sound very graceful," she pointed out. "Or modest."

"I think we skimmed over being graceful at the fire academy. But, tell you what. To make it easier, I'll get on the floor. If you step up onto my back and take Aidan's hands for balance, I'll get up on my hands and knees and you should be high enough so one of the guys can get you under the arms and lift you out with no problem."

"You don't mind?"

"Trust me. It won't be the worst thing that's happened to me on the job."

Her gaze flicked to the scar that ran down his jaw, but she didn't ask. Instead, she walked to the opening and handed her leather notebook up to Aidan. "*Please* don't lose that or drop it down the elevator shaft or anything. It's my entire life."

"Don't lose this, Scotty," Aidan said, handing the book over to another firefighter. Then he took Olivia's shoes from her and set them aside. "I'm going to lay on my stomach so I can reach out and give you something to hold on to while you step up on Derek. Then Chris here is going to get you under the arms and lift you so you can reach the lip. You ready?"

She nodded, and Derek got down on the floor as if he was going to do some push-ups. This still wasn't going to be all that graceful, she realized as she stepped onto his back. "Am I hurting you?"

"Nope. You ready?"

She reached up and Aidan grasped her hands. "Okay. But no looking up."

His chuckle vibrated through the bottoms of her feet. "I won't. I promise."

His back muscles flexed and she barely had time to register his strength as he lifted himself—and her—before somebody grabbed her under the arms and lifted her. She got her knees onto the lip, but they didn't let her go until she was on her feet and several feet away from the elevator shaft.

"Lieutenant Rick Gullotti," one of the older of the group said to her, and she shook his hand. "Are you injured at all? Do you need medical attention?"

She wouldn't mind Derek's hands on her some more, but she definitely didn't need an ambulance. "I'm not injured. Thank you—all of you—for getting me out."

He nodded and then turned back to the elevator. She stepped into her shoes, thankful her ankle didn't offer up more than a slight twinge. And the firefighter who'd been called Scotty handed over her journal. "Thank you."

Her phone chimed with a text from the driver. *Two minutes and then I'm leaving.*

Olivia hesitated. She wanted to stay and thank Derek. Maybe she'd work up the nerve to ask his last name or give him her business card.

But if she got in the car right now, she could still salvage her day. Rescheduling one appointment was bad enough. Depending on traffic, she could make the next one and maybe not even be late. And it was a big client she'd been trying to land for a while. Waiting for another Lyft could derail that.

Coming right now, she messaged back.

"I really have to run," she said, "but thank you for everything."

"All in a day's work," Scotty said.

She looked at the elevator, hoping Derek would be out already, but Aidan was in the process of pulling Derek's coat and helmet out of the elevator. "Tell Derek I said thank you, too."

"You sure you can't wait a couple more minutes?"

She wanted to. She really did, but she shook her head. "I have a meeting. But tell him I said thank you."

She walked toward the front door as fast as her sore ankle allowed, feeling a little like Cinderella fleeing the ball.

Once she was in the back seat of her ride, she knew she should check her email account and see if anything needed her attention as she always did while in transit from one appointment to the next.

Instead she leaned her head against the leather and closed her eyes, regretting her decision already. Not that leaving was the wrong decision. Success came from making a plan and executing it, and right now her focus was one hundred percent on her business. Dating was *not* part of her plan yet.

She opened her eyes as the car pulled away from the curb and she caught a glimpse of two fire trucks parked down a side street as they passed by. It would be a while before she forgot her firefighter, she knew. His laugh. His eyes. The feel of his hands on her skin.

And now she'd probably never see him again. Sometimes making the right decision really sucked.

Chapter Two

Olivia let herself into her sixteenth-floor apartment and, once the door closed, leaned against it with a weary sigh.

Getting stuck in the elevator had thrown off her schedule and when your business was helping others manage *their* schedules, you busted your ass to catch up so you wouldn't be late or appear rushed. She'd managed it and she'd done it with a smile on her face and not a hair out of place, but now she was both physically and mentally drained.

And when Kelsey stuck her head out of the second bedroom, which they'd made into an office, Olivia felt a rare pang of regret at not having rented a separate space. Usually having Kelsey here worked well. Two of her employees worked remotely except for staff meetings once or twice a month, but Kelsey was not only vital to almost every aspect of her business, but she lived in a tiny apartment with two other women and working from home wasn't a viable option. It would be a waste of money to lease office space just for the two of them—especially since so much of Olivia's work was done on-site—so the home office worked well.

Except for the nights Olivia was exhausted and

wanted the apartment to be her sanctuary and not her office. It had been a splurge, especially considering the view she had. She loved it, despite the number of times her parents had reminded her that renting was setting money on fire. She should invest in a property and, when she was ready to start a family, sell high and upgrade. But the location, the total lack of maintenance responsibilities and the view had deterred her from making the fiscally responsible decision. It didn't happen often, but it had been worth it.

"You look beat," Kelsey said as Olivia stepped out of her heels and walked across the pale maple floor to get herself a glass of water. Hydration had been one of the sacrifices she'd made to get back on schedule.

"Of all days to get stuck in an elevator." Usually she'd go into the office with Kelsey and review the day before prepping for tomorrow, but she crossed to the living room area and sat on the sofa. The thick area rug felt like heaven under her feet, and she inhaled deeply before slowly exhaling.

"What happened?" Kelsey sat in one of the two armchairs facing the sofa. Those and several glass tables made up the seating area, which was set up to take advantage of the view of the water outside the tall windows. There was no television. It was in the bedroom, since she only watched a few shows and preferred to enjoy them while curled up in bed. "Today was so crazy, you haven't even told me about it yet."

Olivia shifted onto her hip so she could tuck her legs on the sofa. Kelsey had become a friend as well as an employee shortly after she'd started working for her two years ago. Even though there was still work to be done, she didn't mind relaxing for a few minutes.

When she was finished telling the story—except the part about him massaging her ankle—she took a long drink of water. "I didn't want to hold the door for him, but I'm glad I did. I probably would have totally panicked if I was stuck in there alone."

"Was he hot?"

"What?"

Kelsey snorted. "The firefighter. Was he hot?"

"Yeah." She answered without thinking, and it was too late to take it back, so she smiled. "Not my usual type, but definitely hot."

"Why didn't you jump him when you had the chance?"

Olivia almost choked on her water. "When did I have the chance?"

"You were stuck in an elevator with him, right?"

"Not for *that* long." Thank goodness. She'd been more and more tempted with every second she'd been trapped with Derek.

"You haven't been on a date in forever. It probably wouldn't have taken very long."

"Remind me to curtail your access to my personal life."

"You don't really have one, which is my point."

"Even if I wanted to jump the man and had time, there are security cameras in the elevators."

Kelsey shrugged. "Nobody pays any attention to those."

"They probably do if there are actually people stuck in the elevator at the time."

"Maybe." She smiled, though. "But it might have been worth it."

Worth essentially making a sex tape for the security staff? And whoever they decided to share it with, including possibly the entire internet? Not likely. But Olivia felt heat in all the right places as she remembered the way the hot firefighter with questionable taste in movies had looked at her while his hand stroked her leg.

"You're blushing right now." Kelsey pointed at her, her eyes wide. "You're thinking about having sex with him in the elevator, aren't you?"

"I am not."

"Then what were you thinking about?"

"The way he looked at me, not that it's any of your business."

"Aw. That's so romantic, though not nearly as fun as sex against the elevator wall. Did it have mirrors?" When Olivia glared at her, she shrugged. "Fine. But you should have at least given him your business card."

"Trust me. A prospective client, he wasn't."

"You're hopeless, Olivia. It's totally normal to offer a business card to somebody, and it would have given him a way to contact you *and* made him feel like that contact wouldn't be totally unwelcome."

"It doesn't matter now." Kelsey was right. It would have opened the door without lighting up a neon sign announcing her interest. "I'm never going to see him again."

"You could if you really wanted to. Isn't bringing a firefighter a pie or something to thank him for rescuing you a thing?"

"I'm not really up on damsel in distress etiquette, and technically he didn't rescue me. He was stuck with me and he got rescued, too."

Kelsey frowned. "Good point."

Maybe they could be done with this conversation

now. It was ridiculous and yet it was also making her wonder if she *could* see him again.

Even though it made no sense, she couldn't remember the last time she'd been attracted enough to a stranger to think about him again, never mind talk about him. Technically she'd talked about him because she was telling Kelsey about the elevator incident, but when she'd asked if the firefighter was hot, Olivia could have shrugged it off. Kelsey would have believed her boss hadn't even noticed the man in the elevator with her in that way.

Ouch.

"So you could bring the pie to the other firefighters and he works with them, so you'll probably see him." Obviously Kelsey *wasn't* done with this conversation. "Oh, I know! You could reach out to him because you lost something and you're hoping one of the firefighters found it."

"Not only is that ridiculous, but there's no point."

"Sex is the point, Olivia. You tell everybody how important for productivity it is to maintain a healthy physical and emotional balance in your life. And orgasms are an important part of both, so…"

"So I have plenty of orgasms, thank you very much." Olivia put her feet back on the floor and reluctantly stood. "And I'm better at giving myself orgasms than any guy I've dated has been, so *not* dating is actually more efficient."

She expected Kelsey to laugh at her, but her friend actually looked sad. "But it's lonely."

"I'm too busy to be lonely." It wasn't quite true, but she'd gotten where she was by making a plan and sticking to it. In approximately five years, when she estimated she'd be able to ease up on the reins of McGovern Consulting, she'd be glad that the past version of her had focused on building her business so future her could find and maintain a healthy balance of work and family. "And speaking of being busy, let's finish up so you can get home and I can find my yoga pants."

"You know," Kelsey said as she followed her to the office, "I won't suddenly forget you're my boss if I see you in yoga pants."

"You already know that's not going to happen unless we go to a yoga class together. And I don't have the time or patience for that."

Kelsey sighed, which made Olivia smile. When they were finished reviewing what they'd accomplished today and making a bullet-point list for the morning so they could hit the ground running, Kelsey would go home. Olivia would close the office door and heat up one of the precooked meals she bought every week because she had neither the time nor inclination to cook and had learned the hard way eating junk on the run was bad for her health, her waistband *and* her productivity. She'd surf the internet and catch up on news while she ate, which was a bad habit she should break…someday.

Then she'd slip into yoga pants and a soft, slouchy sweatshirt. There was no work once the comfy clothes were on, and years of training her mind were why— no matter how exhausted she was—she didn't change until the day was done. The evening was for relaxing and charging her batteries so she could be at her best the next morning. Sometimes she read, sometimes she watched television.

And sometimes she stared at the TV and had no idea what the show was about because her mind was on a sexy firefighter with the scar and the smile and the rough hands that warmed her insides like hot chocolate on a cold day.

Why didn't you jump him when you had the chance? She wouldn't have in a million years. It wasn't in her nature. But alone in her bed, she let herself imagine the firefighter offering her comfort. Kissing her. Backing her up against the elevator wall.

It was a harmless fantasy, she told herself. She'd never see him again.

It had been a slow shift so far and Derek was stretched out on the couch, close to nodding off while channel surfing. As the new guy on this crew, he didn't get control of the television very often, but everybody was occupied elsewhere so he'd been looking for something good to watch. He hadn't found anything.

The woman from the elevator was the only reason he wasn't asleep. Every time it was quiet, she popped into his head. *Olivia.* A week later, and he was still kicking himself in the ass for not getting her contact info.

Hey, I meet a lot of people in my line of work. You got a business card in case I find somebody who needs... whatever it is you do again?

It was for the best he hadn't opened his mouth, since he probably would have said something stupid. And a woman like that probably would have shot him down, anyway. Or she might have gotten a kick out of having a fling with a firefighter, but she wasn't going to stick around for a guy like him. While he wouldn't mind a casual fling now and then, he had the kids to think about.

But none of that stopped him from thinking about Olivia. A lot.

"Hey, Derek," Grant said on his way through to the kitchen. "Amber and the kids are downstairs. I was on my way up, so I told her I'd let you know."

"Thanks." He tossed the TV remote on the table and got up off the couch.

His ex-wife had sent him a text earlier telling him she was going to try to stop by, but she hadn't been sure when.

When he got down to the bay, he saw Amber standing just inside the open bay door, talking to Danny Walsh. They'd been divorced before he moved shifts to this crew when Jeff Porter retired, but Derek had worked out of this house for most of his career so she knew a lot of the guys and their families.

He looked at his kids, his day already better. It had only been a couple of days since he'd dropped them off, but seeing them was the best thing about his life.

While eight-year-old Isaac favored Derek, ten-year-old Julia was the spitting image of her mother. She had Amber's curly black hair and dark eyes, and she had mimicking her mother's facial expressions down pat. And his ex-wife and daughter's matching smiles when they saw him lifted his mood instantly—bright, cheerful reassurances the hard decision to divorce had been the right thing for their family.

"Dad!" Isaac tore his attention away from the apparatus long enough to spot his father and ran in for the hug.

"Hey, bud." He swung his son into his arms to kiss his cheek, groaning a little at his weight. "Another growth spurt? What's your mother been feeding you?"

"Doughnuts."

"Isaac!" Amber rolled her eyes while her kids laughed. "That was just today, because we were running errands."

"He got taller, so that's why he weighs more," Julia said in her serious way. "Not because Mom gave him junk food."

Derek chuckled and ruffled her hair. "I know, sweetheart. I was teasing."

It was a habit left over from the pre-divorce family dynamic, though one they thankfully saw a lot less often these days. Their little girl had taken on the role of mediator in an attempt to fend off parental bickering. Derek and Amber had rarely fought. Neither of them had been emotionally invested enough in the marriage to care enough to really fight. But the sniping at each other and constant minor arguments had worn them all down.

"Dad! Don't mess up my hair," she squealed, but then she laughed when he did it again. And so did Isaac and Amber.

So now, whenever he felt shitty because he wasn't there to kiss them goodnight every night or he'd missed the moment his little tomboy suddenly cared about her hair, he clung to these moments. Those two smiling faces that lit up when they saw him, and the woman he could honestly call one of his best friends again. Hell, he even liked Jason, the guy Amber had married two months after their divorce was finalized.

"I wanted to remind you about the Village Hearts meeting next week," Amber said. "And I was talking to myself out loud and reminded myself to remind *you*. Isaac heard me and suggested we stop by instead of sending you a text."

Village Hearts was a charity near and dear to both their hearts, and when they'd split, they'd both been adamant about staying involved. Derek did more of the behind-the-scenes volunteering, while Amber volunteered directly with the kids. Since that was how they'd generally done it in the past anyway, they were both happy with the arrangement. Amber had always been the calendar keeper who reminded him about things, though, and that was a harder habit to break.

"Did you put a reminder in my app thing?" he told her, holding up his phone.

She gave him an exasperated look. "The app thing is called a calendar. And I showed you how to add reminders."

And he'd tried to pay attention, but she talked fast and he wasn't as tech-savvy as she was. "Show me one more time."

He pulled up the app on his phone and Amber walked him through setting a reminder for the meeting. She'd hooked their apps together shortly after the split, and everything to do with the kids went into the shared calendar. And when it came to the kids' stuff, she'd set it to remind Derek when anything fell on him. Sometimes she'd even set multiple reminders that started going off several days and then hours in advance. But she refused to manage *his* digital calendar for him, no matter how much he tried to sweet-talk her into it.

"Got it?" Amber asked, jerking his attention back to her.

"I think so." Nope.

"If you'd use it more often, you'd get better at it," she said. "You don't have anything in there other than the kids' calendars and your Tuesday and Friday tours."

He shrugged. "That's all I've really got going on. I mean, I hang out at Kincaid's sometimes, but grabbing a beer with the guys isn't something I need to schedule."

And he did have a paper calendar at home. He was pretty sure it was under a stack of mail he needed to go through. The problem with the paper calendar was that it didn't have a built-in reminder. If you didn't look at it, the appointments didn't exist.

The alarm sounded, making Isaac jump. Derek had just enough time to kiss them both quickly and then Amber was pulling them out of the way as the guys ran for the trucks.

"Don't forget that meeting!" she yelled at him as he stepped into his gear.

He gave her a wave and then winked at his daughter as Ladder 37 started to roll. He wouldn't forget the meeting. Village Hearts was too important to him, although it wouldn't hurt to have his phone remind him.

That brought his thoughts right back to Olivia of the elevator. He still wasn't sure exactly what she did, but it sounded like scheduling and calendars and reminders might be something she was very good at it.

It was a damn good thing kicking himself for not asking for her business card was only a figure of speech or he'd be covered in bruises.

Chapter Three

Olivia pulled open the frosted glass door of Broussard Financial Services at precisely 5:50 in the evening. Ten minutes wasn't early enough to be rude to the hosts of the meeting, but would ensure she was on time and prepared for the scheduled six o'clock start.

Her heels clicked on the floor as she walked to the receptionist's desk, where a woman was on her feet. It looked as if she was preparing to leave for the day, but she paused when Olivia entered.

"Hi, are you here for the Village Hearts meeting?" When Olivia confirmed she was, the woman smiled. "It's in the boardroom, which is down that hall and on your right. You can't miss it. Jess is already in there."

"Thank you." Olivia wasn't sure exactly who Jess was, but she took a deep breath and concentrated on her posture as she followed the receptionist's directions.

She wasn't usually nervous going into meetings, but she wasn't here to sell McGovern Consulting's services, which she had complete confidence in. While volunteering with a charity was work-adjacent, as it was an excellent venue for professional networking, it was new to Olivia and new things triggered a low-level buzz of anxiety.

There were several people in the boardroom, but it was a blonde woman about her age or a little older in an elegant pantsuit who stepped forward to greet her.

"You must be Olivia McGovern." She offered her hand, which Olivia shook. "I'm Jessica Broussard Gullotti, but please call me Jess."

Broussard Gullotti. She'd seen one of those names written in bold letters on the frosted glass on the way in. But the second…it sounded familiar, but she couldn't quite place it. "Pleased to meet you. I'm excited to be here."

"And we're excited to have you. It tends to be a little thin around here when it comes to the so-called boring stuff, but I guess as long as everybody shows up when it's time to donate or help out the kids, I won't complain."

Jess gave her a brief rundown on Village Hearts, a lot of which Olivia already knew from the overview Kelsey had put together for her. They offered support for families with children suffering long-term health crises—whether due to injury or illness—by helping take care of the children's siblings. Whether it was helping with school pickups and transportation, babysitting or just setting up some fun playdates, Village Hearts would help.

"We can also help parents find other charities and organizations to help with their child and their financial situation," Jess said, "but when a family is overwhelmed by having a child with a serious health issue, it's easy for the needs of their other children to get overlooked, especially the little ones."

"It takes a village," Olivia said.

Jess grinned. "Exactly. Let me introduce you to some people."

There were whirlwind introductions, since the meeting would be starting, but Olivia didn't sweat it. She was pretty good at making names-to-faces connections and, while taking notes in her notebook during the meeting, she'd jot down some observations about each person, which would help cement the hasty introductions in her mind. Thanks to Kelsey's notes, Olivia already knew that George and Ella Orfanakis were in charge. Her parents had started the charity when Ella needed a liver transplant as a child and they'd struggled to maintain a sense of normalcy for her younger brother, Frankie, who was also on the board.

The last person to meet was across the room, and Olivia doubted there would be time for introductions, since George was taking his seat at the head of the massive conference table. But when the man turned to grab a cookie from a tray and she could see slightly more than his profile, she sucked in a breath and clenched her fingers around her notebook.

It was the firefighter from the elevator. *Derek.* The man she'd been spending more than a little mental time with each night as she fell asleep, because he was a safe fantasy. She was never supposed to see him again.

"And that guy scoping out the baked goods is Derek Gilman. He's a firefighter, actually. He works with my husband, Rick."

Gullotti. That's where Olivia had heard the name. Rick Gullotti was one of the men she'd talked to briefly after being pulled out of the elevator.

Praying her face wasn't as hot as it felt, she forced a smile. "We've met, actually. Derek and I were briefly stuck in an elevator together and your husband helped get us out."

"Wait, you're—" Jess stopped talking for a second, her gaze flicking to Derek and back before she spoke again. "I heard about that. I'm glad it wasn't anything more serious."

"Me, too," she said, hoping her response wasn't too wooden, but she was too busy trying to figure out what was happening to care all that much.

Seeing Derek was a shock. And Jess's reaction was odd, as if Olivia had been the topic of somebody's conversation. But most of all, her own response to seeing the firefighter was downright alarming.

She probably shouldn't have spent quite so much time remembering how good his hands had felt on her skin. And she definitely shouldn't have been imagining her back pressed up against the elevator with her legs wrapped around the man.

He chose that moment to turn in her direction. His eyes met hers and he froze with a cookie halfway to his mouth. Olivia's cheeks felt hot again and she gave him what she hoped was a polite, *nice to see you again* smile. Derek returned the smile, and then started across the room toward her.

"Let's get started," George said in a loud voice, startling her.

Derek didn't look away from her as she obediently took a seat, and for a long and strangely nerve-racking moment, she was afraid he was going to sit next to her. Considering what she'd imagined him doing to her last night, she wasn't sure her nerves could handle that.

But he stayed on his side of the table and took a bite of his cookie while George called the meeting to order. Of course he started by introducing their newest member, even though she'd already met everybody one-on-one, and thanking her for her involvement. Once the spotlight was off her, Olivia opened the leather cover and sifted through the notebook inserts crammed into it until she found the slim one she'd added for Village Hearts.

Prepared to take notes, including adding a question mark to anything she needed to catch up on, she listened to George go over some statistics from the last month.

It didn't take but a few minutes before she realized Derek sitting across from her might be worse than if he'd sat next to her. He was in her peripheral vision and she was keenly aware that he was watching her while he listened and ate his cookie. Not staring, exactly, but he spent a lot more time looking at her than he did looking at George.

She might have assumed he vaguely recognized her and was trying to place where he knew her from if not for the slightly weird way Jess had reacted when she said she'd been stuck in the elevator with him.

Wait, you're— And then the quick glance at Derek as she cut off her sentence.

"I don't feel like we did a great job at promoting the auction fundraiser last year," Ella was saying, and Olivia jerked her attention back to the business at hand. It wasn't like her to get distracted like that. Of course, she wasn't usually presented with a distraction like Derek while she was trying to focus.

"I feel like there was a disconnect in the images we put out," Ella continued. "The poster made it clear the charity supports children, which is great. But for this particular event—a dinner and dancing while auctioning off some very nice items—I feel like we need to be targeting wallets more than hearts, I think. It's hard to explain. We had a good turnout, but I'd like to attract some bigger spenders."

"There's a wide range of items, though," Derek said, and Olivia's skin tingled at the sound of his voice. She'd imagined that voice whispering some pretty dirty things in her ear since the last time she saw him. "We don't want to make it look like such a high-end event that the core community doesn't bother showing up."

"That's a good point," one of the other women said. "We want to appeal to people with deep pockets who aren't necessarily involved with Village Hearts, but it's important to celebrate the everyday people who do the work, too."

"I would suggest splitting your marketing campaign," Olivia said, and all heads swiveled to her, but she kept her gaze on George and Ella at the end of the table. "It sounds like your promotion for last year was considered successful, so I'd continue that. Make marketing materials geared toward the children and some of the more fun, affordable items going up for auction, along with a date night for a good-cause theme. Those are the images your core community, as Derek called them, will be sharing on their social media accounts."

Ella was nodding and nobody jumped in, so she kept going. "At the same time, I'd set up some promotions specifically targeted toward people who support similar charities, along with donors to local hospitals and others whose donations come from their accountants' advice rather than the heart. A more elegant advertisement, pushing the dinner and any high-end auction items. Rather than the word-of-mouth, organic sharing the Village Hearts community and their friends and family will generate, this marketing would be driven by keywords and very specific ad targeting."

When she was finished speaking, nobody said anything for a moment and Olivia forced herself not to fidget while she waited for feedback from the rest of the room. She didn't think she'd stepped on anybody's toes, but it wouldn't matter. Once she made a commitment to something, she followed through, so she wouldn't hold back ideas or information to save anybody's ego.

"Wow." George leaned back in his chair, tapping his pen on the table. "That sounds great. I've gotta be honest, though. I didn't understand all of that, and I think we did okay with Facebook last year, but I don't think any of us really know the level of stuff you're talking about."

"I have a social media and marketing manager on my staff," Olivia said. "McGovern Consulting would be happy to donate two hours per week of her time, as well as an hour of my assistant's, to help with promotion for the auction. It doesn't sound like a lot of time, but they're very good and very fast."

"That's a generous offer," Ella said. "If you're sure..."

"I am." Olivia had already spoken to Kelsey and Brynn about it. While they'd be paid the same whether they were working on something for McGovern Consulting or Village Hearts, she wouldn't throw a new twist in their workflow without asking them first.

"I'll touch base with you later in the week about the accounting and tax docs related to that," Jess said.

Olivia nodded. "And we'll need to give Brynn, my marketing manager, admin access to the organization's Facebook page."

"I'd be the contact person for that," Ella told her. "If you give her my contact info, we'll get her added."

"Perfect," George said. "Let's go over the list of items we have so far, so we can see how much more we need to drum up."

Olivia turned to a fresh page and wrote in a header so she could take notes to pass on to Brynn. The items they'd be auctioning off would impact the marketing, so the more information she had up front, the better.

But as she tried to focus on George, she caught Derek watching her again, and this time she glanced over. He didn't look away. He just gave her a warm smile that made his eyes crinkle at the corners, and she smiled back.

Derek was trying like hell to focus on the meeting, especially since Amber would expect a full report, but Olivia from the elevator was sitting across the table from him and she had a habit of tapping the end of her pen against her bottom lip when she was thinking.

Her mouth was a hell of a lot more interesting to him than whatever George was talking about.

It's a good thing he hadn't already taken a bite of the cookie in his hand before he turned and saw her or he probably would have choked on it. He'd known somebody new was showing up, but he hadn't bothered to ask for a name, assuming they'd be introduced at the meeting. And even if he had known, he hadn't gotten Olivia's last name in the elevator and he would have told himself it was a coincidence. That there was more than one Olivia in Boston.

But it was her—the woman from the elevator who'd been in his mind constantly since then—and he was on his way to talk to her when George, with the worst timing ever, chose that moment to start the meeting. Not getting a way to contact her had been a colossal mistake, but he was going to remedy that before they left tonight. He hoped.

For now, he forced his attention away from Olivia and back to the business at hand because he handled a lot of the business of the auction items. When it came to divvying up the work, he preferred that to being involved with the dinner or dancing plans.

"I've been promised four tickets to a Patriots game, but we haven't nailed down which game yet." George paused, looking at Olivia. "That's usually one of our biggest ticket items."

"I'll make a note of that. The Patriots…that's football, right?" When all heads turned her way at once she blushed. "My parents didn't watch sports and I haven't really paid attention except for seeing news clips and overhearing conversations."

"How can you be from Boston and not know who the Patriots are?" George asked and her blush deepened.

"She *did* know," Derek said. "They play football, just like she said, and we have four tickets to auction off. I've also got gift certificates to some local restaurants and a weekend stay at an inn on the South Shore."

"Oh?" Ella perked up.

Derek shrugged. "It's not a wicked-expensive inn, but it would be a good weekend getaway for a working couple. It's really nice, but in an affordable area for dining out and stuff like that."

"Sounds good," George said, but Derek's attention had already shifted back to Olivia, who was taking what appeared to be very diligent notes. He wondered if she knew she was cute as hell when she was concentrating.

"That sounds great, but I think we also need to get more donations that will appeal specifically to the people we want to bring in," Jess said. "We need items that will give the white-collar people with expendable income an excuse to relax. A deep-sea fishing charter for a group of four. A day at one of the more exclusive spas. Gift certificates from restaurants where *they* live. We have a great assortment of affordable, practical things for our core community, but we need to reach out for donations outside of that circle if we want to maximize Olivia's marketing plan."

"I agree," Derek said, and they all nodded. "At this point, I think everybody needs to email me your lists of donations to date. I'll make a master list and then we can figure out where we have gaps."

"A master list would help in planning the marketing, too," Olivia added.

"We can touch base on that," he said, looking directly at her.

She didn't look away. "Definitely."

Yes. Now he had a valid reason for contacting her.

After quick updates on the catering company handling the dinner and making a decision on the DJ for the dance, George decided to call it a night.

Usually Derek would take his time leaving, chatting and scoping out any leftover snacks, but he was betting Olivia was the kind of person who'd say a brisk goodbye and rush off to whatever was next on her agenda. Hanging around scavenging cookies probably didn't jive with her productivity gig, and he wanted to talk to her. He wasn't sure about what, but he'd spent the last week and a half or so regretting not having a way to contact her. Her showing up to volunteer for Village Hearts was some kind of a sign and he wasn't going to waste the opportunity.

He'd been right about her making a quick exit and after he gave Jess a quick wave—which got him a knowing look—he followed Olivia out of the board-room. Once he was past the glass windows, he had to do almost a half-jog to get close enough to call her name without raising his voice.

"Hey, Olivia," he said, and the click of her heels stopped as she turned back. "I'll walk out with you, if you don't mind."

"I don't mind at all." She waited until he was next to her and then resumed walking. "I was hoping to get a chance to talk to you, anyway."

"Really?" He stepped forward to open the frosted glass door for her.

"I never thanked you for keeping me company in the elevator. I was so behind schedule that day that I just rushed off without saying a proper goodbye. Or a proper thank-you."

He chuckled. "It was my pleasure to keep you company, even if I didn't really have a say in the matter."

He didn't miss the way her cheeks blushed a little at the words *my pleasure*. "You didn't have a say in being in the elevator with me, but you went out of your way to be good company. I probably would have panicked if you weren't there to keep me calm."

It was kind of his job, but he stopped himself from pointing that out. It would be a conversational dead end. "I enjoyed it, actually. It wouldn't have broken my heart any if it had taken a little longer for the guys to get the door open."

She gave him a sideways look, the corner of her mouth curved into a playful smile. "And here we are, about to tempt fate again."

For a moment, he was confused, until he realized they were at the elevator. "Feeling lucky?"

"Either way, it's a win."

Derek wasn't great at flirting, but it didn't take a genius to figure out she wouldn't mind being stuck in the elevator with him again and that was *definitely* a win.

Once they were in the elevator and the doors had slid closed, though, she looked nervous. She leaned against the back wall with her leather journal clutched to her chest. Her face was a little flushed and the deep breath she took was a little shaky.

"So what did you think of the Village Hearts crowd?" he asked, hoping to distract her in case she was having any kind of anxiety issues about being in elevators after getting stuck in one. He knew it happened.

"They all seem nice and they're enthusiastic. I'm looking forward to working with everybody."

"George can be a little tough to deal with at times, but he means well. I'm sorry about the football thing."

"I probably should have just told him I'm not from Boston."

"No shit? Sorry. I mean, really? You don't have much of an accent. Where are you from?"

"Virginia, but I went to college here and decided to stay. That's probably where I learned to match the team names with the sports." She shrugged as the elevator came to a stop and the door opened. "And you don't have to apologize for swearing. It doesn't bother me."

"Why didn't you tell him?" He followed her into the main lobby of the building, aware that with every step they took, his window of opportunity was closing.

But he was second-guessing himself now. One, it didn't seem right to hit on her the first time she showed up to help out with a charity that meant a lot to him. She'd already shown she had a lot to offer them and he didn't want to scare her off. And secondly, while it might look like she was flirting, it was still hard for him to believe a woman like her would be interested in dating a guy like him.

"It's probably stupid," she said, "but I didn't want him to know I wasn't from Boston. I'm already new to the committee and I didn't want to be an outsider, too. Not that it matters, really, but he seems like the kind of guy who'd hold it against me for no good reason."

"I'd like to say you're wrong because I've known George for years, but he can be a jerk sometimes. And he was kind of rude to you."

"Thank you for jumping in." She smiled, and the warmth in her eyes made him wish she'd smile all the time. "I wasn't really sure what to say because I didn't want to make a big thing out of it, but I also didn't want to apologize for not being a sports fan."

Derek couldn't imagine not having sports in his life, but he damn well wouldn't expect Olivia to be sorry about it.

"Ignore him when he's like that. He'll warm up to you."

Once they'd walked out of the chill of the climate-controlled lobby into the steamy evening air, he saw by the way she turned that they'd parked in different directions. But she paused and looked at him. "My car's this way."

"I'm the other way, but I can walk you."

"Thank you for the offer, but I can actually see it from here. I'll be fine. I should give you my card, though, so you can contact me." She opened her notebook and he saw a pocket with a small stack of business cards, but she pulled one from a separate pocket. She handed it to him and he saw that she'd handwritten a telephone number on it. "That's my cell phone. I should warn you up front that I rarely answer calls, but I'll respond to voicemail messages as soon as I can. The same with text messages if I'm with a client."

He pulled out his wallet and tucked the card away. Later he'd put her number into his phone so he wouldn't lose it. "If I'm on a call, the same warning applies to me, I guess."

She laughed. "I don't imagine answering a text is a high priority if you're fighting a fire."

"Nope. So don't take it personally if I don't respond right away."

"I won't if you don't." She took her time securing the elastic band around her notebook, and then she pressed her lips together for a few seconds before meeting his gaze again. "I try to be strict about not working after seven o'clock, so if you want to call and chat about something, any time after that's a good time."

His pulse jumped, but he tried to keep his expectations in check. He wasn't sure if that was an invitation or if she was simply being practical. "I don't want to interrupt your relaxing time with Village Hearts work."

"I think I'm going to enjoy working with you all enough that it won't be like work at all. You can call me anytime, Derek." She paused, and then gave him a smile that lit him up almost as much as it lit up her face. "You'll just have a better chance of talking to me after seven."

"I'll keep that in mind." As if he could forget it. He was on the verge of asking her if she'd like to go somewhere and get a drink, but in the time he took second-guessing whether that would be too pushy at this point, a couple of other people walked out of the lobby and Olivia started moving away from him.

"I'll talk to you soon?" she asked, lifting her hand.

"Definitely," he said, and she gave him a smile before turning to walk away.

Derek allowed himself a few seconds of watching the sway of her hips and listening to the click of her heels on the sidewalk before he headed for his own car. That was when he realized he hadn't given her *his* contact information, which meant he'd have to make the first move.

But he had her number and a good reason to reach out to her. It was enough for now.

Chapter Four

After a restless night, Olivia wasn't her usual focused and driven self in the morning. She was even wishing she hadn't given up caffeine her third year of college. Right now she could go for a coffee. Or a soda. Anything that would help wake her up and get her going.

She'd gone to bed at her normal time, but then she'd tossed and turned as she did her best *not* to think about Derek. Now that she'd not only seen him again, but would be seeing him on a fairly regular basis, her sexy firefighter wasn't exactly a safe fantasy anymore.

It was a point driven home hard when they'd gotten in the elevator together after the Village Hearts meeting. Every dirty thing she'd imagined him doing to her in that first elevator ran through her mind like an X-rated highlight reel and all she could do was stand against the wall and clutch her notebook like it was a physical barrier between her and doing something stupid. She *had* to stop imagining them naked together if they were going to see each other often.

And she was a little cranky about that.

Maybe that's why, when Kelsey let herself into the apartment and said good-morning to her, as she always did, Olivia pointed a half-joking but accusatory finger at her. "Did you know?"

Kelsey's eyes widened at her unusual tone. "Did I know what?"

"Did you know Derek Gilman would be at the Village Hearts meeting last night?"

There was a long pause. "Remind me who Derek Gilman is?"

"The firefighter. From the elevator."

The look on Kelsey's face told her two things. One, she hadn't known. And two, now that she did, Olivia was never going to hear the end of it. "Oh em gee, *your* firefighter is involved with Village Hearts?"

"He's not *my* firefighter." At least not when her eyes were open and she was fully dressed.

"He could be. Especially since you'll be *seeing him again.* A lot."

Olivia winced. "Don't remind me."

"Did he remember you?" When she nodded, Kelsey grinned. "So he's probably been thinking about you and kicking himself for not getting the business card you should have given him."

"I don't think so. And so what if he remembered me? It's only been like a week and a half since he saw me."

"But think about how many people he sees in his line of work. I doubt he remembers every person he rescues. Did you talk to him?"

"Yeah." She didn't mention they'd ridden the elevator down together again because she didn't want to give Kelsey any more ideas than she already had.

"And did you give him your business card this time?"

"I did. We'll be working on a few things together, so it only made sense to give him a way to contact me."

"Maybe I'll get to meet him," Kelsey said. "Since I'll be helping with the promotional stuff."

"I doubt that will be necessary." Olivia could only imagine what would happen if Kelsey saw them together. She didn't think her assistant-slash-friend would embarrass her in front of the guy, but Olivia would know what she was thinking and that would be enough to make her self-conscious.

When Kelsey took a sip of her coffee from the extraordinarily large travel mug she used, Olivia sighed and put her breakfast dishes in the dishwasher so they could get to work. She was aware that Kelsey was busy with her phone, but she didn't think much of it until she gave her a look with eyebrows raised.

"He doesn't say much on Facebook, but people tag him in pictures a lot. And you're right, he's definitely hot."

"I'm not really comfortable with you invading his privacy like that." And because she'd said it, she had to stay where she was instead of going to look over Kelsey's shoulder at her phone screen.

Kelsey looked up at her and shrugged. "If he cares about people invading his privacy, he should make use of his privacy settings."

"Good point." She still didn't move, though. "That's kind of a gray area, isn't it? Just because he doesn't either understand or doesn't care about privacy settings doesn't mean I should creep on his profile."

"You're not. I am," Kelsey said, using her finger to scroll down her screen. Then she glanced at the clock. "And technically I don't start working for another three minutes, so you're not paying me, either, if that was going to be your next argument against me looking at this photo of a sweaty, shirtless Derek playing football in somebody's backyard."

Okay, that got her moving. She ignored Kelsey's laughter as she yanked her phone out of her hand.

And yes, a sweaty and shirtless Derek was worth the possible—but probably minor—violation of her own personal sense of ethics. Especially a shirtless Derek who was not only running with a football, but laughing as one of the guys who'd helped get her out of the elevator tried to grab him. She could tell that if there were a few more frames, they would show the guy missing him.

"Do you want me to save the photo and send it to your phone?"

"No." That would definitely be creepy. She handed the phone back to Kelsey before she could succumb to any more temptation she'd feel guilty about later. "Did you finish editing the podcast?"

"Of course. Once you've reviewed it and it's good to go, I'll send it to Wes."

The podcasts weren't Olivia's favorite part of her job, but her agent and Brynn had convinced her they were worth doing. They helped sustain interest in her first book, which focused on organization and working efficiently for college students, and helped generate interest in the book she was working on now, which was more business-focused. And Brynn did a lot of the heavy lifting. She'd designed the podcasts with something of a radio show format. She did the intro and asked questions that were sent in by listeners or via social media and then Olivia answered them, offering suggestions for solving problems under the planning and organization umbrella.

The bonus in Brynn being the host, so to speak, was that it kept Olivia positioned as the expert on the topic. She'd rolled her eyes the first time Brynn said it, but the number of subscribers kept growing and the questions kept coming, along with invitations to speak and to be quoted in industry publications. Kelsey did the editing because hers was a fresh ear and she enjoyed it.

Wes was the fourth member of the McGovern Consulting team and, like Brynn, was a part-time employee who worked remotely. He did the technical stuff, like maintaining the website and uploading the podcasts and—much less frequently—videos to her YouTube channel. Brynn maintained the face of their social media, but Wes was their behind-the-scenes guy. Olivia had managed the nuts and bolts of her online platform herself in the early days and she'd enjoyed it, but it hadn't been long before it was more practical and cost-efficient for her to hire that work out.

Once she'd signed off on the podcast and done some other administrative tasks in the office, Olivia left to take care of two follow-up meetings. She always went back two weeks after setting up a system to answer any questions and make sure they were using the system efficiently.

Kelsey left early because Olivia had scheduled several hours at the end of the day to work on her book and she preferred to be alone when she did. She considered the work she did to be very interactive—the clients' workflow and personalities determined the best method for working more efficiently—so presenting information in a more generic format wasn't easy. But her first book had been a bestseller and continued to sell well, and her agent felt this one would, too.

Once she'd closed her notebook and turned her laptop off, she ate a quick meal while flipping through the information she'd received from Village Hearts. Kelsey had printed the email and attachments for her, and some papers she set aside to look at later. But she scanned through the contact list.

She hadn't gotten Derek's number last night, even though they'd talked about how he didn't respond when he was busy. Maybe he'd simply assumed he'd call first and she'd save it then. And once others had started leaving, she'd taken the opportunity to walk away before the standing there got awkward and she did something stupid, like kiss him goodnight.

Because, despite her certainty that dating wasn't a priority right now, she'd wanted to.

There were no telephone numbers on the list, though. Olivia had been added to a shorter list at the top and then, after a divider, was a multipage list of names. She assumed those were all the volunteers who helped out in some capacity, and it annoyed her slightly that there were no descriptors attached. Just names and email addresses. It didn't make sense to give contact information without any indication of what one would contact a person for.

One name on the second page caught her eye. *Amber Gilman.*

It wasn't a common last name, so two of them involved with one charity probably meant there was a connection. Sister? Mother?

Wife?

No, it couldn't be a wife. At least she didn't think so. The lack of a wedding ring or a telltale pale strip where one was supposed to be probably didn't mean anything, since she wasn't sure if firefighters usually wore wedding rings or not. But he seemed like such a good guy and she didn't want to believe he'd flirt with her if he was married. Nor did he seem stupid enough to flirt in front of a bunch of people who must know Amber. Assuming he even *was* flirting. It had been subtle and she wasn't sure now if it was just wishful thinking on her part.

She might be his ex-wife.

Olivia wrinkled her nose and set the paper aside. She didn't really have room in her life for any relationship right now—which was why finding a guy still wasn't part of her life plan—but she definitely didn't have time for a messy relationship. And divorces were messy. They made families messy and, in her parents' case, so hostile every aspect of life for every member of the family was tainted by their anger. There had been zero chance of Olivia going to college in Virginia because she was sick of choking on the tension between her parents. Her aunt and uncle's divorce had been almost as bad, and her cousin had the police to her house at least six times during hers.

Maybe it was his sister or his mother, she told herself as she changed into leggings and a sweatshirt and settled on her bed to watch television.

At twenty after seven, her phone rang. She didn't recognize the number on the screen and normally she let unfamiliar numbers go to voicemail, but the chance it might be Derek—and the accompanying spike in her pulse rate—made her reach for the phone.

She answered on the third ring. "Hello?"

"Hey, it's Derek. Are you busy?"

"Not at all." The sound of his voice made her forget about the unknown Amber, and she relaxed against her pillows. "If I was busy, I wouldn't have answered the phone."

"No multitasking?"

"Don't get me started on the evils of multitasking. Trust me, all my attention is on you." There was a long pause, and she winced when she replayed the words in her head, and then kept going to fill the silence. "What's up?"

"I was looking over the list of prizes we have so far and trying to think of some more items that would appeal to the people Jess was talking about. And it seems like you work in that world, too, so I figured we could brainstorm together?"

"I love brainstorming," she said, and then wondered if it sounded weird. But it was true. Pen, paper and people just throwing ideas down was a great way to stimulate the more creative parts of the mind. "Were you thinking now, or did you want to come up with a time that's good for both of us?"

"I was actually thinking this kind of thing would be a lot easier to discuss in person. Are you open for dinner at all?"

Olivia's pulse quickened, but she forced herself to ignore any non-professional reaction she might have to his invitation. Of course it was easier to brainstorm in person. She'd eaten countless meals with people for exactly that reason.

It was silly to get excited just because the question had been asked in a deep voice that belonged to an undeniably sexy man.

"Let me look." She picked up her planner—which usually sat on the bed next to her until it was time to sleep—and scanned quickly through the days. "We're far enough apart so we wouldn't want to eat too late, but I have meetings right up to the end of the work day. Saturday I'm speaking at a local business conference, so Sunday's my only totally open day."

"Sunday works, unless you left it open on purpose. It sounds like you don't have much free time, so I don't want to butt in on it."

She *didn't* have much free time, but Sunday was only open because other people liked having the time off. "No, it's fine. Sunday's great. You can just text me where and when sometime between now and then. I'm not picky."

"Sounds great. I'm looking forward to it."

So was she, she thought as they ended the call. Even though she could tell herself it was a work-related meeting, she was going to be alone with Derek for longer than the time it took an elevator to go down—even with an unexpected stop—and *that* was the part her nerves were focusing in on.

Not a date, she told herself. She wasn't even looking to date. She was already busy all the time, she had a book to finish, and she'd learned young that success came from making a plan and sticking to it.

She feared Derek Gilman was going to be one hell of a distraction. But as long as he was a diversion and not a derailing, she'd be okay. Probably.

On Sunday evening, Derek watched the door, his stomach in knots for stupid reasons he couldn't shake. The restaurant was one of his favorites—a family-owned place that served up food that wasn't fancy, but was damn good—but it probably wasn't the kind of place where a woman like Olivia McGovern usually ate.

He hadn't even been sure they had wine until he got there and, now that he'd looked at the list, he had no idea if the wines were any good or not. Judging by the price, they probably weren't fancy. And no, he didn't know if Olivia drank wine, but he assumed she did. Women like her seemed to.

Women like her. He tried to kick that thought out of his head. Sure, she had expensive clothes and shoes. And her hair and makeup and nails were flawless. And maybe that made him feel a little like he was from the wrong side of the tracks. But that was on him, not her. *She* seemed really genuine, and she was smart and funny and driven and...

Holy shit. She was goddamned beautiful.

Derek didn't wait until she got to the table. He stood as soon as she appeared in the door, and the way her face lit up when she saw him tightened the knots in his stomach until he felt as if his insides were vibrating with the tension.

He felt himself returning her smile as she crossed the dining room and could only hope it was a friendly-but-professional smile and not a goofy grin.

She wasn't wearing a suit tonight. Not that he minded seeing her long legs showcased by the skirts and the high heels, but her legs looked amazing in slim navy pants, too. Her white T-shirt would have been casual, except it was a little shimmery and she was wearing jewelry that dressed it up. And in place of the high heels were strappy sandals that showed off her feet and bright purple toenails.

For some reason, that amused him. He would have

guessed she'd choose a classic color or muted pastel for her toes, and he liked that unexpected pop of color.

"Thank you," she said as she settled in the chair he pulled out for her. "I'm sorry I'm late."

Derek glanced at the ornate clock hanging over the door as he sat down. "I hadn't even noticed, since it was literally two minutes."

"On time is late," she said, and he was pretty sure she was serious. "Just ask my parents."

He wasn't sure how to respond to that, but then her mouth curved into a smile and he realized she was kidding. Or maybe she wasn't kidding about her parents or punctuality, but she had a sense of humor about it.

"About the only thing I'm not late to is work," he said. "It drove my ex-wife crazy."

While her smile froze for a few seconds before she turned to rummage in the leather bag she'd hung on the back of the chair, Derek mentally face-palmed himself. He hadn't even made it a minute before mentioning the ex-wife. Women *loved* that shit.

Not that they were on a date, but still. It was a bad habit.

"How long have you been divorced?" She set the leather notebook she'd had in the elevator on the table in front of her, but didn't open it yet.

"It's been final almost a year."

"Do you have children?"

It was a natural question to ask a guy who'd just told you he was divorced, but she looked stiff and awkward as she asked it, not making eye contact. "Two. Julia's ten and Isaac is eight."

Her smile was definitely forced. "One of each. That's nice."

Tamping down on the impulse to pull up photos of the kids on his phone, he decided to turn the conversation back to her. "How about you? A significant other in your life?"

"Nope. Not part of the life plan yet."

He laughed. "I can actually see you not only having a life plan, but actually writing it down."

Olivia put her hand on her notebook in what looked to him like a defensive gesture. "Of course I do. If you don't write it down, it's a thought, not a plan."

She wasn't joking. But before he could respond, the server showed up to take their beverage order. After glancing at the wine list, Olivia asked for a lemonade and he had to fight the urge to apologize to her for his choice of restaurants. Maybe the wine choices didn't impress, but the food would.

He hoped. Maybe she was used to places that served those tiny portions of things nobody could pronounce with a fancy sauce smeared around the plate like a kid's finger painting. This wasn't that kind of place.

After a minute of reading the menu, instead of wrinkling her nose in disdain, she looked across the table at him with big eyes. "It's like all of my favorite comfort foods in one list and everything sounds amazing. How am I supposed to choose?"

"I wish I could help you narrow it down, but everything *is* amazing."

"The drink choice was easy," she said, looking back at her menu. "I have to call my mother later and I always make myself a calling-Mom cocktail, which I don't want to put on top of wine. But I might need a few minutes with this menu."

He chuckled, relief flooding through him. He didn't

drink wine, so he wasn't sure why the fact she wasn't a wine snob after all should be a big deal, but he was still glad she wasn't. "Take your time. There's no hurry."

His favorite was the chicken parmesan, but he liked to save slurping up red sauce-coated pasta for at least the second or third date.

Dinner, he corrected himself. This wasn't a date. The second or third *dinner*.

When the server returned, he ordered the meatloaf dinner and Olivia, after making him and the server laugh at her indecision, went with the herbed stuffed chicken.

"A favorite of mine," he said when they were alone again. "You won't be disappointed."

"I bet everything on that menu is your favorite."

"I wouldn't bet against you." After taking a sip of his coffee, he leaned back in his chair. "So tell me, how did you get involved with Village Hearts?"

"I've wanted to be involved with a charity for some time, as they're a great way to make professional connections while giving back to the community, but it's a tight circle. I've had Kelsey, my assistant, keeping an eye out and when she heard about this one, it seemed like the right opportunity. How about you? I mean, I know firefighters are very supportive of charities, but how did you come to be with this one? Do you get assigned to them?"

"My son was born with a ventricular septal defect."

She'd been lifting the lemonade glass to her mouth, but now she paused and set it down without taking a sip. "I'm sorry."

He smiled. "Thanks, but he's fine now. When he was born, though…it was rough. Amber and I were pretty much consumed by Isaac and being at the hospital and we didn't have a lot of energy left to give Julia. Thanks to our families and Village Hearts, she got to keep being a happy two-year-old while we went through hell."

Maybe it was a trick of the dim lighting, but it looked as if Olivia's eyes were glistening. "You must think I'm awful, talking about professional networking when it's obvious Village Hearts is deeply meaningful to you."

"I don't think you're awful at all," he said quickly because it was true, but also because he didn't want her to cry. "And I don't care why people support Village Hearts, just that they do. I asked Jess to be a part of the board, actually. It wasn't because she had any personal connection to the charity, but because she's freaking amazing with money. Growing and maximizing funds is wicked important when you're as small as we are. And if you're an expert in planning and working efficiently and whatnot, trust me. I want you."

I want you.

The words hung between them for a long moment, and he thought maybe she blushed, but then she pulled her leather notebook close and opened it. It looked as if she'd already clipped some pages together because it fell open to a fresh page and she pulled the pen out of the leather loop.

He wasn't sure if she'd opened it because it would be easier to get started before their meals came or if it was a pointed message to remind him this was something of a business meeting, but it threw him off. Either way, it wasn't the time to find out if she'd like to get together outside of their mutual involvement with Village Hearts. And if he was smart, he'd wait until they were done here, since he didn't want any awkwardness if he'd been misreading their chemistry to spoil their meals.

They got a lot done before the food showed up. She was a smart woman and together they brainstormed some great prizes they'd like to solicit. Derek would pass the list on to Ella, since she was really good at schmoozing people, and because Jess and Olivia worked in those business circles. Using connections could come in handy, but they tried not to put their volunteers in potentially awkward positions professionally.

Olivia slid her notebook back into her bag before reaching for her napkin, which Derek took as a sign they could ease off the charity talk and maybe get a little more personal. There was a lot he wanted to know about her—namely *everything*—but he kept quiet as she ate the first bites of her dinner.

"I am definitely *not* disappointed," she said and, even in the dim lighting, he could see the humor and warmth in her eyes.

"So I've been wondering something. Why Boston? A woman as smart as you could have gone anywhere in the country if you didn't want to stay in Virginia, so why were we lucky enough to get you?"

The hint of pink on her cheeks told him she wasn't immune to the sincere flattery. "Staying in Virginia wasn't an option. I have a very…toxic family, I'm sorry to say. I mean, I love my parents and they love me, but once they stopped loving each other and divorced, things took a turn for the unpleasant."

That probably went a long way toward explaining why hearing him mention his ex-wife had made her smile freeze up, and why finding out he and Amber had children had made her look uncomfortable. A lot of people their age had marriages in their rearview mirror, so it shouldn't have been that much of a surprise. But if her parents' divorce had ruined her family, she might think he had a lot of toxic baggage of his own. Quite the opposite, but he didn't want to get into that now.

"I'm sorry to hear that. My divorce was amicable and still hard for the kids at first, so I can't imagine what that's like. So when it was time to strike off on your own, you obviously chose Boston for our sports teams, right?"

She laughed, as he'd intended. "It's an awesome city with a lot of history, and they had the fields of study I wanted at a school I was accepted to—business and psychology, which is probably an odd mix. And a friend from school got accepted to the same school, so we got to start fresh on a new adventure without being alone."

"It's no fun being alone so that worked out well."

"Yeah. Unfortunately, she really hated it here and dropped out halfway through the first semester. She went home and got her degree while living at home."

"I'm glad you stayed."

It was probably the most overtly flirtatious thing he'd said yet and he could tell by the way her expression softened that she didn't miss it. "I am, too."

He asked her how she'd started her business, and she talked about freelancing and YouTube and such. And she'd written a book, which blew his mind, and traveled sometimes to talk at conferences. A lot of the computer terminology went over his head, but she was obviously intelligent, passionate and driven. He liked that about her.

Once she'd declined dessert and he'd paid the bill— over her objections and he didn't give a rat's ass if it *was* a business expense—there was no reason to stay, but he would happily have sat across the table from her all night.

"My Lyft will be here in a few minutes," she said, which answered the question of what she'd been doing on her phone while he signed the credit card slip.

"Did anybody tell you about the fundraiser next Saturday?" he asked as they walked toward the door.

"Brynn shared a graphic about a fundraiser at a bar. Is that the one you mean?"

"Yeah. It's more than just a bar, though. Kincaid's Pub is owned by Tommy Kincaid, who retired from Engine 59. His son, Scotty, helped get us out of the elevator. So it's almost more like a family hangout than a bar to us." Even as he said it, he realized that they might love Kincaid's, but he had a hard time picturing Olivia there. Definitely not her kind of place. "All the net proceeds they make Saturday from five o'clock until close will go to Village Hearts."

"That's very generous of him."

"Tommy's a good guy. I know you've got a busy schedule, but I'd love it if you could stop by." Her kind of place or not, he wanted to see her again.

"I usually block out Saturdays to write, but I can probably sneak out for a while to support the cause."

He held the door open for her, and then let it go when some idiot stumbled on the sidewalk. Without thinking, he hooked his arm around Olivia's waist and pulled her closer to him and out of the guy's path as the door swung closed behind him.

"Thank you," she said in a soft voice. A little drizzle was falling, and the moisture sparkled on her upturned face.

"Not to downplay the fundraising aspect," he said, "but I should probably clarify that when I said I'd love it if you stop by, I was speaking on behalf of myself, not Village Hearts."

He couldn't miss the curving of her lips into a smile, since he was staring at her mouth. She hadn't moved out of the curve of his arm and, with her face turned up into the light rain, he hoped like hell it was an invitation because he was going to kiss her.

"Since writing a check and going back to work is the most efficient way for me to support a fundraiser, if I'm there, it'll be because of you."

He tightened his arm around her waist and his gaze dropped from her eyes back to her lips as they parted slightly.

As he lowered his mouth to hers, Derek felt the same fear and exhilaration he'd felt the one and only time he'd jumped out of an airplane. If it ended badly, it was really going to hurt, but he knew the experience would be worth the risk.

Tentatively at first, to give her the space to back out if she wanted to, he brushed his lips across Olivia's.

She didn't back out. She put her hands on his shoulders and rose up, pressing her mouth against his. Relief and hunger swept through him as he kissed her, and he wrapped his arms around her, pulling her close as his tongue dipped between her lips.

Her fingertips brushed over his back and then her hands curled, bunching his shirt in her fists. He cupped her face, deepening the kiss. Her skin was damp from the rain and he knew he should stop and let her go, but he didn't want it to end.

Then she made a sound deep in her throat, a hungry

sound that told Derek she didn't give a damn about the rain. She wanted him.

And he wanted her so badly it hurt, but it wouldn't be tonight—it was too soon, and the first date and he didn't want to screw it up by going too fast—so he was going to take every second of this kiss he could get.

It was definitely too soon when she pulled back, breaking the contact. "I'm pretty sure that car just sitting there, with the driver trying really hard not to look at us, is my ride."

Her voice sounded as shaky as he felt inside. It was hard not to ask her to send the driver away and let him drive her home, but he was trying damn hard to remember the reasons he didn't think they were compatible. In the aftermath of that kiss, though, he couldn't come up with a single one.

"Thank you for dinner," she said.

"It was definitely a pleasure." He opened the back door of the car for her, but she paused with one leg inside and they locked eyes over the top of the door.

"Definitely," she whispered.

He winked at her as she got into the car. "Sweet dreams, Olivia."

The look she gave him just before he closed the door confirmed that he wasn't the only one who knew sleep might be hard to come by tonight.

Chapter Five

"I never thought I'd be one of those women getting kissed on a sidewalk in the rain." The squeak of an office chair swiveling startled Olivia, reminding her too late that she wasn't alone. "Did I say that out loud?"

"You kissed him?"

"I was mumbling to myself. How did you even hear that?"

"You're my boss. When you talk, I listen." Kelsey smiled. "Especially if you're talking about kissing."

"Well, I'm done talking about kissing. I have to get through this material."

A last-minute cancellation by a potential client had opened up an unexpected window of time, so she was taking the time to research an upcoming productivity suite that encompassed paper and digital planning. The cornerstone of her business was finding systems that allowed for individual workflow within the centralized structure, so continued success meant staying on top of the evolving software. A lot of entrepreneurs in the market would reach out to her for beta testing or an endorsement, but she didn't bother with apps that simply digitized written pages for future reference. An app that analyzed a handwritten page and updated a central digital system interested her.

But today her mind didn't seem to find her work nearly as interesting as it found reliving Derek's kiss. She'd lost count of the times she'd read the same few paragraphs on her screen, and now she was talking to herself about it.

And to Kelsey, since she was in the room.

"I want to hear more about last night," Kelsey said. "And I'm not going to stop bugging you about it, so the most efficient thing for you to do is spill the details so we can both get back to work."

"Or I can take my laptop to another room and work in peace." When Kelsey just folded her arms and cocked an eyebrow, she caved. But only a little. "The food was amazing. We got some brainstorming done for the benefit. And he kissed me goodnight."

"Was the kiss better than the food?"

"Yes." She didn't even have to think about it. "And that's saying something, because it was the best herbed stuffed chicken I've ever had."

"And when are you going to see him again?"

"There's a fundraiser at a bar on Saturday—you know, the one Brynn made the graphic for—and he made it clear he'd like for me to go, and not just for Village Hearts." She inhaled slowly, held the breath for a few seconds and then let it out. She needed some damn clarity. "I'd planned to write Saturday and…I'm just not sure."

"You *want* to go. It's written all over your face. Just go for it."

"He has an ex-wife. And two kids."

"Okay." Kelsey looked as if she expected more of an explanation, but Olivia wasn't sure she could put her reservations into words. "If you want to date a guy your age who doesn't have an ex or any kids, you're seriously shrinking the dating pool."

"I don't want to date *anybody* right now. That's the point."

Kelsey made a sound that translated to *hmm, maybe I don't believe you.* "You met him. You liked him. You saw him again. You agreed to have dinner with him. And you kissed him, on the sidewalk in the rain, no less. You're thinking about him instead of focusing today. I'm pretty sure you *do* want to date him."

"And you just proved my point." Olivia stood and stretched her back. "Thinking about Derek has killed my focus this morning and *that's* why I don't want to date anybody. In a few years, I'll be able to step back a little and have the time and attention to give to a relationship."

"I know you, Olivia. By the time you're ready to step back, your potential dates will not only have ex-wives and children, but grandchildren, too."

"You're exaggerating badly, but it doesn't matter. When I do have a family, I don't want to feel torn between them and my company." If you piled too much on, things started sliding and everything could crumble. "I'm going to see if we have anything for lunch and then prep for my afternoon meeting. No more dating talk. I need to focus."

"I'm having a yogurt in about twenty minutes, when I finish this, so I'm all set." Kelsey swiveled back to her screen and Olivia grabbed her phone and walked to the kitchen. There wouldn't be many lunch options, since she usually grabbed something on the run if she had time between meetings and Kelsey seemed to live on Greek yogurt and protein bars. Luckily, there was always extra yogurt since her assistant liked a variety on hand. Only having mango when you were in the mood for strawberry was a tragedy, apparently. There were three blueberries, so she grabbed one and pulled back the top.

Then her phone buzzed and she couldn't deny the way her pulse quickened when she saw Derek's name on the screen. Her attraction to the man wasn't going to be scheduled in a neat little box in her planner.

She *should* let it go to voicemail and eat her yogurt so she could get ready for an afternoon of follow-up visits, but she couldn't resist him and picked up the phone and said hello.

"Oh…" He paused for a few seconds. "Hi."

"You sound surprised."

"I am, a little."

She laughed. "But you called me."

"I did, but I wasn't expecting you to answer at this time of day."

"A potential client managed to double-book himself and even though he clearly needs some help with his scheduling organization, I'm the one he rescheduled. What's up?"

He chuckled. "I spent half the morning rehearsing the voicemail message I was going to leave and had no backup plan for if you actually picked up."

Her stomach clenched when the obvious reason for him deliberately calling at a time he didn't anticipate her answering flashed through her mind. He just wanted to leave a quick message telling her he'd had a good time and enjoyed their kiss, but that he had a lot on his plate and wasn't looking for a relationship right now. But he hoped she'd still pop into Kincaid's for the fundraiser to support the cause.

The disappointment was an almost physical ache, but it was for the best, so she'd make it easy for him. "I'd hate for all that prep time to be wasted, so pretend I didn't answer and tell me the message. *Beep.*"

"Hey, Olivia, it's Derek. I just wanted to tell you I had a great time last night—it was the best night I've had in a long time, actually—and I can't wait to see you at Kincaid's, so I really do hope you'll come." There was a brief pause, and then a low chuckle. "That was it, so I guess this is where I'd hang up."

"Don't," she said quickly, but then she had no idea what to say next. She was still processing the fact he hadn't been taking the easy way out in dialing things back before he saw her in person again. "I…I had a good time, too."

"Does your cancellation leave enough time for lunch?"

She wanted to say yes—she *really* wanted to say yes—but if she factored in the time it would take them to meet somewhere, it didn't. They'd barely have time to chug a coffee, never mind eat anything. And she'd be off her game all afternoon because Derek had that effect on her. Especially if he kissed her again.

And she really wanted him to kiss her again.

"I can't today. Or at all this week," she said honestly. "My schedule's pretty booked and I didn't…"

I didn't see you coming.

She didn't say the words out loud, but she felt them deep inside. She'd built a good, solid life and career with careful planning and execution and then Derek Gilman had come out of nowhere. And she still didn't know what to do about that.

"I figured as much," he said, "but I'll repeat the part

about how much I hope you'll make it to Kincaid's Saturday night."

"I'll be there," she said, wincing as she made the statement without leaving any wiggle room for getting her priorities back in order and changing her mind.

"Good. I can't wait to see you again."

The way his voice lowered as he said the words made her body sizzle with anticipation and her hand tightened around the phone. It was all too easy to imagine that voice in the dark, his breath hot against her ear as he told her all the naughty things he wanted to do to her.

"Olivia?"

"I'm still here," she said in a breathy rush that didn't give her time to think about what she should say. "I can't wait to see you, either."

"I'll let you get back to work, but I'll talk to you soon."

"Bye, Derek." The phone beeped to let her know the call had ended and she set her phone back on the counter. Carefully, since her hand was shaking slightly.

"I guess you probably heard that," she said in a barely raised voice.

Kelsey's laughter rang through the apartment. "Hell yeah, I did."

Friday was a pain-in-the-ass day. While Derek didn't wish catastrophic events on anybody, the constant in-and-out for stupid shit wore on his nerves after a few hours.

Like idiots who managed to forget they put pizza rolls in toaster ovens and filled their offices with smoke, setting the alarms off and forcing an evacuation.

"You've gotta be kidding," Derek said, yanking the

plug out of the wall. "How do you not set a timer for pizza rolls?"

"I don't," Gavin said. "But mostly because I stare at them until they're done. I wonder if they have any more of these, less well done."

"Seriously?"

He shrugged. "I'm starving."

"You're always starving. Let's get this out of here so we can clear the place."

Once they were done and gave the all clear to the guys in ties and rolled-up shirtsleeves standing around outside smoking and talking on their phones, they headed for the trucks.

"Hey, are you guys going to reimburse us for that toaster oven?" one of the guys called after them.

They all paused, but it was Rick who spoke. "What's that?"

"The door broke when you dropped it on the sidewalk, so are you going to buy us a new toaster oven? That one's garbage now."

Rick chuckled. "Sure thing. Send a bill to the mayor's office and let me know how that works out for you."

The guy was still calling them names when they climbed—laughing even though they probably shouldn't— into the trucks. And the mood only improved when they got back to the house and Scott told them he had a line on some Red Sox tickets.

"Who's in? The guy thinks he can get me six seats if we need them."

"I'm in," Derek said, at almost the same instant Gavin did.

"My name better be on one," Aidan yelled from the other side of the bay.

"I'm out," Grant said.

Gavin whipped his head around so fast, Derek was surprised he didn't give himself whiplash. "What the hell are you talking about? You never miss out on games."

"I'm saving my money."

"For what?"

"Something."

Derek probably would have minded his own business at that point, but Gavin didn't seem to have any qualms about forcing the issue. "It's the Yankees at Fenway, dude. What could possibly be more important than that?"

"I'm saving up to buy a ring for Wren, okay?"

"No shit," Gavin said, and then he grinned and stuck out his hand. "Congratulations, man."

Grant shook his best friend's hand, but Derek didn't miss the way his brow furrowed. "Thanks, but there's nothing to congratulate yet. I need to find a perfect ring and then, you know…ask her."

"Guys are dropping like flies around here," Chris said. "Pretty soon there won't be any single guys left to stand outside and flirt with the pretty women."

"Hey," Derek said, holding up his hands. "I'm not getting married again anytime soon."

Rick looked up from the clipboard he'd been writing on. "Really? Because I've heard a few things about that woman you were stuck in the elevator with."

That got everybody's attention in a hurry. "You sure as hell didn't hear that I'm marrying her."

"No, but rumor has it you were making googly eyes at each other during the last Village Hearts meeting."

"Googly eyes? Are you fucking kidding me with

that?" Derek laughed. "There is no way in hell Jess used those words."

"No, but she said there was so much sexual tension between you she was surprised the air wasn't sizzling, and that made me want a steak so I stopped listening after that."

"She was hot," Scott said, as if Derek needed a reminder. "You guys were stuck in there for a while, too."

"While I tended to her injury." That was an exaggeration and it did nothing but remind him of how soft her skin was.

"She's a little out of your league, though," Scott continued.

That struck a nerve, though he did his best not to let it show. Yeah, she was out of his league. No matter how much he tried to tell himself it was a bullshit phrase that didn't mean anything, it really did. While the chemistry between them might sizzle like a steak when they were together on neutral ground, he was a burger and she was filet mignon. Wrapped in bacon.

"Good thing I'm not looking to play ball, then," he lied.

As he'd hoped, the playing ball reminded them they'd been talking about Red Sox tickets and—other than a lingering, skeptical look from Jess's husband—they jumped back to that topic.

Derek tuned them out and then headed upstairs. The way this day was going, it wasn't going to be long before somebody threw a cigarette butt in a trash can without putting it out or got upset because a cat was sitting in a tree, so he was going to grab a snack while he could.

She's out of your league.

They lived two very different kinds of lives, and it

wasn't just about the money, although that was a big part of it. Her life was her own, to plan and live exactly how she wanted it and she seemed to like it that way. His life wasn't his own and hadn't been for a very long time.

Since he surprised her with the call during the day on Monday, they'd spoken on the phone every night. On Wednesday night, he'd put his cell phone out of reach and tried to focus his attention on the TV screen to make the time pass. He felt as if he was rushing into something that could be a dead end, and he was determined to put a little space between them. Maybe cool things off.

But when his phone rang, he couldn't help walking over to it and as soon as he saw her name on the screen, he'd forgotten about his doubts and answered. They talked about their days and expanded on the ideas they'd brainstormed at dinner. Last night they'd discovered they both watched a legal drama series and they'd watched together—almost perfectly timing hitting play on Hulu. Her voice on the phone as she tried to guess at the show's twists and turns wasn't quite as good as having her on the couch next to him, but he hadn't minded.

When it was just the two of them, whether they were having a dinner or talking on the phone, it was easy to forget that nothing about their lives seemed compatible. And tomorrow, when he finally got to see her again at Kincaid's, he knew he'd forget everything but her the second she stepped into the bar.

One kiss and it was too late, he thought as he stared into the pantry with no idea what he was in the mood to eat. It was too late to go back and let her leave the charity meeting without a word from him. Or, hell, to go back to the day they got stuck in the elevator and take the stairs instead.

It was too late to wonder if he should get too serious because he wasn't sure if he and his kids could ever fit in her life. And it was definitely too late to take back that kiss because he knew, no matter what happened, he didn't really want to.

Even though he knew he didn't have much of a shot at going the full nine innings, when it came to Olivia, he wanted to play ball.

Chapter Six

Olivia couldn't remember the last time she'd been to a bar. Probably in college, which was when she'd discovered that in Boston, any establishment with a television and a liquor license was a de facto sports bar if a game was on the screen.

She might have missed Kincaid's Pub entirely if Derek hadn't given her such good directions on top of the street address printed on the promotional materials. Her Lyft driver had found the address with no problem, but it had taken her a few seconds to spot the small sign over a glass door flanked by two high and long glass windows in a very unassuming building. Clearly Kincaid's didn't feel a need to announce their presence to the public at large.

But when she stepped inside, she was met by the kind of establishment she'd been expecting. Brick and wood, with sports photos and fire memorabilia hung on the walls. There was a massive U-shaped bar, and the place was probably only a few more customers shy of their occupancy limit.

Even though it was probably an exercise in futility, she looked around for Derek. She also kept an eye out for Jess or anybody else she'd recognize from the board, but mostly she was looking for him.

Her thoughts had been spinning out of control since she left him at the restaurant. She'd even had trouble concentrating on work all week, which was problematic, to say the least. And every night, she waited for his call. She started thinking about it as she put her work away— or even before then, if she was honest with herself—and changed into her comfy clothes. Would he call? She'd found herself practically vibrating with anticipation as she waited. And on Wednesday night, when he hadn't called, she'd thought maybe he was with his kids and tried to put him out of her mind. That hadn't worked and when she thought it was late enough so small kids would be in bed, but not *too* late, she'd taken a deep breath and called him before she could change her mind.

It was the same feeling she'd had when she pulled open the door to the bar tonight. Compelled to go in and see him, but knowing she had to do it quickly before she could change her mind.

He kissed me.

He has children and an ex-wife.

I don't have time for a relationship right now.

I want him to kiss me again.

His having an ex-wife had thrown her for a loop. Hearing he had children had thrown her for a loop. And his kiss had definitely thrown her for a loop. Basically her emotional state was a bad carnival ride, and if she didn't find a way to get off, she was going to make herself sick.

But when their eyes met across the room and she watched his face light up as he saw her, she was ready to hand over her ticket and get right back on the ride.

There was something about looking at him that made her breath catch in her chest. There were probably guys in the crowd around her who were hotter in a general sense, or younger or more what she'd always considered her type, but she didn't care. Ever since getting stuck in the elevator with him, her type had been narrowed down to Derek Gilman.

Rather than just waving her over, he said something to the guy he'd been speaking to and started making his way through the crowd toward her. Since people kept trying to talk to him, she knew it would take a minute, so she opened the wallet case she'd put on her phone for the night while she waited. There was a donation bucket at the end of the bar and she reached between two customers to drop some cash in.

By the time she was done, Derek had reached her. "You made it."

"I told you I would. This is quite a place."

He looked around, and she could see the affection he had for it on his face. "Yeah. It's a little worn around the edges, but it's comfortable and homey."

"Like a favorite old pair of jeans."

"Exactly like that." He gave her a skeptical look. "Are you telling me you not only have jeans, but have a favorite old pair?"

She laughed. "Of course I have jeans. And yes, a favorite old pair that are worn so thin in the butt and the knees that I'm afraid to wear them out in public without tights under them. Who doesn't own jeans?"

His eyes dropped, sweeping over her pale blue, summer-weight sweater and black capris. She'd opted for black ballet flats over sandals tonight because she wasn't sure what to expect as far as the bar atmosphere, but she wasn't risking open toes.

"You just don't strike me as a jeans kind of woman, I guess."

It was a weird thing for him to say. "What does that even mean? Do you picture me running around doing errands and cleaning my apartment on the weekends in a skirt and high heels?"

She expected him to laugh, but he leaned closer so he could lower his voice. "When I picture you, you're not doing errands or cleaning your apartment. Or wearing a skirt."

Olivia's cheeks flushed with heat—along with other parts of her body—but she didn't look away. She just smiled and raised one eyebrow. "And the high heels?"

He blushed and gave her a sheepish grin, as if he hadn't expected her to respond in such a direct way. "I do like the shoes. But I wouldn't mind seeing you in those jeans, either."

She usually only wore them in the colder months, but she'd make an exception if a little denim could keep that look in his eye. "Maybe."

"I know they stocked up on the usual beer," he said, holding up his half-full glass, "but I don't know if there's a wine list. To be honest, I don't even know if they even *have* wine."

"A beer is fine. Whatever you've got." When his eyes widened, she laughed. "Yes, I drink beer. Not often, but on occasion. And one time, back in college, I even drank beer while wearing jeans."

It was his turn to laugh, and more than a few heads turned at the sound. "I deserved that."

Once he'd managed to push through the crowd at

Under Control

the bar to get her a beer, he nodded toward the back. "Jess and Rick are back there. And…well, pretty much everybody else."

As much as she'd like to find a relatively quiet corner and have Derek's company all to herself, this was a fundraiser, not a date. "Let's go say hi."

He led the way, and she said hi to Jessica and was reintroduced to her husband, Rick. There were so many names she knew she'd never remember them all, except maybe Aidan and Scotty, from the great elevator escape. Derek seemed to know everybody, of course, and when somebody yelled his name, he raised his hand in greeting.

And when he dropped his hand, it came to rest at the small of her back and Olivia felt as if she was standing at a crossroads. While Olivia only really knew Jess, these were Derek's friends and coworkers and it was something of a *claiming* gesture. Anybody looking at them would assume they were a couple, or on their way to being one.

Yes, they'd kissed. They talked on the phone every night this week. And she wanted him to kiss her again. But being an actual couple was a commitment and the part of her brain still embracing logic over libido shied away from that possibility.

She could stick to her carefully structured plan for herself and step away from his touch. Temptation didn't *have* to be acted upon, and often shouldn't be. Or she could throw caution—and a lifetime of lessons learned—to the wind and lean in. Logically, she knew which was the right choice. She should move away.

She leaned in.

Not a lot. But she shifted slightly toward him, leaning against his hand, and his fingertips pressed a little more firmly in response.

She'd worry about her carefully structured plan tomorrow. Which was probably what she'd told herself yesterday. But with Derek's arm around her and a beer in her hand, she didn't care.

As far as Derek was concerned, the fundraiser was a success. He didn't need to wait for the official accounting to know they'd raised a lot of money for Village Hearts. And everybody was having a fun time, with not a single fight breaking out. While Tommy ran a pretty tight ship, anything could happen with a full house.

And, maybe most important to him, Olivia was having a good time. While she probably only saw the fundraiser aspect, for Derek it was more than that. These people were like family and Kincaid's Pub was like an extension of home for most of the firefighters in the neighborhood, but especially for Engine 59 and Ladder 37. While he shied away from thinking too much about *why*, her liking the people she was meeting tonight mattered to him.

He didn't stray far from her side over the course of the night, but sometimes she'd wander away in conversation with somebody and then he'd hear her laugh. Or he'd glance over to find her watching him and they'd share a smile. It felt good to have that connection again, and he could imagine them coming here often. Playing pool. Laughing. Enjoying the company of friends and each other.

If only she didn't live on the other side of the city.

Scott walked over to him, an almost empty mug of

beer in his hand. "You waiting to shoot some pool or is this just a good vantage point for watching Olivia?"

"Is it that obvious?"

"Some guy actually asked me if I knew you, because he was concerned about the way you were staring at her."

Derek snorted, but then he forced himself to turn his body so she wasn't directly in his line of sight anymore. "Is Jamie here? I haven't seen her."

"No, she had to work. Did you and Olivia come together?"

"No."

"You leaving together?" He scowled at Scott, who only held up one hand defensively. "Just making conversation. You guys are obviously a thing."

"We're not really anything." *Yet.*

"Bullshit. Anybody who's seen you together knows you're a thing."

Derek took a long swallow of his beer, unable to resist turning his head enough to catch a glimpse of Olivia over the rim of his mug. "You're the one who said she's out of my league. And she is."

Scott laughed, drawing attention Derek didn't want. "Dude, I was just busting your balls when I said that."

"Doesn't make it wrong."

"You can't be fucking serious right now. She seems like a cool chick and you guys obviously hit it off, so don't be stupid."

Scott shook his head and walked away before Derek could say anything else. Not that he would have, anyway, because Olivia was making her way back to him. As usual, seeing her made every thought except how much he wanted her fly out of his head.

"He looked annoyed, and you look serious all of a sudden," Olivia said, nodding her head in the direction Scott had gone.

"He's always annoyed, and I was missing you."

She laughed and leaned against him. "I was ten feet away."

"Having a good time?"

"Yes. Everybody's been really nice, once they got the elevator jokes out of their systems." Her chuckle let him know she'd taken it all in fun. "And Cait has the best stories. Being an EMT sounds…interesting."

"Firefighters have better stories," he felt obliged to say.

"You'll have to tell me some, then, because I find it hard to believe you can top Cait's."

The more opportunities he had to tell her stories, the better, as far as he was concerned. "Challenge accepted. And remind me to start with the story about Cait pushing a firefighter down the stairs."

The sound of a glass shattering brought conversation around them to a halt, and then they watched as Lydia—the bartender and Aidan's wife—said something to a red-faced patron and pointed to the framed photo of Bobby Orr on the wall.

"What's going on?" Olivia whispered.

"If you break a glass, you have to kiss Bobby Orr."

"That doesn't sound…hygienic."

"Well, you kiss your fingertips and then press them to the glass. Which, now that I think about it, isn't much better. But bad things happen if you don't do it. Trust me."

She snorted as the customer pressed his fingers to the glass and the crowd—jinx safely averted—went back to their conversations. "I don't really believe a lot in luck or superstition."

"Nope, you're definitely not from Boston."

She laughed. "My entire life is built around the premise that anything can be accomplished with a well-executed plan. Luck has nothing to do with planning."

"Not everything can be planned."

"Everything that matters can be."

"I don't know about that." He put his arm around her shoulders, dropping his head close to hers. "You didn't plan to get stuck in an elevator with me."

"So you think that was luck?" She turned toward him slightly, so he could see the smile tugging at the corner of her mouth.

"It was definitely something," he said, and then he kissed her temple. "I'd like to take you out on a proper date."

She smiled. "A *proper* date? What constitutes a proper date for you? You picking me up at my door with flowers? A restaurant with cloth napkins?"

"There are restaurants with cloth napkins?" He tucked her hair behind her ear, his gaze lingering on the sparkly blue stone in her earlobe. It wasn't as dark as a sapphire and it almost matched her eyes. "I mean, like an actual date. Not using brainstorming as an excuse to have dinner with you or this fundraiser as an excuse to hang out with you here. And definitely not being stuck in an elevator."

"Cute first date story, though. And yes, I'd like to go on a proper date with you."

"Now comes the fun part."

"Scheduling it." She held up her hands. "And I don't even have my planner with me."

"Should I have my people call your people?" he teased.

"No. Definitely don't call my people or I'll never hear the end of it."

"When I brought the kids back to their mom's for the night so I could come here without hiring a sitter, I told them I'd take them for pizza and bowling tomorrow night to make up for it." It was on the tip of his tongue to ask if she'd want to come along, but he stopped himself. He hadn't even told the kids he might be dating somebody, and he wanted to see if the relationship had any chance of sticking before he introduced her into their lives. Wanting it to and making it happen were two different things. "Tuesdays and Fridays are out for me, obviously."

"How about Monday night? I know it's short notice, but my last meeting of the day will be with a custom home builder in Brookline, so I could meet you somewhere on the way back through the city."

He wasn't sure that totally lived up to his idea of a proper date. Picking her up and surprising her with reservations somewhere nice was more of what he'd had in mind, but there were the logistics to consider. If he turned down a Monday meet-up, it would probably be the following weekend before he saw her again and he didn't want to wait that long. Short notice worked for him.

"That sounds great. Do you want me to pick the place again?" When she grinned sheepishly, he laughed. "You want to go back to the *same* place again?"

"I'm not done with that menu," she confessed. "But no planner this time. Just us."

"I like the sound of that. How did you get here tonight? Do you want me to—" He stopped talking, trying to remember how many beers he'd had. And if he couldn't remember, it was more than two. "Shit."

"I guess the better question is how *you* got here tonight. And how you're getting home."

"Gavin and Cait picked me up, and she's not drinking. I was going to borrow his truck, but…I can ask her to drive us, if you want."

"I'm fine with a Lyft, I promise."

"Isn't that a pain in the ass? And expensive?"

She shrugged. "Sometimes. I have a car, you know."

That's right. She'd driven to the Village Hearts meeting. "What kind of car?"

"A silver one," she said, and he laughed. "A silver Audi, actually, but I spent so much time trying to find addresses and then trying to find a place to park and then walking back to the address I was going to—and too often being late because of it—that I realized it was more efficient and even cost-effective in the long run to let somebody else drive."

"Unless you're coming all the way across the city," he pointed out. She held up her now empty glass and he nodded. As much as he wished one of them had a vehicle so they could go somewhere else—like maybe his place—making sure nobody drove drunk was important to everybody at Kincaid's, so he liked that about her.

"I think I'll go ahead and order a ride now," she said. "It's getting late and I have a rule about not falling asleep in the back seat of strange cars."

Derek didn't want to think about that. He didn't even want to think about her being awake in a strange car, but it wasn't his place to dictate her transportation. And he wasn't in a position to offer an alternative at the moment. "That's a good rule."

Once she ordered a car, the clock was ticking on their night and they spent most of the remaining time circulating through the crowd so Olivia could say goodnight to the other members of the board and the members of his crew.

When it was time to go outside, he walked out with her. Their fingers were interlocked and it felt so good to walk hand in hand with her that he was tempted to ask her to cancel the car and just walk with him for a little while.

But then an image of her asleep in the back seat of a stranger's car flashed through his mind and his fingers tightened around hers.

"You okay?"

"Yeah." He knew it was probably the safest way for her to travel if she didn't want to drive herself, but that didn't mean he had to like it. "Of course I'm okay. I finally have a good reason to look forward to a Monday."

She laughed, and he let go of her hand to wrap his arm around her shoulders and pull her close. Going in for the kiss was easier than jumping out of a plane this time, but the feeling it gave him was no less exhilarating.

When he heard a car pull up and slow, he reluctantly ended it. "Send me a text when you know about what time you'll arrive Monday. And please text me when you get home tonight so I don't lie in bed worrying about you falling asleep in a stranger's car."

She laughed. "I will. Enjoy your pizza and bowling night."

Once she was in the car, he waved and then shoved

his hands in his pockets. He knew once he went back inside, the guys were going to grill him about Olivia. Especially Scott, probably, since he'd made it clear he thought she was out of Derek's league. And they'd probably ask a lot of questions he didn't know the answers to yet.

But the one answer he did know made him smile as he pulled open the glass door. Yes, he and Olivia were officially *dating*.

Chapter Seven

Derek was never going to get used to ringing his own damn doorbell. It wasn't his anymore, and hadn't been for a while, but the small cape had been his for a long time. Standing on the front step, waiting for somebody to answer the door would never feel right.

Amber had met Jason two weeks after Derek moved out and they'd hit it off immediately. Even Derek had to admit they were perfect for each other. At first he'd felt some jealousy and sometimes even anger, but seeing them together had gotten easier with time. Amber deserved to be happy, and Derek knew living in a happy home was the most important thing for his kids. And he'd seen the difference it made in them, and especially in Julia.

He wouldn't mind having some of that happy home stuff for himself, though. Eventually.

Jason answered the door. "Hey, Derek, come on in."

It was never easy walking into the living room—and maybe never would be—but like everything else about the divorce, he took comfort in believing they were all better off for it. And the new furniture helped. It wasn't really *his* living room anymore.

"Amber's in the kitchen, doing her grocery list. The

kids will probably be a few more minutes because they have to finish putting their laundry away before they can go."

"Thanks. How are things?"

"Good. And you?"

"Good." That was usually as far as they got in conversation unless Amber or the kids were part of it—not because of animosity, but because they didn't have a lot in common—so Derek went into the kitchen.

"The kids are almost ready."

"Laundry. Jason told me. Do you mind if I help myself to a soda?"

She chuckled and shook her head. "Of course not."

He went to the fridge and grabbed a soda. She didn't care if he got himself a drink and he knew it, but it didn't seem right to go into the fridge as if it was his own, just as it didn't seem right to walk in without ringing the doorbell. Amber didn't feel the same way, since half the time she walked into his apartment without knocking, but it was different. His apartment was just his apartment. This house was Jason's house now.

"So, I heard you were kissing Olivia McGovern at the pub," she said out of the blue, and he almost choked on his drink.

"What?"

"You heard me."

He wasn't sure why she sounded…maybe not mad, but at least a little unhappy. It shouldn't be jealousy, since she literally had a new husband. "Yeah, I heard you."

She looked at him while the seconds ticked away, until the silence became too much for her. "And?"

"And what?"

Maybe they got along better now than the last few years of their marriage, but she'd given him a few lectures when she first started dating Jason about how her personal life was only his business when it involved their children. He'd had some trouble wrapping his head around the concept since everything she did affected their children—especially bringing a man he didn't know into their lives—but they'd eventually found a balance. This was the first time he'd been on this end of the boundary blurring, though.

"Derek."

"What are you after here, Amber? Yes, I kissed a woman at Kincaid's." He refrained from pointing out she was doing a lot more than kissing the man in the other room because it wasn't relevant and he wasn't getting into a pissing match with her.

"No, you kissed a woman who's brand-new to the charity and, from what I'm hearing, is going to be a huge asset. I just don't want you to scare her off."

"Thanks. That's really flattering." Then he chuckled, because he knew what she was getting at. "Olivia's not a woman who scares easily, I don't think. And it's not like she walked through the door and I pounced on her. We'd met once, before either of us knew the other was with Village Hearts, and we had a brainstorming dinner together before the fundraiser at the pub."

"Oh." Then she smiled. "Oh?"

"Aren't you the one who was preaching boundaries when it came to dating other people?" he asked, but with no heat in his voice.

"Wait. Are you actually *dating* this Olivia woman? I mean, I want things to go smoothly for her with the charity, but I want you to find an awesome woman to date even more."

He knew she did. While she didn't push at him, he knew Amber wanted him to fall head over heels in love with a woman. Mostly because she genuinely wanted the best for him. But also because a little part of her felt guilty that she'd found the love of her life and was living happily ever after with him and their children while Derek was alone.

"I guess we're in the early days of actually dating, you could say. There was the kiss, and we're going to go out again tomorrow night."

"That's really great, Derek." She smiled, but it quickly faded and she got that pinched look between her eyebrows. "So I heard she lives in some fancy high-rise in the Back Bay or someplace like that?"

Jess sure hadn't wasted any time running to Amber with gossip. He knew they'd become very good friends through Village Hearts but had the woman been texting her *from* Kincaid's? And he couldn't really do anything to discourage it. Not only had Jess become a very valuable asset to the charity, but she was his lieutenant's wife.

"Some place like that." When the pinch turned into a frown, he knew she'd fast-forwarded right to the hard questions that didn't need to be asked yet. Yes, it would make co-parenting a lot harder if he was that far away, and Olivia certainly wasn't going to give up a fancy high-rise apartment to move into his not-fancy, post-divorce apartment with him. "I said *early* days of dating, Amber. You're not only putting the cart before the horse, but you don't even *have* a horse yet."

"I don't even know what that means," she said, and

they were laughing when the kids came in with their backpacks.

Since going out for pizza and bowling would be fun enough, they were just going to hang out at home until it was time. He'd managed to find a three-bedroom he could afford by sacrificing overall size and living with the building's need for a remodel, and it always struck Derek as odd that it felt empty and huge when he was alone and not nearly big enough when the kids were with him.

They'd just finished a light lunch when his son threw him a curveball.

"Will you be the new baby's stepdad?" Isaac asked, and Derek paused, having absolutely no idea what his son was talking about.

"What new baby?" he asked at the exact same time Julia shrieked her brother's name.

"It's a secret, stupid," she hissed at him.

"Don't call your brother stupid," he said automatically. But his mind was spinning.

"Mom said not to tell anybody yet." Julia looked at him with a serious expression. "I don't know why they told Isaac. He never keeps secrets."

Amber was pregnant. He sat back in his chair, trying to process how he felt about that in the time he had before he opened his mouth. And that wouldn't be long, since both kids were staring at him, waiting for his reaction.

For some reason, he hadn't even considered the possibility. After Isaac was born—and even after he was healthy and the fear was behind them—Derek and Amber had agreed that two kids were enough for them. Neither of them had gotten around to any permanent measures to make that happen, but they'd taken precautions to ensure there wouldn't be any surprises.

But Jason didn't have kids of his own. They'd fallen in love and gotten married, so the next step for a lot of people was having a baby. Derek should have seen it coming, but he hadn't. And now he had his two kiddos looking to him for his reaction.

"A new baby is exciting," he said finally, sidestepping Isaac's question. He'd give Amber a heads-up that they needed to figure out how to explain the biology and legalities of the impending new dynamic in very simple terms. "Are you excited?"

They both shrugged, but Julia did the talking. "It'll be weird. Babies cry a lot."

"They're cute, though," Isaac mumbled. "Everybody loves babies."

"Everybody loves both of you, too," Derek said, ruffling his son's hair. "Loving a baby doesn't mean less love for you."

"Will you love the new baby, too?"

"The baby is going to be your little brother or sister, so yes, I will care about the new baby. But I will never love anybody more than I love the two of you. I promise." They both smiled at him. "And your mom and Jason will give the baby a lot of attention because little babies *need* a lot of attention because they can't do anything, but your mom loves you like crazy, too."

"I'm glad you don't have a girlfriend, Daddy," Julia said. "I don't want you to get married and have new babies, too."

Ouch.

"Can we play video games now?" Isaac asked.

Even though he usually held out a little longer because he liked hearing about all the stuff he missed, today he nodded his approval on the first ask. He wanted out of this conversation. "For one hour, then we'll start getting ready for bowling."

As he watched them powering on the video game console and arguing over who got to be player one, he thought about Amber and how the new baby was going to change everything. Especially for Julia and Isaac.

Jason was a good guy and he genuinely loved his stepchildren, so Derek didn't think they'd get pushed aside for his own child. It was still going to be a huge adjustment for the entire family, though, and especially for the kids.

I'm glad you don't have a girlfriend, Daddy.

Obviously now wasn't the time to bring up the subject of Daddy having a new girlfriend. He leaned his head back with a sigh and closed his eyes. If the kids were feeling insecure after the news of Amber's pregnancy, he'd wait a while before talking to them about Olivia, he decided.

It didn't feel right, almost like living two separate lives. But he'd make it work for now and hope that, when the time was right, Olivia and the kids would meet and hit it off because his kids were his entire life, but he was really starting to like having Olivia in it, too.

The restaurant could have been burning down around them and Olivia wasn't sure she'd be able to tear her gaze away from the man sitting across the table from her.

For the last hour, they'd talked and laughed, taking their time with the meal. They'd had a drink first, and then picked at an appetizer before ordering their dinners. And he'd told the server they'd like a few minutes to relax before looking at the dessert menu.

Olivia didn't care if they stayed all night. At some point in the evening, he'd unbuttoned the cuffs of the light blue button-down shirt he was wearing and folded them back.

She'd long ago admitted to herself she couldn't resist the combination of heat and humor in his expression whenever they were together, but she was surprised by how much the sight of his hands and the tanned skin of his forearms against the pale fabric turned her on. His hands were rough and callused, and he'd recently scraped a couple of knuckles on something. And all she could think about right now was how much she wanted those hands on her.

"Tell me how you got your scar," she said, trying to distract herself. "I mean, if you don't mind. If you don't want to talk about it, that's okay. I was just curious."

"I don't mind talking about it, but you'll probably be disappointed. Most people expect it to be from some kind of line-of-duty act of heroism."

"I'd be lying if I said I didn't make that assumption. Not that it was an act of heroism, necessarily, but that you got hurt while working."

"When I was twelve, I was helping my dad lay new sheathing and shingles on our roof and I slipped. I managed not to fall off, but I caught the edge of the nail I'd been pounding on the way down to the edge."

She winced, trying not to imagine what that had looked—or felt—like. Especially when it was so pronounced this many years later. Of course, he didn't strike her as the kind of guy who was big on creams and sunscreens. "Ouch."

"It was the first time I ever swore in front of my mother."

"I bet she didn't mind."

He laughed. "I don't think she even heard me. She was too busy yelling those same words at my old man for having me up there in the first place."

"I gather she'd told him so?"

He grinned. "Oh, she'd definitely told him so."

"Did you grow up here?"

"On the north shore. My parents still live there, and I have a brother and a sister. Both younger and, trust me, they were never allowed on the roof."

She laughed, wondering what it was like to have siblings. Being an only child was not only lonely at times, but she didn't have anybody to split her parents' focus with. There was no *hey, look what my sister's doing* when it got too hot under the magnifying glass.

"What about your family?" he asked. "Other than in Virginia and no longer married to each other, of course. Are you still close? Siblings?"

While she was curious about his family, hers was probably the last thing she wanted to talk about tonight. "It's just me. And I'm fairly close with both of them, I guess. Separately. I talk to them on a regular basis. My dad remarried, to a woman who had three kids from a previous marriage. All younger than me and I was already away at college, so I know them, but we're not close. And did I see strawberry shortcake on that dessert menu?"

She could see he noticed the deliberate subject change, and was thankful when he let it go. "You did, and it's delicious. They make the biscuits themselves. And the whipped cream."

"I shouldn't. I really shouldn't."

"Then I will, and you can sneak as many bites as you want."

They ate it slowly, as if they had an unspoken agreement to stretch it out as long as possible. But when she put down her fork because the ice cream had melted and joined forces with the strawberries to turn the last of the biscuit into mush, Derek pushed the plate to one side.

"After-dessert coffee?" he asked her as the server approached.

She groaned at the idea of putting anything else in her stomach, but she didn't want to leave, either. "One. But decaf."

Once the dessert plates were cleared and they'd fixed their coffees, Derek leaned forward. He rested his forearms on the table when he did it, which brought her attention right back to them. "I'm out of ways to keep you here, so don't be surprised if it takes me a *really* long time to drink this."

"Me, too. Baby sips." And unable to resist the urge anymore, she reached out and stroked his arm, from his wrist to the edge of the rolled-up cuff.

"This probably sounds weird, but you have really great arms and I've wanted to do that all night."

"Trust me, you're welcome to touch any part of my body you want."

"That would be a scandal this restaurant would never forget."

She watched the words sink in—the admission she wanted to touch him in places she couldn't touch him in public—and for a moment his expression was so intense, she thought he might haul her across the table and onto his lap.

"You're worth the risk of being on the eleven o'clock news for."

It was the weirdest and yet most romantic thing a man had ever said to her, and Olivia shivered. "I bet handcuffs are a lot sexier in theory."

"And there's a good chance I'd know the officers responding and never hear the end of it." The muscles in his forearm twitched under her trailing touch. "I'm on tomorrow, so it's an early alarm for a twenty-four-hour shift."

"I have an eight-o'clock meeting in the Seaport." She didn't even want to think about what time she'd have to get up in order to leave this part of the city in time to make it home, shower and get dressed, and make the meeting by eight. Dark o'clock, and in the height of summer, that was saying something.

"We can make this happen." He pulled out his phone. "I don't have the kids next weekend. Amber's hosting a couple of Village Hearts kids for a few days and they'll be there through the weekend. Since they don't have school, I'll just grab Julia and Isaac Wednesday morning and bring them home Thursday night instead."

Olivia wanted to ask how that worked—if he'd have to fight his ex to change up the schedule—because he didn't seem to get that tenseness in his voice when speaking of his ex that her parents and almost everybody else she knew did. But she didn't want to interrupt where this conversation was heading by discussing his failed marriage.

Since she'd come straight from a meeting and therefore had it with her, she reached into her bag and pulled out her planner, clearing the space in front of her to set it down.

"Hey, I thought there was a no planner rule for tonight."

She paused in the act of opening it and gave him a guilty smile. "I know, but I had it with me for the meeting. And since I have it, I may as well use it. Plus, you used your phone. Same thing."

"I'm teasing you. I don't care if you have it open all the time as long as it gets my name in there." He leaned over and tapped the very small empty space at the bottom of the Saturday box. "Just write it in. *Have great sex with Derek.*"

"I'm not writing that in my planner."

"Why not? If you don't write it down, it's a thought, not a plan. Isn't that what you said?" He gave her a grin that had her smiling back. "And put *great* in block letters."

"Managing expectations isn't one of your better skills."

"Sure it is."

Why did he have to look at her like that? Like he really had an expectation that sex between them would be great?

Because it probably would, she told herself. "You're setting the bar pretty high for yourself."

"I work well under pressure. Very, *very* well."

She did it. She pulled out the pen—with the heavy black ink that couldn't be erased if she changed her mind—and wrote him in. *Have GREAT sex with Derek.*

He made a low growling sound of pleasure that made her want to accelerate that particular appointment. "You might want to write *sleep late* in the Sunday block, too."

She laughed. "Now you're pushing it."

"There," he said when she closed the book. "That was easy."

Easy? She was already making a mental to-do list. Shaving her legs, for one thing. And she couldn't remember the last time she'd bought sex-worthy underwear. There was also the *what to wear* question. Was he going to take her out to dinner first, or was she just supposed to show up at his door, naked under a trench coat?

"Waiting until Saturday won't be easy, though," he added, and she had to agree. "And you keep coming all the way over here, so I think it's time I come to you."

Other than Wes for the occasional on-site staff meeting, there hadn't been any men in Olivia's apartment. She didn't date often and certainly hadn't gotten to know a guy well enough to bring him into her space. But when she thought about Derek in her apartment—in her bed—it felt right, so she nodded.

"I'll tell them you'll be parking in my guest spot and text you the info. And I'll leave your name downstairs." When he arched an eyebrow, she just shrugged. "I wouldn't exactly call it security, but I like knowing somebody's keeping an eye on who comes and goes in the building. And I'll cook for you."

"Really?"

She laughed. "Let me rephrase that. I'll have to think about the cooking, but I promise to provide a meal for you. How's that?"

"Sounds perfect." He reached over with his free hand and covered hers, sandwiching it between his arm and his hand. "Did you drive yourself or take a Lyft?"

"Lyft." She'd considered driving herself, but she talked herself out of it because it would have made things more awkward if she decided to go home with him. It had been a very strong possibility until work rained on the parade.

"Then go ahead and order a ride and then I'll kiss you on the sidewalk until it shows up. Maybe I'll get lucky and it'll get a flat tire."

Olivia, it's your mother. Call me.

Olivia stared at the phone sitting on the counter next to her as though it were a snake about to strike. The text had come through while she was in the shower, and she hadn't responded to it yet. It hadn't been very long since her last call to her mom, so the message had been a surprise and when it came to Adam and Deborah McGovern, there were very few *pleasant* surprises.

It seemed to her that if it was an emergency, her mother would have said so. If it wasn't, she could have simply referenced the topic in her text message. Call me so I can complain about your father and make you feel guilty for moving to Massachusetts. Deb didn't text very often, so she tended toward being abrupt and to the point, but Olivia wouldn't have minded a hint to what she was in for.

She didn't have time to call her right now. She had to leave for her first meeting in twenty minutes and if her mother was in the mood to talk, she was impossible to shake. Drinking her customary calling-mom cocktail so soon after eating breakfast wasn't an option, either.

Lunch, she thought. She wouldn't have a cocktail, but maybe she'd splurge on something fattening and eat while they talked. It was one of her mother's pet peeves, so ending the conversation early might give added value to the calories.

"I omitted one of your appointments."

Olivia looked over as Kelsey walked out of the office with her leather notebook in hand and scowled. "*Everything* goes on the master calendar."

"I used my discretion." She set the open notebook in front of Olivia and rested the tip of her index finger on the page.

Have GREAT sex with Derek.

"I admire your optimism," Kelsey said, clearly struggling to keep a straight face.

Olivia closed the book with a snap. She hadn't even thought about it when Kelsey arrived and, as always, took the planner into the office to update any new information from the day before. "In that case, I appreciate your discretion. And yes, I'm feeling optimistic, although the wording was Derek's idea."

"Wait. You scheduled this *together*?" She laughed. "That is so you. I guess the date went well last night?"

"Obviously."

"And you're not seeing him again until Saturday?"

"It's an almost forty-minute drive on a good day and in Boston, there are very few good traffic days. And he works today. Tomorrow and Thursday he'll have his kids. He works Friday." She put her hands up in a questioning gesture. "And you know as well as I do, I don't have room to take three hours out of my schedule on a weekday."

Kelsey cocked her head. "Three hours with an hour and a half for travel time? That's just plain sex. If you're having great-in-block-letters sex, it's going to take longer than that."

"Remind me to schedule something that requires me to leave before you get here on Monday morning."

"You'll have to come back eventually. You live here."

"Remember that whole 'I appreciate your discretion' thing?"

"Don't worry. I won't tell a single soul all the details you're going to tell me. Speaking of, his place or yours?"

"He's coming here."

"That's a big deal for you. You must really like this guy."

"I do."

"I bet we could come up with a reason for me to be just leaving as he arrives and I could meet—"

"No."

Kelsey laughed and went back to the office, while Olivia started getting ready to leave. And when she picked up the phone, she made a conscious effort to put her mother's text out of her mind. She couldn't afford to be distracted this morning. The hopefully new client she was meeting today had the potential to bring her a lot of business and she was bringing her A-game.

Several hours later, exhausted but thrilled to have been able to text the generate a contract text to Kelsey, Olivia bought a slice of pizza and a water before walking the short distance to a small park. Pizza was a particular weakness of hers—something that could be eaten mindlessly with one hand while watching TV or reading—so she only bought it by the slice for special occasions. This slice was part reward and part fortification.

She'd considered putting the call off until evening so she didn't ruin her current mood, but she didn't want to be on the phone with her mom if Derek called. He was working, but if he had down time, he'd probably call. So she took a few slow breaths to center herself and then tapped her mom's number.

"Hello, Olivia."

"Hi, Mom."

"I was beginning to wonder if my text got through to you and it doesn't tell me if it did or not."

She knew it didn't. She had the read receipt function turned off because people tended to be put off if they knew she'd read their text message but hadn't responded right away. People like clients. And her mother.

"I was in meetings. I called as soon as I could. What's going on?" Then she took a big bite off the end of the pizza slice, knowing from experience that she'd have plenty of time to chew before her mother took a breath.

"Your father's trying to kill me." And that was all she said, which left Olivia in the awkward position of trying to chew and swallow fast without choking. "Olivia? Did you hear me?"

"I'm here," she managed to say. Then she had to take a quick swig of water before she could say more. "Dad's not trying to kill you, Mom."

"He is."

"He's not. If he was capable of killing you, he would have done it years ago." As soon as the words left her mouth, Olivia wanted them back. Deb didn't like sarcasm any more than she liked her ex-husband. "I'm sorry. Why don't you back up a little bit and tell me what's going on, but an abridged version because I have a meeting soon."

"His stepdaughter wants to teach at the beauty school and you know Camilla, who opened it, is a dear friend of mine, and he had the audacity to ask me to put a good word in for her."

"And that's trying to kill you how?"

"You know how my blood pressure is, Olivia. Don't be sarcastic."

"Mom, he's just trying to use connections to help his stepdaughter out. You know as well as I do that's how the world works."

"I am *not* one of his connections. I want nothing to do with him or that woman he married. You remember what she called me."

"You said some pretty ugly things about her when they started dating, even though your divorce was already final." Olivia sighed, and then winced because her mother probably heard it over the line. "And her daughter has nothing to do with anything."

She already knew that diplomacy wouldn't work. As far as her mother was concerned, there was Team Adam and Team Deb, and then there was Olivia, who was the tug-of-war rope between them. And Deb's dismissive snort proved her right.

"Okay, Mom," she said in a firm voice, because this was ridiculous and she wanted to eat her pizza. "Imagine if I could land an important client, but I didn't get the contract because he was a friend of Marge and she doesn't like you any more than you like her."

"That's different."

"It's not. It's punishing a child for the decisions the parent made." *Not that they did anything wrong.* But she wasn't saying that out loud. It didn't matter that the divorce was in their rearview mirror. Her father's ex-wife and his current wife would go to their graves hating each other.

Olivia wanted nothing more than to hang up on her mother at that moment. She'd been dealing with the emotional fallout from the divorce and ensuing passive-aggressive warfare for years, but it was different now.

She was dating a man with an ex-wife and children. The thought of being the Marge to Amber's Deborah made her mouth go dry, and her stomach soured.

He hadn't said a bad word about his ex-wife yet, she reminded herself. And they'd found a way to work with Village Hearts amicably enough. But the thought that the animosity might be there, under the surface and waiting for a trigger—like Derek bringing another woman into the mix—before blowing up in their faces was a real fear.

"If you don't want to put in a good word for her, then don't," she told Deb, wanting desperately to get off the phone now. "But don't try to block her. If Camilla mentions her, simply say you don't know her at all, which is the truth. You're better than this, Mom."

"Fine. But I don't like it. And I don't like the fact your father seems to think he can ask me for a favor."

"That *is* a little surprising. But it's for his stepdaughter and he obviously cares about her. Now, I really have to run. I'm going to be late for a meeting."

Since punctuality was something Deb prized above all else, it worked. "Thank you for listening, honey. I'll talk to you soon."

When she'd tucked her phone away, Olivia leaned back against the bench and took another bite of her pizza. She'd earned this slice and she was going to enjoy it.

She also wasn't going to worry about Derek's ex-wife... too much. Yet. She was still getting to know him. He hadn't even hinted around about her meeting his kids, so he wasn't there yet, either. Borrowing trouble was a waste of mental and emotional energy.

And she wasn't going to let any of it ruin their date on Saturday. The pizza was an excellent treat, but she had no doubt great-in-block-letters sex with Derek was going to be so much better. She wasn't letting doubts or anything else spoil it.

Chapter Eight

Derek's small and *very* used car looked out of place in the line of luxury sedans and SUVs in the guest parking lot of the very tall and very shiny building Olivia lived in. He didn't bother looking for a silver Audi, since she'd told him residents parked in a private underground garage. But the woman at the front desk was friendly enough and gave him directions to the elevator after checking his name in her computer.

He stood outside her door without knocking for a moment, though. This was all very much out of his league, as Scott had said, and it was making him jumpy no matter how much he told himself it didn't matter. The address, the concierge, the view from the floor-to-ceiling window at the end of the hall when he stepped out of the elevator. All of that was just *stuff,* but it was very expensive stuff.

And it was the kind of expensive stuff Olivia was used to. She didn't seem to care that he wasn't, but maybe she hadn't realized yet just how much he wasn't used to it. She liked him and he liked her, and that's what he needed to remember, but seeing this world she lived in made it hard.

He was lifting his hand to knock when the door

opened, and he belatedly realized the woman down-stairs had probably told Olivia he was on his way up.

"Hi," was all he said, because she looked so damn pretty, and then he looked down and realized she was wearing jeans with high heels and his brain stopped functioning.

"I was worried you got lost," she said, stepping back to let him in.

"I was looking out that window," he lied, not want-ing her to know he'd been working up the courage to knock. "Nice view."

"The view's why I pay too much to live here," she said. "I have the same view in the living room and from my bedroom. Come on in."

The click of those black high heels across her floor made his dick so hard, he wasn't sure he'd be able to follow, but he managed. And she was right. The view of the water from her living room was worth the suffering.

"This is quite a place." He'd pictured something warmer, with a lot of decorations and throw pillows and color. But he supposed a woman whose job was ef-ficiency would probably keep clutter in her life to a min-imum. And it still suited her. Simple and elegant, and you could host a formal dinner party—albeit a small one—or curl up in sweatpants and watch a movie.

"Thank you. It's in a good location for me, and Kelsey and I use the second bedroom as an office, so I don't need to lease space that I'd rarely be in."

He nodded, but he didn't care about office space or Kelsey or any other damn thing right now. All he cared about right now was Olivia.

"You know," he said, closing the space between

them, "this is the first time you and I have been alone together behind closed doors."

"I was beginning to wonder if you have a thing for sidewalks."

"I have a thing for *you*, no matter where we are." He hooked his finger into the front pocket of her jeans and pulled her to him.

She cupped her hand behind his neck and when she pressed her body against his, she smiled. "Seems like you have a thing for jeans with high heels."

"I do now." He slid his hands down the curve of her ass. "But you've put me in a tough position because—"

"I haven't even started yet."

He chuckled. "I want to get you out of these jeans, but I'm also enjoying the sight of you in them."

Her fingernails scraped lightly over his neck before sliding into his hair. "I felt a little silly when I put them on. Jeans with high heels aren't something I usually wear around the house, just so you know."

"You will be when I think of you."

"Oh? Do you think of me often?"

He groaned and cupped her face in one hand. "I can barely think about anything *but* you since the day we met."

Then he kissed her and for the first time, he held nothing back. He claimed her mouth, his kiss growing deeper and more demanding until she whimpered and dug her fingernails into his back.

He wanted to bury himself in her—right here, on her floor—but he forced himself to ease back. She resisted for a few seconds, moving with him, but then she released him and opened her eyes.

She was gorgeous, with her lips moist from his kiss

and her cheeks flushed. The deep breath she took was a little ragged, and he fought the urge to kiss her some more. There would be plenty of time for that.

"What?" she asked. "Why are you looking at me like that?"

"I'm not sure how you feel about me walking through your door and pouncing on you. We can hang out for a while. Maybe watch a movie or something if you want." Then he frowned because that's what was missing. "Wait a minute. You don't have a TV?"

She laughed. "It's in my bedroom because that's where I really relax."

"Your bedroom." He nodded, pressing his lips together for a moment. "I can and will exercise restraint, but I can't lie. Watching a movie in your bedroom isn't going to be relaxing for me."

"I'm not as certain as you are about my ability to exercise restraint, so I doubt we'd make it through the opening credits anyway."

It was incredibly hot, the way she didn't feel a need to be coy about the fact she wanted him as much as he wanted her.

"I did promise you a meal, though," she added.

"Not hungry." He popped the button of her jeans open.

"I can put it in the oven now, so it'll be waiting when…we're finished with the tour of my bedroom."

"How long is it supposed to bake?"

"About thirty minutes."

"It'll burn."

She grinned. "There you go putting pressure on yourself again."

"I told you. I work well under pressure."

"Prove it."

* * *

Note to self: Don't challenge Derek Gilman.

Olivia wanted him. She wanted him naked and in her bed and in *her*. She'd imagined this moment so many times since that day in the elevator—though not always in this setting—and now that it was finally happening, she wanted it to *happen*.

But Derek was lingering at her bedroom door, watching her. And she knew he was going to make sure dinner would have burned to a crisp if she'd put it in the oven.

"You coming in?" she prompted, hoping to move things along. Her body ached with the need to feel his hands on her.

"Just looking for a minute. Now when I talk to you on the phone, I'll be able to picture you in this room. On that bed."

"Get over here and you'll be able to picture me naked on this bed."

That got him moving, though he still wasn't showing the sense of urgency she felt. She expected him to go straight to pulling her shirt over her head so he could get to the boobs, but he ran his thumb over her bottom lip.

"I love kissing you," he said, his gaze fixed on her mouth. "I could happily do nothing but kiss you for an hour."

"Don't even think about it." But he was thinking about it. She could see it in his eyes.

"Do you have us on a schedule? Was there an agenda for tonight written down in that planner of yours?"

"You know what it says in my planner because you made me write it."

"Have great sex with Derek," he said, and then his mouth curved into a wicked grin. "But a plan's only as good as its execution. And the key to a successful execution is attention to detail."

"Expediency is good."

He shook his head. "It's not good to rush things. You don't want me to miss anything, do you?"

Though she had no doubt he was going to take as much time as he wanted teasing her, she could do a little teasing of her own. She pulled her shirt over her head, tossing it aside, and when Derek sucked in a ragged breath, she felt sexier than she ever had before.

"You're cheating," he said in a husky voice.

"I could put it back on."

But his hands were on her already, running over the ivory lace to cup her breasts. "Nope. But I'm taking the jeans off of you myself."

"I'm looking forward to it."

She caught the flash of his grin before his mouth closed over hers again. His thumbs stroked her nipples through her bra while he kissed her, and she cupped the back of his neck with her hand before sliding her fingers up into his hair.

"Did I mention I could kiss you for hours?" he said against her lips.

"You can kiss me all you want as long as you can multitask."

He lifted his head so she could see his amused expression. "What happened to the evils of multitasking?"

Tugging his shirt out of his jeans, she gave a guilty laugh. "Okay, it's not *always* a bad idea."

His shirt joined hers on the floor and Olivia ran her hands over his broad chest as his mouth claimed hers again. Tongue dancing over hers, he kissed her harder and she scraped her fingernails over his taut back.

Her bra was next in the pile, and she sighed when his hands skimmed over her naked breasts. His hands felt rough against the soft skin—but not painfully so— and she moaned as his thumbs flicked over her sensitive nipples.

Reaching down, she popped the button on his jeans and smiled at the sound he made. He caught her bottom lip between his teeth for a few seconds before leaving a trail of hot kisses down her neck and chest. With his hands pressed against her back, he closed his mouth over her nipple and sucked hard enough to make her gasp as he backed her toward the bed.

Her knees hit the mattress and still he didn't stop. He switched his attention to her other breast, licking and biting until she fisted her hand in his hair, which was just long enough to catch between her fingers.

He chuckled and paused long enough to slide his jeans down and pull them and his socks off. But when she unbuttoned and unzipped her jeans, he shook his head. "I told you I'm taking those off."

Since he was standing there looking hard and delicious in nothing but snug gray boxer briefs, she wasn't about to argue with him. But she wasn't going to wait all night, either.

She didn't have to. With her knees already against the bed, all he had to do was kiss her again and push her back onto the mattress. His hands were at her breasts and she stroked his back, her fingertips kneading the muscles that flexed as he moved.

Then he stood and took a step back, looking down at her with so much heat, she was surprised she didn't burst into flames. He lifted one of her legs, running his hands down the denim until the black heel was in his hand.

"I do love these shoes," he said, and the rasp in his voice left no doubt of that. "But they're in the way."

He slid the shoe off and tossed it aside before repeating it with the other leg. Then he tucked his fingers in the waistband of her jeans and tugged. She lifted her hips so he could wiggle the denim over her hips.

"Careful," he said. "I don't want to be the one who rips your favorite old jeans."

Right now, she didn't give a damn about jeans. She wanted them off her. She wanted the ivory lace panties off her. And she wanted Derek *on* her.

Once he'd dropped the jeans on the floor, he reached for the panties, but he didn't pull them down. Instead he ran his fingers over the lace in a light, teasing touch that made her squirm.

"These are so pretty, I almost hate to take them off," he said.

"I can take them off, don't worry."

But when she reached down, he grasped her wrists and lifted her hands over her head as he bent over her body. "I've got this."

He kissed her throat and then slowly—so slowly she wanted to pound a fist on his back to hurry him up— made his way down her body. Her breasts slowed him down even more, since he took his time sucking each nipple in turn. He released her wrist to cup her breasts and then pinch her nipples between his thumb and finger as his tongue flicked over the tips.

When she moaned, arching her hips, he started moving again. His mouth blazed a trail down her stomach, and when she tried to wiggle free, he put his hands on her hips to hold her down. Then he ran his tongue across the elastic edging of the panties and she sucked in a breath.

"You're torturing me on purpose," she said in a strained voice.

His chuckle against her lower stomach vibrated through her. His fingers brushed over the lace, making her whimper, but he took his time. He stroked her through the flimsy fabric until she grabbed his shoulder, her fingernails pressing hard into his skin.

When his mouth closed over the lace, a shuddering sigh escaped her lips and she let go of his shoulder to slide her fingers into his hair. He hooked his finger under the leg elastic so the back of his knuckle brushed over her naked flesh and she had to remind herself not to hold her breath.

When she growled in frustration, he pulled back and slid the panties down over her legs. She was vaguely aware of him fishing a condom out of his jeans and the anticipation quickened her pulse. *Finally.*

Derek slid his arm under her and lifted her just a little, pushing her farther back on the bed. But instead of moving over her, he slid his hands to the inside of her thighs. She made a sound—surprise or need or both—as his mouth closed over her.

Her frustration melted away as he took his time tasting her. The sound he made, echoing the hunger and desire she felt, inflamed her and she put her hand on his head, holding him close. His tongue flicked over her clit as he pushed one finger slowly into her, testing and twisting, before he sucked hard enough to make her hips buck.

But she wanted him. She wanted to feel him inside

her, and she scraped her fingernails over his shoulder. "Now, Derek. I want you now."

He groaned and gave her a punishing bite on the inside of her thigh, but he stood and peeled off his briefs. She only had a few seconds to appreciate the view— he was *definitely* ready for her—before he opened the condom wrapper and rolled it on.

Slowly kissing his way from her thigh to her neck, pausing only briefly at her breasts, he moved over her and settled between her thighs. His gaze locked with hers as she reached between their bodies to close her hand around him. He groaned, his eyes closing for a moment as she savored the hard length of him, and moved his hips.

He took his time entering her and she could feel the effort of his restraint in the slight tremble of his muscles. Slowly, he pushed deeper into her. Pulling back, then pushing forward. She rocked her hips, her hands on his hips, until he filled her.

Derek paused, his breath slightly ragged as he smiled down at her. "How you doin'?"

She skimmed her fingernails over his back and felt him twitch inside of her. "Doing great, and about to be even better."

He grinned and then his hips moved in a hard thrust. She gasped, and her hands grasped his arms. "Yes. More of that."

Olivia lost herself in the sensation of him as he complied, moving in and out with hard strokes. The heat of his skin against hers. The feel of his firm muscles moving under her hands. The sound of his breath and the way their gazes locked together.

Then he hooked an arm under her leg and shifted

his position so he could thrust harder and deeper. She was so close—so ready—and she moaned low in her throat as she reached down and pressed the heel of her hand against her clit. He groaned as the arch between her thumb and finger closed lightly over his erection, and he drove into her.

The orgasm took her breath away, and she dug her fingertips into his hips as her back arched off the bed. Maybe she screamed or said his name. She didn't even know. All she knew was the explosion of pleasure.

He came almost immediately after, groaning and grinding as he pulsed deep inside of her. Then he collapsed on top of her, his breath coming in short bursts against her neck. He kissed her skin as their bodies trembled in the aftermath.

After a few moments to catch his breath, he kissed her neck again and then lifted his head to kiss the side of her breast as he secured the condom and slid out. Olivia gave a satisfied moan and wrapped her arms around him, holding him close for a few more seconds. She didn't want him to move yet.

But after a few minutes, when she could feel his breath slow and wondered if he might fall asleep, he kissed her before sliding away. "I'll be right back."

While he was gone, Olivia stretched, enjoying the delicious ache of a body that was deeply satisfied. Then she pulled back the covers and oriented herself properly on the bed, so her head was on the pillow, and closed her eyes.

Derek climbed onto the bed and pulled her close, but he didn't yank the covers up over himself. Instead, he propped his head on his hand and smoothed her hair away from her face as he smiled down at her. "Do you want me to go?"

While she appreciated that he'd asked because she hadn't been sure how she'd feel about it when the time came—though she'd stocked up on breakfast foods, so maybe she'd had a hunch—now that he was in her bed, she wanted to keep him there. "I want you to stay."

He buried his face in her neck, nipping gently at her skin. "Good, because I'm not done with you yet."

Seconds ago, Olivia would have guessed she was about as sated as a woman could be, but as soon as he said the words, her body responded. "You were right. If I'd put dinner in the oven, the smoke alarms would be going off right now."

Derek woke before Olivia did, opening his eyes to a bedroom awash with light. He had room-darkening drapes in his apartment because sometimes he needed to sleep during daylight hours, but he didn't mind the sun streaming in this morning. Olivia was warm against his body, her breathing slow and even, and he was content to lie there.

It was almost unnaturally quiet this high up in a luxury building, though. Sunday mornings in his neighborhood weren't quiet. Doors slamming. Cars starting. Kids playing. Lawn mowers running. People yelling at neighbors who mowed their lawns too early on a Sunday morning.

He loved his messy, loud, slightly—or maybe not too slightly—tattered-around-the-edges neighborhood. It suited him and though he hoped to upgrade to a nicer apartment or a small house at some point in the future, he couldn't imagine himself living anywhere else. And he sure as hell couldn't imagine himself living in a place like this. If Olivia hadn't worn him out, he wasn't sure he could even *sleep* in a place like this.

And even though it was way too early in the morning and far too premature in their relationship to be worrying about it, he couldn't help acknowledging that after seeing her here, he couldn't picture her living in a place like his.

It wasn't long before Olivia stirred. After opening her eyes for a second, she closed them again before making a sleepy sound and nestling against him.

"Good morning." Her only response was another sleepy sound, so he kissed the top of her head, letting go of the pessimism that had been on a slow but steady roll through his mind. "Not a morning person?"

"I usually am, but I also usually go to sleep when I go to bed."

"Regrets?"

She laughed softy, and her breath was warm on his skin. "Not a single one. Well, except for the food situation. I think I promised to provide you with a meal. A midnight raid on the fridge isn't a meal."

"You didn't specify *which* meal."

"Good point. And I just happened to buy everything I need to make a good breakfast for two."

He slid his hand down her arm. "Just happened to, huh?"

"Just in case." She pushed herself up, taking the sheet with her, much to his disappointment. "And now that I'm talking about it, I'm starving. Time to get up."

"I'm going to jump in your shower for a quick minute if you don't mind."

Her shower blew his mind, though, and he was in

there for a lot longer than a quick minute. Multiple shower heads. Water hot enough to produce billows of steam. And water pressure that felt almost as good as a massage. It was so good that he didn't even mind that her shampoo and body wash smelled a little less masculine than he was used to.

When he reluctantly dragged himself out of the shower, he pulled on his jeans and went to find Olivia.

She was in the kitchen, the place smelled like bacon, and Derek couldn't remember the last time he'd been this damn happy this early in the day. Or at any time of the day, honestly.

He stepped up behind her and kissed the side of her neck. "Where do you keep the coffee?"

"I don't drink coffee, remember?"

He froze, unable to comprehend how a person transitioned from waking up to being a fully functioning human being without caffeine. "But I see a Keurig. Why do you have a Keurig with no coffee?"

"Herbal teas," she said matter-of-factly.

"On a scale of you-don't-care to you-never-want-to-see-me-again, how bad is it to do a walk of shame to a coffee stand and back?"

She laughed. "Kelsey keeps coffee in the cabinet over there, so you can help yourself. I swear her blood type is caffeine-positive."

Crisis averted, Derek brewed a mug of coffee and brought it to the table. After talking a sip, he set it down and walked to the tall windows to look at the water.

"I didn't think the view could get any better," Olivia said. "But you shirtless is definitely an added value."

He grinned at her over his shoulder. "I don't know if I could stand here in less. I might be too shy."

"You are definitely not shy. And nobody can see you."

"Is that an invitation?"

"Depends on how burnt you like your bacon."

"Nope." He sighed and shook his head. "Can't mess with the bacon."

"Then leave your pants on and breakfast will be ready soon."

They'd worked up an appetite, so he did as he was told. Sitting at the table, he drank his coffee and wondered again what it was like to live in this building. Everything felt hushed to him, but he supposed a lot of that was superior construction. But did she know the other people who lived in the building? Or even on her floor? Were there polite nods in the elevator instead of block parties? A discreet email sent to the building management with a noise complaint rather than a threat shouted across three yards?

Derek had a hard time wrapping his mind around the fact this wasn't a fancy hotel. Olivia lived here. This was the home she'd chosen for herself and it represented the world she belonged in.

She's out of your league.

He couldn't picture Julia and Isaac in a place like this, either. For a little while, maybe. They'd be on their best behavior and sit quietly with their tablets or talk to each other. But where did kids play around here? Where did dads take them out to play catch or to teach them how to ride a bike?

Logically he knew there were a lot of very happy people raising very happy children here. But he couldn't picture himself here. Or his kids. No matter how hard he tried, he couldn't see what that looked like.

"You look so serious," Olivia said, setting a plate down in front of him.

He smiled up at her, shaking off the unwelcome but very persistent doubts. "Just spaced out. This looks amazing. Thank you."

She leaned down and kissed him before going and getting her own plate, which had more fruit and less bacon to go with the eggs and toast. "It's fun to cook once in a while. I'm not very good with dinner foods, but I've always enjoyed making breakfast and I don't have a reason to do it very often."

"There has to be a reason to make breakfast?"

She laughed as she sat down and picked up her fork. "I make eggs and toast a lot, but I usually skip the bacon."

"That's the best part."

"But cleaning up after making bacon is *not* the best part."

"I'll help you clean up, but then we should go back to bed for a while and recover from all that work."

She gave him a look so hot, he was surprised it didn't make the bacon sizzle in his hand. "I like a man with a plan."

Chapter Nine

Derek sat on the hot street, leaning against the hot metal side of Ladder 37, wishing it wasn't so damn hot and drinking the ice-cold water one of the volunteers who manned the canteen truck had handed him.

The hottest days of summer were a shitty time to fight fires in full gear, but those were the days people were most tempted to move their barbecue grills into the shade of a covered deck. Sometimes it worked and sometimes it set a triple-decker on fire and three families were displaced.

And made tired firefighters cranky as hell.

"You look beat, Gilman."

He looked up, squinting against the ball of fucking hellfire that was the sun today, as Gullotti lowered himself to the street next to him. "Hey, LT. We clear?"

"Yeah, but we're blocked in. As soon as the other trucks get packed up and move, we can return to quarters."

"That house across the street over there has central AC." Derek pointed to the condensing unit on the side of a nearby house. "I'm thinking about introducing myself and asking if I can crash on their couch for twenty minutes. Or four hours."

"Been spending too much off time going back and forth across the city?"

Derek took another swig of water and then chuckled. "A couple of nights this week. Last night, since I'll pick up the kids for the weekend when the tour ends."

After leaving Olivia's place Sunday, he'd made it maybe twelve hours before seeing if she had plans for the evening. She didn't, so he'd gone back to her apartment and they'd managed to eat dinner before falling into her bed. He'd made it home late, but he got enough sleep to get by. Last night, though, he'd nodded off and gotten home in time to only grab a few hours. And, of course, today hadn't been a slow day that allowed for naps between calls. It had been a hellish day in hellish heat and humidity. And there was still a late thunderstorm in the forecast, so he didn't see falling into his bunk anytime soon.

"Speaking of the kids," Rick said. "Has she met them yet?"

"No. I haven't even told them I'm dating anybody yet, actually."

"Do you think they'll hate her?"

He frowned. "Why would they hate Olivia? There's nothing to hate about her."

When Rick held up his hands, he realized he'd asked that in a sharper tone than he'd intended to. "Let me rephrase that. Do you think they'll hate that you're dating, no matter who it is?"

"I don't know." He wasn't going to share Amber's news with anybody yet, since it wasn't his to share and they had a lot of mutual friends. Even though he knew he should be able to talk to these guys about anything, it was a small community and it would get back to her.

"They've had a lot of change already, and since they get less time with me, they might be less inclined to want to share."

"How does she feel about kids?"

He took his time trying to come up with an answer to that one. "I think she has a plan for her life and having kids is still a few years down the road."

"Have you asked her how she feels about *you* having kids?"

"No. It's probably too soon for going that deep."

Rick turned his head to give him a look that might have been almost fatherly if there were more years between them. "I saw you two together at Kincaid's. And you get this look when you talk about her. Maybe you should have that talk before you get in any deeper than you already are."

He knew the LT was right, but it really did seem too soon to ask her straight out if she could see herself settling down with a guy who had two kids. And if he asked the question, he was giving her the opportunity to admit she really didn't. And logically he knew it was better to know that sooner rather than later, but emotionally he didn't want to open that door.

"She knows about Julia and Isaac," he said. "It's not like I'm keeping any secrets."

"But knowing there are kids is one thing. Spending time with them and sharing *your* time with them is another, especially to a woman who doesn't have kids of her own."

"I didn't want to bring her into their lives until I knew it was serious."

"Past tense?"

Derek chuckled. "Busted. Yeah, I think it has the

potential to be serious. But don't forget I just met her a month ago. We don't get to spend a lot of time together and…I guess I'm being selfish. When I'm with her, I want it to be about us. For now."

"You're going to wear yourself out."

"Yeah." After taking another swig of water, he looked over at Rick again. "You mind if I ask you something weird?"

"If it involves a rash or anything parental controls would block in an internet search, I mind. Otherwise, go for it."

"You and Jess…she was raised with money, right? Like maybe not super rich, but she always looks like a million bucks and she was used to nice things."

"Like Olivia?" When he nodded, Rick shrugged. "Yeah, I guess you could say that. And no, she's not buying those shoes on my salary, but she still has all the nice things she wants because she works her ass off. She didn't give up her career for me and I hope you're not thinking Olivia would for you. Especially since Jess built her success at her father's side before branching out but Olivia built hers from scratch."

"Of course I wouldn't expect her to give it up."

"I get that it would be tough, though," Rick continued. "When Jess and I got together, she left San Diego behind because I was here, and her grandparents. But Olivia already has her own life here and blending them together wouldn't be easy."

"I've seen her life and I know mine and…let's just say they wouldn't blend well."

"I guess if you haven't talked about kids, you haven't talked about that, either."

"Not yet." It was going to have to be soon, though. He knew it, even if he was trying not to think about it.

Gavin turned the corner and offered a small stripe of shade as he stared down at them. "I was wondering where you went. Danny said we should be able to get out of here in a few minutes."

Derek pushed himself to his feet, groaning a little, and then offered a hand to pull his LT up. "I've never wanted a shower so bad in my life."

"No shit." Gavin pulled up the hem of his T-shirt and mopped his forehead with it. "It's so hot, I'm not even hungry."

"Great." Rick shook his head. "It's the end times and I'm spending it with you idiots."

Olivia did something she rarely did. She deviated from her schedule to sneak in a visit to Derek. But her appointment had been closer to his side of the city than hers, and she'd make it a quick visit. The accounting review could wait. As much as she protected her evening leisure hours, it wouldn't hurt to look over the documents tonight.

After she found a place to park near the address for the fire station he was in—having taken her own car just in case this kind of opportunity popped up—she sent him a quick message. It was brutally hot and she wasn't going to walk all the way there if he wasn't around.

I'm nearby. Are you around? I thought I'd pop in and say hi. And see your fire truck.

We're here now. I can never guarantee more than two or three minutes, but I'd like to see you.

I'll be there in a minute. So we should get at least two. :)

After grabbing the paper bag off the passenger seat, she locked the car and walked down the sidewalk to the three-story brick building with old-fashioned, side-by-side arched openings for the trucks. The doors were open, so she stepped inside.

Derek was waiting for her, and there was nobody else around. He kissed her hello, and then kissed her again. "Did you write *make Derek's day by surprising him at work* in your planner?"

She laughed. "No, so let's not even talk about my planner right now. I brought a couple of chocolate chip muffins. It's a weird time, I guess. After lunch and before dinner."

"I'd love a muffin. There's a card table and some chairs back there. We can sit for a few minutes."

"Is that your truck?" She'd always thought fire engines were big, but she had no idea how huge they were until she was standing right next to one.

"No, that's Engine 59. Danny, Aidan, Scott and Grant belong to her. Ladder 37's this one. She's mine, though I have to share her with Rick, Gavin, and Chris. And technically Rick's in charge."

"They're always so shiny."

"Polishing the apparatus is pretty much the go-to chore around here."

Once they were sitting, he pulled the muffins out of the bag, along with the water bottle she'd bought. At this point in their relationship, they could probably share if she got thirsty.

The thought startled her, because that somehow

made everything seem crystal clear. She'd found the man she'd share a water bottle with.

He was also a man she was willing to sacrifice her schedule for and who complicated things with his job and his location and his children, which made trying to keep perspective difficult. Why couldn't she have met him in a few years, when she had a couple more books out and had built her client base to the point she could turn people away rather than having to go out and court their business?

"So you just hang around and wait for a fire?" she asked when the silence stretched on. He was focused on his muffin and didn't seem to notice it, but she did.

He shrugged. "Some days it feels like that. But we have a lot of stuff that keeps us busy, and we're constantly inspecting equipment. And then other days, we're lucky when we have time for a sandwich on the run. Today's been a bitch, actually. And the heat's kicking our asses. Half the guys are sleeping upstairs right now."

"You could have told me you were busy if you need to sleep or do something else."

"I'd rather see you than sleep." That made her smile, but then his expression turned unusually serious and her stomach tightened. "And I actually wanted to talk to you about something. And I know I call you at night, but it's more of an in-person thing."

"Okay." She tried to brace herself, but without even an idea of what was coming, she couldn't help the dread that settled in her stomach.

"The kids told me Amber's pregnant."

Olivia took a sip of the water, buying herself a few seconds to think. His tone and expression weren't giving her much to go on right at this moment, but it was obviously important to him if he felt the need to talk to her about it.

If he didn't still have feelings for his ex-wife, then why would her having another baby affect him?

"Are they excited about it?" she asked.

He shrugged one shoulder. "I'm not sure they've figured out how they feel yet. Isaac's probably more excited than Julia, but he's younger and more self-centered, so she probably has a better grasp of how much things will change."

"And how do *you* feel about it?" When he didn't answer right away, her heart tightened in her chest.

"I don't know." He leaned back, looking her in the eye. "I'm happy for Amber and Jason, but the family dynamic... I don't know how to explain it, I guess."

"I guess it's a pretty solid sign she's definitely moved on."

He chuckled, surprising her. "I think that point was made when she married Jason."

"True."

He rested his hand on top of hers. "I'm not hung up on my ex, Olivia. I promise. I'm always going to care about her. We were together for a long time and she's the mother of my children. But even if there was no Jason and no baby on the way, Amber and I would never get back together."

"Okay." She couldn't hold back a burst of nervous, relieved laughter. "I know I shouldn't have gone there in my head, but I don't... You said your divorce was amicable and I know you're still both with Village Hearts. And you never complain about her, which is something

I can't even wrap my head around, so I guess it's hard for me to get a grasp on your relationship with her."

"We're actually friends again, but we weren't for a while. We were unhappy and we didn't like each other anymore, but we called it quits before either of us did something that would escalate it to the kind of hate and hurt it's hard to come back from. We worked at it and over time, we rebuilt the friendship. We just didn't do well as husband and wife, other than having Julia and Isaac."

She nodded, because there was a lump in her throat that made her uncertain of her ability to speak.

This man had been in her life for a month. They'd been dating seriously for a couple of weeks. It wasn't very long, but it wasn't really about the timeframe. It didn't feel like a fling. There wasn't anything casual about their determination to spend as much time together as they could. It felt as if they had a commitment to each other and the relationship they were building.

But he had essentially divided his life into two boxes. In one box was Olivia. In the other was a life she was totally separated from. She'd seen glimpses of it— working with Village Hearts and meeting the guys he worked with—but he hadn't shared the most important things in his life with her.

As long as he kept her separated from them, he was keeping her separated from some of the most important parts of himself and eventually they'd just be spinning their wheels going nowhere.

"I told you about the baby for a reason," he said, his thumb making circles on the back of her hand. "It's a lot for the kids. They've had a lot of change and this is a big one, and I'm kind of the one thing in their lives that hasn't changed."

"You haven't told them you're dating me."

He winced. "I hadn't yet, but I was going to because I want to keep seeing you as long as you'll put up with me. And then, when they told me Amber was having a baby, Julia told me she was glad I don't have a girl-friend."

"Ouch."

"I just couldn't... I will." He squeezed her hand, making eye contact with her. "I'm not putting my life—*our* lives—on hold because Amber's pregnant. When Julia told me she was glad I don't have a girlfriend, I couldn't bring myself to correct her when I could see they were already off-kilter. Isaac was asking me how I'll be related to the new baby. It was just a lot."

Olivia had caught the way he said *our lives* and it was enough for now. Derek was as aware of the separation in his life as she was, and he cared that it was a problem in their relationship. He was trying.

"I get it," she said. "They're already confused, so I understand."

"I'll tell them very soon. I *want* to. Amber and I will help them wrap their head around the baby thing and then it'll be okay. They're good kids."

"I'm sure they are. They have a great dad."

He grinned, and then lifted the back of her hand to his mouth. "Thank you."

She smiled back, but butterflies danced in her stomach. They did every time Derek talked about the two people he loved more than anything else in the world. What if they didn't like her?

What if she didn't like them?

Maybe that wasn't the right question. There was no reason at all she would dislike his children. But what if Derek put them all in the same box and there wasn't enough room? What if they didn't all fit?

"On a lighter note, the guys and I are going to a ball game Wednesday," he said, relaxing in his chair.

Fighting back the panic that had been rising, Olivia forced herself to put her doubts out of her mind. "What kind of ball?"

He chuckled, shaking his head. "The best kind of ball. Baseball. The Yankees are coming to Fenway."

"Oh, I know this one. They're your big rivals."

"*Our* big rivals. You live in Boston now." He winked, which made her laugh and a lot of the tension melted away.

"So baseball's your favorite sport to watch?" she asked.

His eyes lit up and he started talking about his dad and watching the games together. Olivia loved the way his face softened when he talked about people and things he loved, and she was content to sit back and listen until an alarm sounded and he stood abruptly.

"I have to run," he said, but he took the time to kiss her goodbye. "I'll call you when I can."

Before she could even tell him to be safe—the alarm was so loud she could barely think—he was gone. By the time she stood and gathered up their trash, the sirens were wailing and the two trucks pulled out of their bays, swinging wide onto the street.

She couldn't imagine what it was like to spend every workday without structure. There were rules and set hours, of course, but that alarm could sound at any time and they had to drop whatever they were doing and run.

There could be a fire while they were trying to eat lunch or somebody stuck on a roof or in a car accident while they were doing some task or another.

Olivia couldn't wrap her head around not knowing what each day would bring. She'd been young when she learned that deliberate planning of each day, week and beyond kept her focused and working toward her goals. Her parents had drilled the discipline of working intelligently and efficiently into her and it had worked. She not only accepted but embraced it, and now it was literally her life's work.

Which she should get back to, she thought as she looked at the time. She was going to be lucky to make it home before Kelsey wrapped up for the day, and that didn't make her happy. Either Kelsey would wait for her and Olivia would feel guilty, or Kelsey would leave and their end-of-day routine would get tacked onto tomorrow's start-of-day routine. Olivia didn't like their core workflow being interrupted, and she especially didn't like when it was her own fault.

I'm on my way back, she messaged Kelsey. 40 mins to an hour, probably.

You can stay if you want. You know I can handle the end-of-day review.

She knew Kelsey could handle it. While she hadn't been lying when she told Derek she didn't really believe in luck, Kelsey applying when Olivia finally took the huge step of hiring an assistant had been the best unplanned thing to happen to McGovern Consulting. But if Olivia started sliding and dumping things off on her, she was not only straying from her own plan, but she'd mess up Kelsey's workflow, as well.

I know, but he's gone anyway. The alarm went off, so I don't know how long he'll be.

I'll wait. And I'll probably eat all your grapes, just FYI.

Olivia smiled and left the fire station to walk back to where she'd parked her car. According to the navigation app, she should be back in time so Kelsey only stayed an extra fifteen minutes or so. That wasn't bad, but she needed to do better from now on.

Once she'd put on her seat belt and started the engine, she glanced at the leather journal sitting on the passenger seat, where it usually did. She'd had a planner with her at all times since middle school, when she'd struggled both academically and personally until her parents decided she needed structure. The first one was a simple composition notebook she'd kept track of goals and tasks in. This particular leather cover had been a gift from her father when she officially opened McGovern Consulting.

It had always been her anchor. And while sometimes an anchor could feel like it was dragging you down, it was really the thing that kept you from being adrift at sea. Right now, she felt as if the feelings Derek elicited in her—excitement and anxiety and doubts and passion and what-ifs—were tugging at her, like choppy seas.

But just looking at the book that held a plan to keep her on track comforted her. As long as she was anchored, she could weather any storm.

* * *

It was a beautiful day for a ball game. The sun was shining, but it wasn't too hot and they were enjoying a rare break from the humidity.

They'd taken all six tickets they could get—Derek, Aidan, Scott, Danny, Gavin and Grant, who'd decided he could sneak enough out of his ring fund to spring for a ticket. And they spent the time before the game started hunched around Grant's phone while he showed them the rings he'd narrowed it down to.

"Has she dropped any hints about what kind of ring she likes?" Danny asked after they'd seen three.

"No. She's not… I don't know if she knows I'm thinking about this."

"I didn't have to guess what kind of ring Ashley wanted. Every time we walked by a jewelry store, she'd stop and pick one out. Every commercial. Every flyer in the mail. She wasn't shy about it." He smiled. "And she still cried when I proposed to her. I think no matter how much ring shopping they do, they love the ring you give them."

Derek nodded. "I didn't have a lot of money back when Amber and I got married, and I was half afraid she'd reject me because the ring was…let's just say it was more of a chip than a rock. But she loved that ring."

"I don't think Wren would want a big, flashy ring." Grant frowned, and flipped through the pictures again. "But maybe I'm wrong. Maybe she doesn't wear big, flashy jewelry because she doesn't have any. I want it to be perfect for her."

"It will be," Danny said. "Because you're going to know it when you see it. You're going to see a ring and think, *Wren would love that*, and that'll be the one."

"I can't believe we're at a ball game talking about women's jewelry," Gavin grumbled, and they all gave him a hard stare. After a few seconds, he laughed.

"Yeah," Aidan said. "That *was* you who interrupted a Bruins *playoff* game to ask us what we thought of the ring you picked out for Cait."

The game started, which put an end to the ring talk. They'd wait until a few innings had passed and then splurge on nachos and a beer. It was how they always did it.

Derek tried to get to a few games during the season. One or two with the guys and, if he was lucky, a couple with the kids. They were old enough now to sit through an entire game without getting bored and asking to leave in the third inning. It was still a little tough for Isaac because he was younger and he wasn't as interested in baseball as he was in hockey and football. It was Julia who'd curl up on the couch with her dad and watch the Red Sox on TV.

He wouldn't mind bringing Olivia to a game. Usually he didn't like watching games with people who didn't know sports because they asked a thousand questions and he spent more time explaining the game than actually watching it. But with Olivia, he bet it would be different. Teaching somebody about a game he loved so they could enjoy it together in the future was appealing. And she was smart. She'd pick it up quickly and probably enjoy the strategic elements of baseball.

He dug his phone out of his pocket and sent her a text message. Busy?

It was only a few seconds before she responded. In a car, between meetings. Aren't you at a sports thing?

He chuckled, because she was exaggerating her lack of sports knowledge to amuse him. Not that she knew much, but she knew he was at a baseball game. Even she wasn't oblivious to the Red Sox and Yankees rivalry. I wish you were here with me.

I...don't. Sorry. But I wouldn't mind doing something else with you.

That got his attention, but his phone showed that she was already writing another message.

That sounded provocative, but I meant that I wouldn't mind doing anything else but watching sports with you. But provocative also works.

Some crowd noise made him look up from his phone, but since the guys he was there with were neither cheering nor shouting angry insults, he didn't think he'd missed anything important.

After taking a second to skim the calendar app on his phone—clearly Olivia was rubbing off on him—he went back to the messaging app. Why don't you come over Saturday night? We can watch a movie and then do provocative things. I'll make you breakfast.

There was a long pause, which was unusual because she was not only sitting in a car with the phone in her hand, but she typed on her phone faster than most people could type on a keyboard.

The kids are going home late Saturday afternoon, he added. Jason's family is having something in Maine and they're leaving very early Sunday morning.

Do I get to pick the movie?

The immediacy of that response was a pretty strong confirmation he'd been right. She'd been wondering if Julia and Isaac would be there and had been reluctant to ask. What he didn't know was if her answer was dependent on it. And if so, whether it was because of his promise of provocative things, or just their presence in general.

Maybe he shouldn't have told her what Julia had said or that he was reluctant to tell them about her so soon after they got the news about Amber's pregnancy. Maybe she'd been wondering if he'd changed his mind, but it bugged him that she seemed reluctant to ask. They needed to be able to talk about the kids without it being awkward.

We should watch Die Hard, he typed. It kills me that you haven't seen it.

Those provocative things better be VERY provocative. Only a few seconds passed before another text came through. I'm almost to my destination. Enjoy the game and call me later.

Good luck.

When he tucked the phone back in his pocket, unable to keep the smile off his face, he caught the other guys staring at him.

Gavin shook his head. "Sad, man. You are so far gone."

"Bullshit. You're telling me you've never sent Cait a text from a game?"

"Not when we're tied up with the Yankees and we've got runners on the corners and no outs."

Okay, maybe he *was* pretty far gone.

When the Red Sox finally got the win, knocking the

Yankees down yet another notch in the standings, they made the long walk back to the lot where they'd parked in high spirits. They'd probably all head over to Kincaid's and have a beer that didn't cost a day's wages, rehashing the game with Tommy and Fitzy, who would have watched it at the bar.

"You ever gonna get rid of this car, or what?" Grant asked when they reached Derek's beige four-door beater. His Jeep, which he and Gavin had come in, was farther down the row. Aidan, Scott and Danny had ridden in Scott's truck, which was across the lot.

Derek shrugged. "I don't know. I've thought about it, but it's paid for."

"I know a guy selling his truck because his wife's having twins and it gets like eight miles to the gallon. It's not a bad-looking ride for the money he's asking."

"I have two kids."

"Yeah, but it's got a bench seat. Put Isaac in the middle."

And what if, someday, Olivia joined them on an outing? Right now, he had a family of three. But it didn't seem smart to invest in a vehicle that *only* sat three.

The car had actually been the one Amber drove most of the time while they were married. He'd driven a beat-up, small SUV with all-wheel drive they'd bought for short money off her uncle because they needed two vehicles and couldn't afford anything better while still paying off Isaac's medical bills. If the weather was bad, Derek usually drove and if he was working, they'd switch. The SUV wasn't all that reliable, though, so he hadn't liked her driving it.

When they'd separated and Derek wasn't around to shovel and salt the driveway or drive the kids when the roads were iffy, he'd told her they'd switch cars and then trade the SUV in toward a newer model. He'd paid the bulk of the difference, but it had been worth it for the peace of mind of knowing his soon-to-be ex-wife and his children were safer on the road.

"I've always wanted to get eight miles to the gallon," he said, and then he snorted. "Driving from gas station to gas station is my kind of fun."

Grant shrugged. "Suit yourself, but let me know if you change your mind."

He wouldn't. He'd thought about finding a vehicle that was more "him" now that his finances had settled post-divorce. His rent wasn't bad and, other than child support, it was his only big expense. But the car was paid for and the truck that had caught his eye one day when he was driving by a dealership had such a ridiculous price tag, he'd laughed at the salesman.

He wouldn't mind having a heated steering wheel in February, but he hadn't picked the winning lottery numbers yet.

An image of Olivia trying to climb up into a truck in one of her skirts and those high heels popped into his head, making him smile. Of course, if she couldn't quite make it, he'd be more than happy to give her a boost up.

"Kincaid's?" he asked as he opened the door. The hinge creaked and Grant rolled his eyes. The kid was a vehicle snob.

"You know it," Scott said. "See you there."

He'd go and have a beer. Shoot the shit with the guys for a while. But he'd make sure he was home in time to call Olivia. He liked to end his days with the sound of her voice.

Chapter Ten

Since Derek had offered to drive her home and that meant more time with him, Olivia took a Lyft to his address late Saturday afternoon.

She hiked her bag on her shoulder and walked down the driveway to the set of stairs he'd told her would have a garden gnome in a Red Sox T-shirt on the bottom step. That staircase led to his second-floor apartment.

The bag was heavier than usual, since she'd suffered a rare bit of indecision about what to bring. *I'll make you breakfast.* She'd taken that as an invitation to spend the night, but it would feel awkward to knock on his door with an overnight bag. If she was driving her own car, she could have left it in the trunk. In the end, she'd compromised by throwing a few things, including her toiletries and tightly rolled leggings and a shirt, into a zipped tote.

Derek must have heard her footsteps on the stairs or been watching for her, because he opened the door as she reached the small landing where another garden gnome sat, this one wearing a Patriots jersey.

She felt that jolt of excitement and anticipation she felt every time she saw him, and wondered if that would fade with time. She hoped not.

And today's anticipation was heightened by the fact he looked delicious in a white T-shirt stretching across his chest and shoulders, along with faded jeans that hugged his legs. "Hi."

"Hey," he responded, and he kissed her before pulling her inside. "Sorry the place is kind of a mess. Usually the kids do a better job of picking up after themselves, but they left in a hurry because Amber hasn't started packing yet."

She set the tote bag down by the door as she looked around. The place wasn't fancy or big, but it was clean and had big windows. They were standing in a kitchen and dining area that was totally open to the living room, and there were several doors she assumed were bedrooms and a bathroom.

"It's not much," he said, "but the neighborhood's not bad and finding an affordable three-bedroom isn't easy. I didn't want them to have to share a room when they're with me, but I also didn't want to sleep on the couch with my feet hanging over the arm of it."

She laughed. "That could be pretty awkward when you have company, too."

"That wasn't really a consideration at the time."

A framed photo on the wall near the TV caught her attention and she moved closer. He'd shown her some pictures of his kids on his phone, of course, but his phone's camera sucked. This shot of Isaac and Julia had been taken on the beach by somebody who not only had an actual camera, but knew what they were doing with it.

They were in pretend surfer poses, both of them laughing, and Olivia could practically feel the joy radiating from them.

"That's my favorite picture of them," Derek said. "Amber and Ellen—Jeff Porter's wife—took them to the beach last year and she does photography on the side."

"I don't think I met a Jeff at the bar."

"One of his kids had a thing, so he couldn't make it. I took over his shift, actually, when he retired. I used to work Saturdays which sucked with the kids and all. He had a bum knee and…some other issues. But he's doing good now that he's off the job. The pain in his knee is better and he and Ellen and the kids are a lot happier."

There was a lot more to that story, but Olivia didn't pry. "That's good. And you need some glass wipes or something."

She reached up to swipe at some of the fingerprints in the bottom corner of the glass, but Derek caught her wrist and stopped her. He gave her a sheepish grin, his cheeks pink. "That's how I say goodnight when they're with Amber sometimes. I touch the glass on my way to bed."

Olivia's insides turned to mush and she turned so she could wrap her arms around him. Maybe luck really *was* a thing, because there was no other way to explain getting stuck in an elevator with a guy this great. "Like the picture of that hockey player at the bar?"

He chuckled as he ran his hands over her hips. "Kind of. And I can't believe I'm dating a woman who calls Bobby Orr *that hockey player.*"

"I'll write his name down in my book so I'll remember it."

"If you remember all the names of the athletes I talk about, you might expect me to start remembering all the computer stuff and books you talk about, so I'd rather you call him *that hockey guy* for a while."

She laughed and slid her hands under his T-shirt. She loved how his abs clenched under her touch. "I try not to talk about work too much."

"I know, and I don't mind when you do. You get really intense and it's hot."

"Speaking of hot, it's a little warm in here."

He grinned before lowering his mouth to hers and kissing her until there was no doubt it was very, very warm in there.

"I turned the air-conditioning down so you'd get hot and strip all your clothes off," he said, undoing the top button of the long shirt she'd thrown over leggings.

"You did not."

He chuckled as he moved to the next button. And the next. "No, I didn't. The air conditioner's an ancient window unit and loud as hell, so I only turn it on when it's really humid or the kids complain."

"It's not that bad."

"Do you want me to turn it on?"

She undid the bottom button of her shirt and worked her way up until their hands met. "I'd rather strip all my clothes off. And yours, too."

They managed to get most of their clothes off by the time they reached the couch, but she was still wearing her pink lace panties and bra when he pulled her down onto his lap. She was pretty sure he'd timed it that way purposely because he *really* liked lace.

She straddled his lap, making sure the lace between her legs skimmed over the hard flesh of his naked erection. He groaned, his fingertips clenching her hips so hard she was sure they'd leave dents. She didn't care.

He caught one nipple between his teeth, through the lace, and bit down with just enough pressure to make her squirm. Considering her position on his lap, she wasn't surprised when the squirming made him moan low in his throat and lift his hips for more contact between him and the lace.

"God, I want you," he unclenched his jaw long enough to say.

She reached behind her back and unclasped her bra. And she watched his tongue flick over his lower lip as she slowly slid the straps down her arms. His hands replaced the lace—warm and rough—and she sighed as his thumbs brushed over her nipples.

"Oh…shit."

Olivia jerked her head up to see a person standing in the kitchen and it felt as if her heart skipped before going into overdrive to make up for the missed beat. The woman she assumed was Amber—his *ex-wife*—turned around, which left her staring at the door and Olivia staring at her back. "Sorry."

Mortification heated Olivia's skin and, since she was naked, she knew it was visible. When Derek pulled the lightweight throw off the back of the couch, she held it in front of her and scrambled off him, belatedly hoping she didn't do him any permanent damage. With one hand clutching the blanket in a poor attempt to cover herself, she snatched up her clothes and retreated to the bedroom and kicked the door closed behind her.

Even over the pounding of her heartbeat in her ears, she could hear the conversation taking place in the living room.

"You can turn around now," she heard Derek say, which she took to mean he'd put pants on or at least covered himself with a throw pillow. Or two.

"I'm so sorry, Derek," Amber said. "I should have knocked."

"I should have locked the door, I guess."

"I have a key."

Olivia frowned, her fingers tightening on the blanket she was still holding over her breasts. A guy's ex-wife having a key to his apartment didn't seem typical to her. The divorces in her own family had started out with open warfare and settled into lingering, long-term hostility. None of them would have dared give an ex a house key.

No matter what he'd said about their friendship and lack of animosity, it seemed weird.

"Isaac left the book he was reading here," Amber was saying. "And you know how he is. There's no reading something else until he can come back and get it and he doesn't want to fall behind on his summer reading list."

"I tried to get him to read on that tablet you bought him, but he said it's not the same."

"I've tried, too. I mean, Jason and I both read on our phones and Julia reads on her tablet, but he wants the paper books. I even tried showing him that I can carry dozens of books with me all the time and they don't weigh anything. He said that carrying books is exercise and makes him stronger than me."

Derek's laugh rang through the apartment and Olivia sighed. There was an easy familiarity in their discussion—which made sense for two people who'd been married for ten years—and she moved away from the door. After pulling on her clothes, though, she wasn't sure what to do, so she wasted another minute neatly folding the throw blanket and setting it on the foot of his bed.

They were laughing about something again and she put her hand on the doorknob. Unless he really was sitting on the couch wearing nothing but a pillow on his lap, it was a little rude for him not to have popped his head in to check on her. It was Amber who'd busted in unannounced and embarrassed them. Or her, at least. It didn't sound like Derek cared.

Of course he didn't. Amber had seen him naked hundreds of times. Thousands, even.

Olivia frowned at the unexpected jealousy that rose up in her. Derek had an ex-wife. He probably had a bunch of ex-girlfriends, too. Neither of them were virgins, so there were exes. And she was genuinely glad he had a good relationship with the mother of his children. She wouldn't wish unhappiness and conflict on any of them, so she was being ridiculous.

And she believed him when he said he had no interest in getting back together with Amber.

After taking a deep breath in an unsuccessful attempt to center herself, she opened the door and almost walked right into Derek's naked chest.

She looked down to make sure he was wearing pants and then lifted her gaze back to his face. "I was just getting dressed."

"Sorry," he said quietly.

"I'm *so* sorry," Amber called from the living room. "I'm just going to grab Isaac's book and then I'll be out of here."

"It's not a problem," she said, because the mood was pretty much gone, anyway. "Take your time."

"I was just planning to run in and out. I'm not used to Derek having company, so I didn't even think to knock. I will from now on. And a text first would be good, I guess."

When Amber disappeared into the other bedroom, Derek gave her an apologetic look. "I should have locked the door."

Olivia smiled to conceal the mixed emotions she was experiencing. On the one hand, it was nice to hear Derek wasn't in the habit of having women in his apartment all the time. On the other, it seemed odd to her that they didn't have more boundaries.

When Amber returned with the book, Olivia watched Derek shifting his weight from foot to foot, and then he took a deep breath. "So you guys probably figured it out already, but this is Olivia. Olivia, this is Amber, my ex-wife."

The formality of introductions steadied Olivia, and she smiled as she stepped forward with her hand out. "It's nice to meet you."

Amber laughed as she shook her hand. "It's probably a weird way for us to meet, but I'm glad we finally did. And I also want to say thank you for getting on board with Village Hearts. It means a lot to my family."

"It's a great organization and I'm proud to be a part of it." She almost offered congratulations for the baby news, but at the last second thought better of it. She didn't know if Amber was actually telling other people yet, or if Olivia had gotten insider information she should keep to herself.

"Okay, I'm going to run now." Amber held up the book. "Again, I'm sorry for busting in like that, and next time I'll text first."

Once she was gone, Derek walked to the door and

locked it before turning to face Olivia. "That was awkward for you. I'm sorry."

Awkward was definitely an understatement. "I'm just glad it was her and not one of the guys you work with. Or that she didn't wait outside while your son ran up and grabbed the book himself."

He made a face and then crossed the room to pull her into his arms. "That's definitely not how I wanted you to meet her."

"That's not how I ever want to meet *anyone*, but especially not your ex-wife."

"I can almost guarantee it'll never happen again." He kissed her forehead. "I'm sorry."

As embarrassing as the moment had been, she didn't want it to ruin her first night at his place. "Where were we?"

Heat flared in his eyes again, replacing the guilt. "I guess now that you're dressed again, we should do something about food before I get you undressed again. Would pizza make you forget what just happened?"

She pushed back enough to look up at his face. "Have you been talking to Kelsey?"

"Uh, no. Why?"

"Pizza is my ultimate comfort-food-slash-reward." She laughed. "And since I just met your ex-wife for the first time while naked, but didn't cry, it can be both at the same time."

"Pizza and a movie it is."

But he kissed her first, biting her bottom lip gently while his hands slid under her shirt, and it was almost an hour before he got around to calling in the order.

"Would those air ducts really support a grown man like that?" Olivia asked, waving a hand at the television screen. "And that would make so much noise in real life. They'd find him in, like, a minute."

"You're overthinking it."

"It's a valid question."

"Maybe you should write all your questions down in your book and then we can go over them when the movie's over. We can schedule a meeting."

She laughed and slapped his arm, which was wrapped around her. They were on his overstuffed leather couch, which had seen better days, but was surprisingly comfortable. Especially if you were holding an amazing woman wearing nothing but a scrap of pink lace between her legs and your T-shirt.

"I just don't understand why they don't make realistic action movies," she said.

"Because they'd be boring."

She sighed, but stopped talking long enough to watch a few more minutes of the movie. Then she gave a derisive snort and he knew another round of picking apart his favorite movie was about to start.

Obviously she needed a distraction. He slowly slid his hand from her hip to her stomach. She stilled, but kept her eyes on the screen. Her back was pressed up against his body, though, so he could feel the way she tensed up and how her breathing quickened.

He didn't kiss her neck or cup her breast. He just tucked his fingers under the pink lace and kept going. Olivia shifted a little, her thighs parting just enough to give him access to her slick flesh. With his middle finger, he found her clit and circled it. Then he slipped the finger into her, working it from tip to knuckle until she made a low growling sound deep in her throat. Then he went back to her clit.

"Oh my god, Derek. What are you *doing*?"

"Keeping you distracted while I watch my movie." It was a lie, of course. At that moment he didn't really give a shit what John McClane was doing on-screen.

She tried to laugh, but her breath caught in her throat as he pressed the heel of his hand hard against her mound. Her hips moved, grinding against him, and it wasn't long before she arched against him as the orgasm racked her body.

She was so fucking hot. He kissed her hair as her breathing slowly returned to normal and pulled his T-shirt back over the pink lace.

"I see what you're doing here," she said, her voice husky.

"I told you I was distracting you."

"You think if I associate orgasms with *Die Hard*, it'll become my favorite movie, too."

He laughed and kissed the side of her neck. "You're too smart for me."

"It's kind of a long movie. Is there a ratio of orgasms to ridiculous plot points?"

"If you make it to the end, I'll take you to bed and make you forget every question you had about the movie."

She wiggled against him, making him groan. "And if I don't make it to the end of the movie?"

"You'll have to take me to bed and make me forget my girlfriend has questionable taste in movies."

They almost made it to the end, and she not only made him forget his girlfriend didn't like his favorite movie, but she made him forget his own name.

Not enough hours later, he woke and his first thought was *Olivia's in my bed*. He could get used to that.

Between having kids and being a creature of habit in general, Derek didn't usually sleep in, but the room was already bright when he opened his eyes because he hadn't closed the heavy drapes over the sheers. He rolled onto his side to face Olivia, who was sleeping on her stomach with her hair across her face. He was tempted to reach out and brush it back so he could see her face better, but he didn't want her to wake to her face being tickled by her hair.

Derek closed his eyes again, listening to her soft breathing, but he knew there was no chance he'd go back to sleep. Maybe it came from years of having to shake off sleep in an instant when the alarm toned, but once he was awake, he was awake.

He knew the instant she woke up. Her breathing changed and she made a little sound as she shifted in the bed, stretching her muscles without actually moving.

Then she lifted her head a couple inches off the pillow, frowning. "What is happening right now?"

"What do you mean?"

"Outside. There's noise and yelling. It sounds like we're under attack."

He chuckled as her head dropped back onto the pillow. "It's just a weekend morning in the neighborhood."

"I don't like your neighbors. Especially the one mowing his lawn."

She'd probably really hate winter, when his neighbors fired up snowblowers in the pre-dawn hours so they could try to make it to work on time. Hell, she'd probably really hate the late nights after a big game when guys who'd had too much to drink in front of their buddies' televisions stumbled down the sidewalks, hooting and hollering as they made their way back to their own houses. He'd suspected from the beginning this wasn't her kind of place, but he could do without the confirmation.

"Maybe breakfast will cheer you up," he said, hoping to get her out of the bedroom, which he'd chosen because the others were on the back side and quieter for the kids.

She gave him a sleepy smile. "I do like food."

He pulled the sheet down far enough to bare her breasts. Then he bent his head and gently sucked one taut nipple until she squirmed. "I know what else you like."

"I had no idea you're a morning person."

He grinned and pinched the same nipple between his finger and thumb, a little less gently. "I'm a *you* person. Any time of day or night, I want you."

Chapter Eleven

On Tuesday morning, Olivia stared at Kelsey's Keurig, reconsidering her life choices. Not all of them. Mostly just the ones that had led to her giving up caffeine.

She knew there was a good reason she had, but right now she'd be damned if she could remember what it was.

"You'll be sorry if you do it." Kelsey's voice drew her attention away from the coffee-giving machine. "While I'll personally never understand not drinking coffee, you *don't* drink it and the caffeine will make you feel worse instead of better."

"I know you're right, and yet…" Derek was wreaking havoc on her sleep schedule and it was almost worth feeling jittery if it helped get her butt into gear.

"No *and yet*. I'm right, so just drink your juice and read the notes. You have a busy day ahead of you, as usual."

"A long one, too." She groaned, casting another wistful glance in the Keurig's direction. "Don't forget I'm going straight from my last meeting to the Broussard Financial offices to meet Jessica, so I'll be late. We can do the end-of-day review in the morning, I guess."

"I can handle it. Then we'll just do a quick end-of-day

recap before we start work tomorrow." She gave Olivia a firm look. "I've got this. Nothing's going to fall through the cracks."

"I know you can handle it." Olivia frowned, resting her hand on her planner. "With the benefit only about six weeks away, there's probably going to be more of this stuff popping up and it's a little frustrating because they should have started nailing some of this down as soon as it was over last year."

"That's probably why they're so happy to have you involved. Once you've seen it in action, you can map out the way to handle an annual event like that most efficiently, so next year they're not overwhelmed at the end."

"That's my plan."

"Of course it is." Kelsey arched an eyebrow at her. "And does your plan also include seeing a certain fire-fighter after you're done for the day?"

Olivia sighed. "He has to work, unfortunately, so I won't be seeing Derek tonight. Or maybe it's fortunately because I'm so tired and it takes forever to get there and back. But I spent a good chunk of the weekend with him, so it's okay and he'll call me if he gets a chance."

"You guys talk every day?"

"Mostly, unless he's on a call and doesn't get a chance. But even then he usually sends me a text message, at least."

"It sounds like he's into you," Kelsey said, but she sounded hesitant. "But you haven't met his kids yet, right?"

"No, not yet. He talks about them a lot, but they were with their mom so they weren't home." When Kelsey made a sound but otherwise didn't respond, Olivia gave her assistant her full attention. "What's that supposed to mean?"

"Nothing. I was just curious."

"I can tell when you're trying not to tell me something you think I won't want to hear." Kelsey would be the worst poker player ever. "And trying to figure out what you're not saying will distract me, so just out with it, already."

"It just means he's not sure about you yet." Kelsey shrugged. "You guys have been seeing each other long enough so it's clear he doesn't take introducing you to his kids lightly, so the fact he hasn't yet probably means he's not sure you guys are serious enough yet."

It felt pretty damn serious to Olivia. "There's a reason he hasn't told them yet, and we've talked about it and I understand."

Kelsey looked skeptical. "If he's really serious about you, it would have to be a damn good reason for him to be keeping you a secret because he should *want* you to get to know them."

"It is a good reason. And I'm not a skeleton in his closet or anything. You're making it sound more sinister than it is."

"Sinister?" She laughed. "Now you're being dramatic. I'm just worried about you. I've been telling you for a long time to put yourself out there, but I also don't want you to get your heart broken."

"It's a little early to worry about that," Olivia lied. Maybe. It seemed to her as if it was definitely too early in the relationship timeline to worry about her heart, but her mind shied away from imagining what it would feel like if Derek wasn't in her life anymore.

The conversation with Kelsey stayed with her, creeping up from her subconscious throughout the busy day.

It just means he's not sure about you yet.

Sure about what, though? Sure that he liked her? Olivia knew he did. And she had no doubt they were compatible in the bedroom. But there was still that whole part of Derek's life he wasn't sharing with her, and maybe that's where the doubt was lurking.

She needed to meet his kids. Until she did, there was only so far forward she and Derek could go together before they started spinning their wheels.

When she walked through the door of Broussard Financial Services, Olivia tried to shove those thoughts back into her subconscious where they belonged—for now. She was here to go over some details for the Village Hearts benefit and she wanted a clear head. They'd decided after a brief email exchange that it would be more efficient to simply meet in Jess's office for a few minutes than to keep bouncing emails back and forth.

It was quiet in the offices, but Olivia could see a few people still behind glass partitions, working at their computers. And Jess stepped out from a hallway, a smile on her face. "Hi, Olivia. Thanks for coming."

"No problem. With the benefit coming up so soon, it's a better use of our time to nail down these details so we can move on to the next items on the list."

And a mere twenty minutes later, when Jess emailed the results of the session to George and Ella, copying the rest of the board, Olivia felt the familiar rush of checking a job done well and efficiently off her list.

"We work well together," Jess said as she powered down her computer. "I hate to keep repeating how glad I am you're a part of Village Hearts, but I really am."

"I am, too. Are you heading home now?"

"I am. I usually work late on Tuesdays and Fridays anyway, since Rick won't be home waiting for me, but I want to stop by and see my grandparents tonight."

"It must be hard to make it all work."

"What do you mean?"

"You live in the same neighborhood as their fire station, don't you?" Jess nodded. "Isn't it a long commute for you?"

"I'm not going to lie. It's tough sometimes, especially when the weather's bad. But it's worth it." Olivia must have looked skeptical, because she laughed. "You don't look convinced."

"It seems like so much wasted time and your time is…valuable."

"More valuable—financially speaking—than Rick's?"

Olivia's cheeks burned. "I didn't mean to imply that. Speaking strictly from an efficiency standpoint, you commute back and forth through the city every day, while Rick works two shifts a week and they're twenty-four hours long."

"I know it looks like that, but they're always doing something with meetings and covering shifts for other guys and community events. Paperwork. Those assigned shifts aren't the full extent of his job. And I like living near our family and friends. Kincaid's. I love our house, which was my grandparents' house, actually. It's just…home." She shrugged. "I use the commute time for things I can do on the move, and I delegate a lot. Sometimes, if I don't have meetings with clients, I just work from home."

Olivia nodded, trying to process that. It didn't seem like a structured enough plan for a woman with Jess's responsibilities, but it looked as if she was making it work. Somehow.

"So, speaking of family," Jess said, "I, uh, heard you met Amber."

Olivia's face suddenly felt so hot, she actually put her hands to her cheeks. "Yes. We met. I guess she gave you the details?"

"She didn't give me *all* of the details, but the fact your face is the color of a cherry tomato right now is filling in the gaps." She made a *sorry* face. "It probably doesn't help much, but she felt *really* bad about it."

"It was awkward. And weird." She frowned. "In my experience, divorced couples don't have relationships like that."

"It's probably rare for a couple to go back to the friendship they had before it all fell apart, but they managed it. Minus the romance in the friendship, of course. You know they're not hung up on each other, right?"

"I know. I believe that." And she did. "It just threw me a little, I guess. It's one thing for him to tell me they have a good relationship, but she has a key and just lets herself into his apartment and they laugh together. And it's not wrong. I don't *want* them to hate each other and fight over everything. It's just an adjustment for me."

"He's worth it," Jess said quietly. "I haven't known him a long time, but I've known him long enough. I know his family. And my husband sees him on the job, and Derek's a good guy."

"He really is."

"Families—especially parents—can really do a job on us, can't they? My dad was estranged from his parents for most of my life. I came out here from San Diego because my grandfather's doctor left a message for my dad and he wasn't available, so I decided to handle it myself. That's when I learned they weren't bad people and my dad had really been the villain of the story." Jess sighed. "Luckily, he was able to admit it and they'll never be close because a lot of hurt built up over the years, but they have a relationship now. And they all love *me*, so they're trying with each other."

"And you met Rick while you were here?"

"He was my grandparents' tenant and he looked out for them. Since he'd heard nothing good about my dad, when I showed up on his behalf, Rick assumed I was here to scope out whether putting my grandparents in a facility and selling their home would be profitable for Dad and I. He was determined to stop me." She smiled. "And then we fell in love."

"I like happy endings."

"Most stories have happy endings if you can stick through the slaying-the-dragons part." She smiled. "Rick and I are happy. My dad's coming out from San Diego for the Village Hearts benefit, which is practically a miracle. And my grandparents will be there. If it's meant to be, it'll all work out."

Olivia didn't believe in *meant to be* so much as *make it happen*, but she smiled. "I'll keep that in mind. And speaking of your grandparents, I should head out so you can go visit them."

"Thanks again for stopping in, and I'm sure we'll be in touch before the next meeting."

Olivia didn't make it home before Kelsey left, but she'd left her boss a note on the kitchen island detailing what they'd accomplished that day, as well as a list of tasks for tomorrow and an overview of the rest of the week. There was color-coding—in the office versus on-site—and symbols—books, speaking engagements, podcast, and the different stages of client work—and she felt herself relax as she immersed herself in the familiar and comforting structure of her business methodology.

Maybe relationships couldn't be structured and color-coded the way a business plan could, Olivia thought, but there had to be some kind of a plan and there were steps to check off. If she wrote them out, she knew what she'd have to write next to the next box. *Meet Julia and Isaac.*

It was a big step—probably the biggest yet—and thinking about it robbed Olivia of the calm she'd achieved since walking through her door. Whether for better or worse, it would change everything. And no amount of planning could give her any control over the outcome.

By Monday morning, Derek felt Olivia's absence like an almost physical ache. It had been just over a week since he'd seen her in person and, though they talked on the phone every day, it wasn't the same.

He wanted to see her. Kiss her. Hold her hand. Fall into bed with her.

Falling into bed was a little harder to pull off, but he had a plan for the first three. He didn't have the patience to type everything he wanted to say into the phone, so he called her knowing he'd probably go to voicemail, which he did.

"Hey, it's me. I have to pick up a couple of donations for the auction tonight and one's in your neck of the woods. I know you're busy, but if you don't have anything planned for after work, I thought maybe you'd like to ride along? Let me know, and if you want to go, tell me what time you'll be free. Oh, and you should meet me downstairs because I really need to get the donations tonight, if you know what I mean. Talk to you soon."

It was almost an hour before he got a response. Love to. Free at six and I'll meet you downstairs because I do know what you mean.

That made him grin as he tucked the phone away. If he went upstairs to her apartment, he was getting her naked and she'd be naked until it was too late to do the errand he had to get done.

The kids' part-time summer camp had ended for the season, so he picked them up and took them for ice cream. They were only gone a couple of hours, but it gave Amber some time to do errands or housework without them underfoot—or soak in a bubble bath eating chocolates for all he knew—and it gave him more time with them. They'd be going back to school soon and it cut down on their flexibility a lot. He'd get the weekends, but visits during the week were shorter and less frequent because they had homework to do and sleep schedules to maintain.

Once he'd dropped them off at their mom's, Derek had just enough time to shower and change into jeans and a decent shirt that didn't have black raspberry ice cream dripped on it before it was time to cross the city to get Olivia.

Traffic gave him plenty of time to think about how wrong his life was beginning to feel. Kids over here. Olivia over there. No overlap. Planning dates around when he'd have Isaac and Julia. It didn't feel right anymore.

He and Olivia had been living in a bubble. They were two people getting to know each other, having great sex and living for the next time they could see each other.

Last weekend, the bubble had popped.

Despite what had been an incredibly awkward first encounter—especially for Olivia—she and Amber had been introduced. It had gone okay, all things considered. And so would her meeting his kids, he told himself.

Maybe it would be a little rocky at first, since they were already dealing with their mom having a baby. But kids were resilient and they'd adjust, especially if everybody was happy. And he had no reason to think they wouldn't like Olivia, even if she didn't have a lot of experience with kids. She was smart and funny and had great people skills.

But there was a constant nagging worry Olivia might not like Julia and Isaac that he couldn't banish no matter how often he told himself he was being ridiculous.

His kids were awesome. He loved them without reservation or limitation, but that didn't mean they were perfect. They were young. Sometimes they got loud. They made a mess. They argued or whined or pitched fits. Bad moods or mild, fast-moving stomach bugs could ruin plans in an instant. They were cuddles and chaos, and Derek just sighed and rolled with it.

They were his kids and he loved them, so *what're you gonna do*?

Olivia wasn't a fan of chaos. And they weren't her kids, so she could choose to walk away. The problem was that if she walked away from them, she'd be walking away from him, and the possibility had been like an ulcer burning his guts for days.

It was time to trust in what he and Olivia had and rip the bandage off.

She was walking down the front steps of her building when he pulled up to the curb, and he wished again his car didn't look so out of place in her neighborhood.

He really should stop being a cheap son of a bitch and buy something nicer. Not new-Audi nice, but maybe something that would pass inspection if he took it to somebody besides his uncle's buddy.

Olivia didn't even give the old shitbox a second glance, though. She opened the door and slid into the passenger seat, smiling at him.

"Hi," he said before cupping his hand around the back of her neck and giving her a hello kiss.

He'd intended for it to be a quick one, but as soon as his mouth touched hers, he forgot about his intentions and the fact he was barely pulled over, with his foot still on the brake. All he knew was the softness of her lips, the warmth of her breath and the feel of her fingertips digging into his upper arm.

"Missed you," she whispered against his mouth.

She had no idea how much he'd missed her, but he didn't want to stop kissing her long enough to lay it out for her. He devoured her, and her small moan of pleasure made him forget everything until a car horn jerked them back to reality.

Olivia chuckled as she reached for her seat belt. "At least we weren't standing on the sidewalk this time. So where are we going?"

Derek pointed at the navigation screen on his phone as he pulled into traffic and then turned down a side street. "I already grabbed the first donation. Now we're just heading down to the South Shore to pick up a painting. There are some things people will bid higher on if they can look at them instead of just seeing a printed-out picture. And having some cash-and-carry items for instant gratification also helps get people in the bidding mood."

"Wouldn't it be faster to take the highway?"

"Probably." He glanced over long enough to see her skeptical look. "Okay, definitely. But we're not in a hurry and I like spending time with you."

"I like spending time with you, too. I was just thinking that the quicker we get the donations picked up, the more time we'd have to relax…at my place."

"We'll take the highway back," he said quickly. "Hell, I'd turn around right now, but I told George I'd take care of it tonight so Ella would stop nagging him about it."

"I'm glad you called me. I wasn't sure when I'd get to see you again."

Rip the bandage off. "How would you feel about getting together next weekend?"

"I'd love to, but don't you have your kids next weekend?"

"Yeah." Even though the thought of saying them out loud scared the crap out of him, he forced the words out. "I thought maybe we could all do something together. The four of us."

"Oh."

That single word didn't offer up many clues as to how she actually felt about the idea. "Not *just* the four of us, though. Aidan and Lydia are having a barbecue and I'm taking the kids with me. If you go with us, you can meet Isaac and Julia, but there will be a lot of people you know there, too. I was thinking it might be less pressure on you. And them, I guess."

"That sounds fun."

"I think you'd enjoy it. It'll be a little like the fundraiser at Kincaid's, but with kids and a lot more food and less drinking. Okay, it won't really be like the fundraiser at Kincaid's. I just said that to entice you because you seemed to like everybody."

"I did like everybody. I want to meet Isaac and Julia, too, and you're probably right about it being a good way to do that. Probably less awkward for them than the four of us sitting at a table, talking."

Less awkward for all of them, Derek thought. "Good. I'll tell the kids."

"Not that it would change my mind about going with you, but is Amber going to be there?"

"No." He reached over and took her hand, lacing their fingers together. "She knows the guys and she's still friends with a lot of the women, but when it comes to these kinds of things, they're like my family and I got to keep them in the divorce."

"That makes sense, I guess. Jess and Rick will be there?"

"As far as I know."

"Should I plan to meet you there? I have her address, so I'll be able to find it."

"If you come to my place, you could meet the kids first and then we could all ride over together." He wanted to keep her first time meeting his kids casual, but not *that* casual. Some subtle signals to Isaac and Julia that Olivia wasn't just another friend at the barbecue might help the process along. "If you don't mind doing that."

"Of course I don't mind." He glanced over at her, and her smile looked genuine enough. "I'm looking forward to meeting them. I really am."

"It'll be fun. I know you usually work on your book on Saturdays. Am I cutting into your work too much?"

This time her smile didn't look quite as genuine, but

she shook her head. "I'm fine. I'll work on it a little bit each night to make up for it."

"Does that mean you won't take my calls after hours anymore?"

"As if I've shown any ability whatsoever to resist you." She laughed. "As if I've even tried."

He hoped she didn't start anytime soon.

Chapter Twelve

Olivia looked down at the football gnome on the landing, her stomach in knots as she listened to children's voices on the other side of the door.

Today was a big deal—for her and for Derek both—and she was terrified she was going to screw it up somehow.

Before she could change her mind and run back to her car to text him some total lie about a migraine or upset stomach, she knocked and the voices quieted. A few seconds later, Derek answered the door.

His face lit up in a smile when he saw her, but he didn't kiss her like he usually did. To be expected, she thought as he stepped back. "Come on in. You could probably hear the kids from outside. They're a little excited today."

"I'm excited, too." And nervous as all get-out, but she kept that part to herself as she faced the two kids in the kitchen. They were watching her with interest, but she didn't see any traces of animosity, which was a good start.

Derek rested his hand on his son's shoulder. "This is Isaac and that's Julia. Kids, this is my friend, Olivia. She's going to ride over to the barbecue with us."

That made her sound more like a hitchhiker than his girlfriend, but she knew he wanted to keep the introduction low-key, so she went with it. "I've heard these barbecues are always a lot of fun."

Both kids nodded, and then Isaac gave her a little smile. "Do you like cheeseburgers?"

"I love cheeseburgers."

"I like hot dogs," Julia said quietly.

"I like those, too," Olivia said, though she hadn't had one in years. "Food cooked outside on grills always tastes better than regular food."

"Is the bag ready?" Derek asked, and both kids scrambled to race into their rooms. He rolled his eyes. "A change of clothes for each of them in case one of them turns the hose on or there's a condiment catastrophe. Sunscreen. Bug spray. And a small first aid kit. The barbecue staples."

Olivia nodded, but somehow she'd thought eight- and ten-year-olds would be more...self-sufficient. She was an only child with no kids and, having distanced herself from her family, she didn't have little cousins or nieces or nephews around. The movies and television shows she'd watched over the years clearly hadn't educated her on the needs of children.

"I can't believe how much they look like the two of you," she said. "Isaac like you and Julia like her mother. I mean, I could see it in the pictures, but it's so much more pronounced in person."

He chuckled. "I think a lot of it's the facial expressions. I mean, Julia is practically a clone of Amber, for sure. Isaac looks like me, but there's also some of Amber's dad in there. His expressions and mannerisms are all me, though, so…yeah, he looks like me most of the time."

"He's cute."

Derek raised his eyebrow suggestively. "So you must think I'm cute, then?"

"You have your moments."

"We're ready," Isaac announced as the kids reappeared, and Julia held a small gray duffel bag with their last name printed on it in bold black marker.

"Does anybody have to pee before we go?" he asked, and Olivia smiled when he glanced at her to include her in the question.

Nobody did, so he ushered them all down the stairs and to his car. Isaac liked to do most of the talking, she realized, and Julia let him because it meant less talking she had to do. Derek had mentioned she was a little shy around strangers, so Olivia hoped that was the cause and not a silent protest of her inclusion in their day.

"I should warn you, it'll be a lot," Derek said. "It gets loud and there's a lot of joking and laughing. Sometimes there are arguments about the grills. We men sometimes get territorial about them."

"And sometimes they set the grills on fire," Julia added.

Olivia laughed. "Firefighters setting barbecue grills on fire? Did you have to call 9-1-1?"

"God no." Derek actually shuddered. "That's the kind of thing a house would never live down. Ever. We handled it."

"But we had to scrape black stuff off the hot dogs," Julia said. "Nobody likes burned hot dogs."

"That one woman did," Isaac said. "I forgot her name."

"There's a difference between a burned hot dog and a hot dog that was *in a fire*."

"Nuh-uh," her brother argued. "That's how you burn them. With a fire."

The bickering continued for a good part of the ride, and at one point Derek gave her an apologetic look. But Olivia didn't mind. She'd much prefer listening to them discuss charred food than spend the ride in an awkward silence.

The area around the house Isaac told her was Aidan and Lydia's was so surrounded by vehicles, it looked like a commercial parking lot, but Derek managed to find a spot to squeeze his car into. As soon as he cut the engine, the kids were unbuckled and gone, and Derek chuckled.

"Come on," Isaac yelled over his shoulder, but he didn't stop and wait for them.

That was fine with Olivia because Derek leaned across the car and kissed her. "Hi."

"Hi." She laughed. "Most of the time I'm sorry I'm an only child but sometimes…do all siblings bicker like that?"

"Yup. And some are worse. One time, my mom had to pull the car over because my brother and I got into a fistfight in the back seat and because we were wearing seat belts, neither of us could run away or fall down. It was going the distance."

"Okay, so being an only child isn't all bad."

He nodded his head toward the house. "You ready for this?"

A minute later, Olivia decided it wasn't possible to be ready for the scene in the backyard. It was a crowd, and Derek hadn't been kidding about it being loud. But once she relaxed and looked around, she was able to pick out faces she recognized. Jess and Rick, of course, who waved from across the room. The firefighters Derek worked with. And Lydia, who'd been tending the bar with her sister the night of the fundraiser.

They were all very friendly and it wasn't long before she found herself separated from Derek, who was involved in a very heated debate about cooking chicken and foil-wrapped potatoes on the same grill.

"Olivia, right?"

She turned to see one of the guys she recognized as working with Derek. "Yes. Olivia McGovern."

"I'm Grant." He stuck out his hand, which she shook. "And this is my girlfriend, Wren. We were at the fundraiser at Kincaid's, but I don't think we technically met."

She shook hands with the pretty blonde woman she had a vague memory of seeing. "There are a *lot* of people in Derek's life."

"Cutter!"

Grant turned toward the shout. "Sorry, but I'll be back in a minute. They probably want my opinion on grill temps or something. I don't know how many years these guys are going to barbecue before they figure it out."

"You're right about there being a lot of people in their lives," Wren said after Grant walked away. "It can be very overwhelming at times."

"I'm not sure they realize it because they're so much like a family. It's just the way it is for them, so they don't really get what it's like walking into it without knowing anybody. Have you and Grant been dating long?"

"Yeah, it's been a while. I wasn't really looking for

a relationship but then I met him and he made it hard to remember why."

"Funny, that's exactly how I ended up here with Derek."

Wren laughed. "Have you ever dated a firefighter before?"

"No." Olivia shook her head. "To be perfectly honest, I never dated a guy who didn't wear a business suit to work before I met Derek. I thought I had a type, but he proved me wrong, I guess."

"It's hard sometimes, because their job is so dangerous. They tell me it doesn't really get easier, but you get better at dealing with it so it seems easier."

Olivia spent a lot of time trying not to think about Derek's job too much. She knew it was dangerous. But she also knew they were trained well and they always had orders and a plan of attack to follow. She took comfort in that.

"What do you do?" she asked Wren when the conversation lagged.

"I was working in a coffee shop and a small bookstore, but the bookstore was finally able to give me enough hours to quit the coffee shop. I love books, so even though the money's not great, I love my job."

"I love bookstores. I need to make more time for them in my life. It's so easy to click a button on the computer and have a book show up in the mail or on my phone that I forget how much I love browsing the shelves and finding books I didn't know I wanted to read until I saw them."

"That's the best part," Wren said, and then she frowned as the conversation by the grills got very loud. "They sound angry."

"I was warned the grill discussions could get heated." She was smiling as she said it, but she could tell Wren wasn't comforted. Anxiety clouded her expression as one of the guys yelled for somebody to give him his tongs back. "Grant said they'd never figure it out, but I think this is part of the fun for them."

"Anger isn't fun."

"I don't think they're angry. They're just loud and trying to shout over each other."

Then she noticed Julia walking toward her, with a couple of water bottles in her hands. She looked hesitant about talking to them, but she returned Olivia's smile.

"Lydia said to ask everybody if they want something to drink. Do you want a water?"

"I would love a water," Olivia said.

Wren took one, too, but she didn't open it right away. She turned it around and around in her hands, keeping an eye on the grills. That situation seemed to be winding down, and there was a lot more laughter than yelling, so she slowly relaxed.

"I guess we should go mingle," Wren said after a few more minutes of small talk. "And there's so much food on those tables already, I don't even know why they have to grill anything to go with it."

She wasn't kidding. Olivia ate more over the next few hours than she had all week, and very little of it was healthy. The vegetables, maybe, if she didn't count the dip she'd dredged them through. She also laughed a lot, and had opportunities over the course of the day to have brief conversations with Isaac and Julia.

Derek had been right about this being a good time to meet his kids. There was no pressure, everybody was in a great mood, and by the end of the day, she felt a sense of almost belonging that surprised her. By putting his arm around her or taking her hand in his countless times, he'd made it clear to everybody that she was his, and they'd welcomed her with open arms.

The kids couldn't have missed it, either, but neither said anything about it. They either didn't care, or they were holding back questions or opinions until she wasn't around. Or they were too exhausted to talk, she thought when it was time to go and Derek helped his son buckle up. She was almost too exhausted to talk herself, and she hadn't run like they had.

Maybe she hadn't run, but she felt as if she'd cleared a big hurdle. She'd spent the day with the two most important people in Derek's life and there had been no tears or tantrums.

It was a start.

Olivia agreed to go up with them when they got back to his place, and it didn't take long for Derek to get the kids cleaned up and put to bed. It had been a big day with a lot of fresh air and he was surprised he'd kept Isaac awake long enough for a quick shower to wash the sunscreen and bug spray off him.

Julia tried to resist, saying she wanted to read for a little while, but her eyelids were heavy as he kissed her goodnight. If he knew his daughter, she'd fallen asleep with her tablet beside her and her bedside lamp still on by the time he'd gotten back to the kitchen where Olivia was waiting.

She was leaning against the counter, drinking from a bottle of water she must have found in the fridge. She'd gotten a little sun, but not too much since Chris Eriksson's wife was a serious sunscreen pusher and the families of Engine 59 and Ladder 37 were like greased pigs by the end of any outdoor event.

He stole the bottle and took a swig of water before setting it on the counter so he could put his hands on her waist. "So, did you have a good time today?"

"I did. It was fun and, to be honest, I don't spend a lot of time outside just enjoying myself like that. I try to walk a lot, but it's different."

That's not exactly what he wanted to know, but he found himself reluctant to straight-out ask her how she felt about spending the day with Julia and Isaac. They hadn't interacted as much as he might have liked, since kids rarely hung out with adults at barbecues, but what he'd seen had looked positive.

"And your kids are great," she said with a knowing smile. Maybe he wasn't as hard to read as he'd been told he was in the past. Or she just had a knack for it. "I enjoyed meeting them."

"I think they liked you, too."

His phone chimed in his pocket and he sighed. "It's probably from Aidan or Lydia because one of the kids forgot something. You wouldn't believe how often a lost-and-found bag or laundry basket is sent into the station after one of these things."

But when he pulled the phone out of his pocket, he saw that it was from Amber. Do NOT let the kids stay up too late. I know school doesn't start for a few more days, but I'm trying to get them back on a decent sleep schedule now so the first week isn't a nightmare.

"Sorry, it's Amber," he told Olivia. "I'll just be a second."

"No problem."

They played hard today and they're already asleep.
I couldn't have kept them up late if I wanted to. Julia
said they messaged you goodnight.

She did, but the time they tell me they're going to bed
and the time they actually go to bed is not always the
same. I'm glad they had fun and see you tomorrow.

He sent back a thumbs-up emoji and tossed the phone
on the counter. "Sorry. The kids start school next week
and she wanted to remind me they need to get back on
a regular sleep schedule *before* the first day. Isaac gets
a little hard to handle when he's tired."

"Because of his heart?"

He smiled, warmed by the concern in her voice. "Because he's eight."

"Oh." She gave an uncharacteristically nervous laugh
and shook her head. "Did you know you smile when
you're texting her?"

Derek sighed, dreading where this was probably
heading. "I did not know that."

"You do, and for a minute I was jealous, but then
when you told me what she wanted, I realized you smile
whenever you talk about your kids. I guess even when
you're texting."

"They make me happy. It sucks that they start school
soon, since I won't get to see them as much as I do during the summer, but they like school and they start getting bored, so it's good for them."

"Speaking of next week, I'll be out of town for a
couple of days next weekend. It's been on my calendar
for a while, but I realized I hadn't mentioned it to you."

"Oh." Even though they often went several days

without seeing each other, her going out of town was new. "Are you going to visit your family?"

She rolled her eyes. "No. I'm speaking at a conference, so I'll fly into Kansas City Friday and then fly home early Sunday morning."

"Kansas City, huh?"

"Are you thinking about how far away I'll be or the barbecue?"

He traced his thumb over her bottom lip. "I'm thinking about how much I'll miss you while you're so far away…eating barbecue."

When she nipped at the tip of his thumb hard enough to straddle the line between playful and painful, he yelped, but she didn't look very contrite. "Before you even ask, Derek, I'm not smuggling barbecue home in my carry-on bag."

"You could put it in your checked bag. You wouldn't even technically be smuggling it, then." When she tilted her head and looked up at him through her eyelashes, he held up his hands in surrender. "Of course you don't check a bag. That would be inefficient."

"Very. Checking a bag and then standing around waiting for the carousel is a huge waste of time for short trips. And even for longer trips, it's sometimes cheaper and faster to buy toiletries and whatnot when you arrive at your destination."

He put his hands on her hips and pulled her against him. "You're very sexy when you're talking about efficiency."

"I can say with certainty I've never been told that before."

"That's too bad, because it's true. When you talk about your work, you get this look. You're passionate about it and knowledgeable, and you give off this air of confidence that's very sexy."

Heat flared in her eyes and she buried her fingers in his hair. "It's very sexy that you find that sexy."

He leaned in, teasing her lower lip with his tongue before pressing deeper. She opened her mouth to him and he kissed her with all of the hunger that had built up over a day of watching her in the sun, relaxed and laughing.

But when his hand cupped her breast, he felt her hesitation and broke off the kiss. "What's wrong?"

"Nothing's wrong, really. It just feels weird to be kissing you with…you know."

"With my kids asleep in their rooms?" He chuckled softly against her hair. "Behind their closed doors?"

"Yes, it feels weird."

"Parents get to kiss people, too, you know. That's why so many people have more than one kid."

"You're making fun of me," she accused, eyes narrowing.

"Only a little." He buried his face in her neck and growled. "When am I going to get you alone again?"

"I don't know. You work Tuesday and we have a Village Hearts meeting Wednesday. I'm flying out Friday."

"Or we can just go in my room and close the door and be alone right now."

Her growl of frustration was even more impressive than his. "Your ex-wife already walked in on us. I'd rather not have one of your kids do the same on the very first day I met them."

She had a point. The work he'd put into finding the perfect way to introduce Olivia, Julia and Isaac in a way that enabled them to ease into it would be a waste if one of the kids walked in on them having sex. Since, as far as he knew, neither of them had done that yet, it would probably be a little traumatic.

"Can we at least turn the TV on and make out on the couch a little?"

She ran her hand up his stomach, making every muscle in his body clench, and hooked her finger in the neck of his T-shirt. "A little. And the clothes stay on."

"I can work with that."

Chapter Thirteen

Breakfast the next morning was cold cereal, though Derek made them each have a banana on the side, per their mother's wishes. But he didn't have the energy for making pancakes after a restless night of tossing and turning.

Making out on the couch with Olivia had been sweet. But not stripping her naked and then walking her to her car with an erection that wouldn't quit hadn't been as sweet. And the cold shower had not only sucked, but it hadn't really helped.

He understood her reluctance—especially considering the way she'd met the kids' mother—but he hoped she got over it soon because when the kids' schedules got more rigid, so did his. Her not wanting to spend the night with him if his kids were there was going to put a serious crimp on things.

"Have fun yesterday?" he asked, sitting down at the table with his own bowl of cereal and a mug of coffee almost as big as the bowl.

"Yeah," they both said at the same time.

"I like Wren," Julia added. "She was funny."

Derek had noticed that Wren seemed a lot more relaxed when she was talking with the kids than with the rest of them, and she'd seemed to particularly enjoy talking to Julia. His daughter could be shy at times and, though she'd met them over the years, she was still getting to know his current crew on a family level. A few families from the shift he'd worked before Jeff Porter retired had shown up, but Julia had still spent a lot of time sitting in the shade with Wren, reportedly talking about books.

Wren was still a little bit of a puzzle. He'd heard she could come off as reserved—almost walled off somehow—and he'd found that to be true for the most part. But over time she'd relaxed a little and he saw glimpses of the woman Grant had fallen for. When she was with Grant, she was more animated and everybody could sense the connection between them.

Then he wondered if the people around them could sense the same kind of connection between him and Olivia, which sent him back down the mental path to how hard it had been to say goodnight to her.

"When do you think we'll see her again?" Julia asked and, for a moment, Derek was pleased his daughter sounded as excited to see Olivia again as he was. "She likes books a lot."

Of course. They hadn't been talking about Olivia. She meant Wren. "I'm not sure. You know we start doing a lot of stuff for the holidays with the fire department, so you'll probably see her then."

Did Olivia go home for the holidays? By the time Thanksgiving rolled around, they'd be well into meeting-the-parents territory, but he wasn't so sure he wanted to meet hers anytime soon. And his family was hard-core into the holiday, so that might be too high-pressure a setting for Olivia to meet his mom and dad.

Soon, he thought. He'd told them he was seeing somebody, but not much more than that because his mom *really* wanted him to find somebody, so he was reluctant to get her hopes up. But now he wanted Olivia to meet them. To see the house he'd grown up in and, maybe on a second trip, meet his siblings.

"Dad, you're not eating your cereal," Isaac pointed out. "If you let it get mushy because you're dawdling, you still have to eat it."

Another of Mom's rules, he thought, smiling at his son. "I'll eat every bite."

And he took a bite to prove the point, and barely managed not to cringe. It had definitely absorbed enough milk so he'd probably dump it if he didn't have little witnesses he was supposed to be a role model for.

Maybe if he kept talking, they wouldn't notice and he could toss it after they wandered away from the table. "Did you guys like Olivia?"

"I did," Isaac said.

Julia only shrugged but her mouth tightened just like her mother's did when she wasn't happy about a topic of conversation. Or when she wanted to say something she knew Derek wouldn't want to hear.

"She liked you both." Then he stopped talking, not sure where to go from there.

Julia unpursed her lips long enough to talk. "Is she your girlfriend?"

Derek had hoped to ease into it a little slower, but he didn't want to lie. "Yes, she is. Is that okay?"

Isaac's expression said it was anything but okay. His eyes widened and his bottom lip got that soft look that wasn't quite a pout, but sometimes became a tremble. "Are you going to have a new baby, too?"

"No." The word seemed to fall out of his mouth in a rush to reassure his son. "I'm not having a new baby."

But should he add *right now*? He knew Olivia wanted kids someday. They were a part of her written life plan. But what he hadn't given a lot of thought to, until this moment, was if *he* wanted more children. It wouldn't be fair to her to continue a relationship if he didn't want the same things in life that she did.

He had Julia and Isaac and he'd always felt the two of them were just right. But he didn't feel a knee-jerk *no* to the thought of being a dad again, and imagining Olivia holding a little bundle of joy made him smile, so he obviously wasn't closed off to the possibility.

Right now, he didn't need to go into any of that with an already confused little boy. The bottom line was that he wasn't having a new baby and if that ever changed, he'd cross that bridge with them when they came to it.

"You guys know you're still my number ones, right?"

Julia smiled. "I'm your number one. Isaac's number two, like poo."

"I'm not poo!"

Derek tuned out the ensuing sibling battle of words, since he could tell they were keeping it light. And the distraction was a good way to change the subject before the conversation about Olivia turned too heavy. The best way to make his relationship with her part of their normal was to treat it as though it already was. Or so Amber had said. *Don't make a big deal out of it and it won't be a big deal.* The advice sounded simple enough, even if it was a little hard to wrap his head around it.

Because it was a very big deal. Olivia was a very big deal. And the fact he was falling in love with her was a very, very big deal.

* * *

Public speaking wasn't one of Olivia's favorite parts of her job. She didn't mind standing in an office, speaking to a group of employees about the changes she was going to help them implement. But having a stage and a microphone always triggered the butterflies in her stomach.

It was good promotion, and she'd never left a conference without at least one new name in her list of professional contacts turning into a new business opportunity. And, thanks to her current book, buzz about her upcoming book—which was suffering thanks to her personal life, dammit—the podcast and her general positioning as an expert on the topic, they paid her a nice fee.

The stomach butterflies usually calmed down once she really got rolling, and today's workshop was her favorite kind. These weren't CEOs with skyline views from their desks or tech developers. The conference was for small businesses and entrepreneurs, which meant she could focus on the basics of productivity and working efficiently without spending a fortune on high-tech software suites. She loved those, too, of course, but this was where she felt she made the most difference.

After her workshop and Q&A, they broke for lunch and Olivia found herself sitting with several people who'd started their own businesses and were in various stages of expanding beyond their home offices. She ate her salad while listening to the parents around the table swap stories of changing diapers while talking to a client via headset and a naked toddler streaking across the background of a video conference.

She couldn't imagine the chaos and she was in awe of the fact these people had managed to build their businesses to this point while living and working *in* that chaos.

"How do you do it?" she finally asked the woman closest to her. "Juggle your business with having three kids, I mean."

The woman looked surprised for a moment—maybe because Olivia was supposed to be the expert at the table—and then laughed. "I gave up sleep."

Olivia knew the woman was exaggerating, though probably not by a lot. It had been a common thread throughout many of the conversations she had, and it made her nervous because sleep was vital to productivity. And it seemed like, to feel as if they were giving everything they could to their business *and* their families, a lot of parents compromised by sacrificing self-care. Sleep. Leisure time. Social lives. Their senses of self.

It wasn't sustainable, so it wasn't a compromise Olivia saw herself being willing or able to make. That was one of the reasons children weren't a part of her plan until she'd built her business to the point she could take a step back. Not too much, because she *was* the business. But there was always new tech and new systems, as well as updates, so once she had enough big corporate clients, she could go into maintenance mode instead of hustling for new clients. She'd have more time to focus on writing. And children.

After lunch, Olivia mingled for a while. She had a list of things to accomplish at the conference besides her workshop—people she wanted to meet and some industry news she wanted to learn—and once she'd checked them all off, she retired to her room.

Then she changed into yoga pants, opened her laptop, and tried to spend more time writing than she did glancing at the clock, counting down the hours until Derek might call. He'd asked her schedule and when she'd told him she planned to hole up in her room and get some writing done, he'd said he wouldn't disturb her because he knew he'd already thrown her off her schedule.

He had, but she'd still told him it was okay. He'd insisted she needed to make use of the time because he intended to distract her more when she got home. She was looking forward to that, but in the meantime, she missed hearing his voice.

She decided to compromise and call him when room service brought her dinner. While she usually avoided it at all costs, she knew Derek wouldn't mind if she ate her dinner while talking to him. And neither of them would have to feel guilty about her lost work time because she didn't eat in front of her manuscript.

She hit his number and it rang three times before it was answered. "Hello?"

Olivia's mind blanked for a second at the little girl's voice, but she recovered quickly. "Hi, Julia. It's Olivia."

"It's Olivia," the girl echoed, very loudly as if yelling across the entire apartment. "My dad has his head in the cabinet and he told me to get his phone."

"I told you to bring me my phone, not answer it," she heard Derek tell his daughter.

"Why does your dad have his head in a cabinet?" she asked, seeing an opportunity to talk to Julia even if it was only for a brief time. Every little bit would probably help.

"We have a leak in the sink and Dad says that the plumber the landlord uses is a—"

"Julia Marie," Olivia heard Derek yell, which made her laugh.

Julia giggled, too, and for a few seconds, Olivia got to share in her amusement. It was nice, she thought. Maybe it was a small thing, but this was Derek's life—his *real,* everyday life—and being a part of it, even over the phone, made her feel closer to him.

"Your dad can call me back later if he wants," she said. "After he gets his head out of the cabinet."

"He said some bad words, so it'll probably be a long time before he gets it fixed."

"Julia!" Derek's voice sounded closer. "Say goodbye to Olivia and give me the phone."

"Are you really in Kansas?" Julia asked instead.

"Close. I'm in Kansas City, which is actually in Missouri." So they talked about her, then. Enough so his kids knew she was traveling.

"That doesn't make sense. But Daddy said they have good barbecue."

"He wanted me to sneak some home in my suitcase."

"Ew. That would totally mess up all your clothes." They giggled together again. "Daddy wants the phone, so bye."

"Bye, Julia." She heard the low murmur of Derek's voice and then what sounded like a door closing. "Hey, you."

"Hi. I guess I caught you at a bad time?"

"I can use a break. And I just told them they could have a half hour of video games or tablets and then locked myself in my room, so I'm all yours. Although, if I remember correctly, *you* are supposed to be working on your book."

"I'm eating my dinner while we talk, which is rude,

but I get to talk to you without losing work time. I'm a problem solver, remember?"

"I don't care what you're doing while you talk to me as long as I get to hear your voice." There was a pause, and then a low chuckle that seemed to vibrate right through the phone and into her body. "I mean, there are other things you could be doing while talking to me."

"I've got a bacon-wrapped filet mignon and perfectly sautéed vegetables in front of me. Don't make me choose between them and phone sex."

"That would be cruel and possibly not end well for my ego." He paused for a few seconds. "I miss you."

That made her laugh. "You've gone longer than this without seeing me."

"Yeah, but you're so far away. You *feel* far away." She heard his sigh over the line. "Usually when I talk to you, I can picture you. I can see you sitting on your couch, looking out at the view. Or sitting cross-legged on your bed or—my personal favorite—lying on the bed with a smile lighting up your face."

She smiled as he talked even though she missed him as much as he said he missed her.

"But right now," he continued, "I can't picture what you're doing and it makes you feel far away."

"I'm sitting in the room's desk chair in front of the room service cart," she told him. "The bed has one of those generic white comforters that feels like it weighs fifty pounds, and all I see out the window is dark sky. But if I get up and walk across the room, I have a lovely view of the mechanical equipment on the flat roof below me."

"Not quite what you're used to."

"I might be a little spoiled."

She thought he'd laugh, but there were a few seconds

before he spoke again. "Nothing wrong with that. Have you met a lot of people?"

Did he really think she was spoiled? She didn't think so. She didn't have an expectation of being given nice things. She worked hard and invested in things that kept their value.

"I did meet a lot of people," she finally said, letting the topic swing toward work. "It's a small conference, so a lot of face time. And I made some likely contacts, so it was worth the trip."

"I'm glad it was productive, even though I miss you. I could pick you up at the airport tomorrow."

"Your kids do not want to get up early on a Sunday morning and get dragged to Logan. They just started school, so enjoy the time with them."

He made a sound that perfectly summed up the frustration she felt. "Let me take you to dinner tomorrow night, then. After I drop them off with Amber, I can head over. You can pick the place. Somewhere nice, and then we'll go back to your place and catch up on everything we missed."

Olivia shivered because she knew he didn't mean a recap of her trip. "I can't wait."

"Finish your dinner and get back to work, then, and I'll see you tomorrow. I…" He paused and she heard him clear his throat. "I hope you have a good flight."

"Goodnight," she whispered, and then he was gone and she was left staring at the phone in her hand.

And wondering what he'd really been about to say.

Derek battled a bad case of the nerves on the elevator ride to Olivia's floor, but this time it had nothing to do with the fancy building or breathtaking view.

He'd almost told her he loved her. The words had actually started coming out of his mouth, but his brain had finally caught up with his mouth and put a stop to it. He wasn't sure if he'd covered well or not, since the panic made it hard to think.

Not that he didn't want to say the words. He loved Olivia. There was no sense in trying to deny it anymore. But he didn't want to tell her over the phone, when she was fourteen hundred miles away, give or take a few.

He wanted to be holding her when he said it. He wanted to watch her face and see her reaction to the words in her eyes. And now that he'd been thinking about it since his near slip on the phone last night, it was *all* he could think about and he was afraid he was just going to blurt it out at an awkward moment.

As he knocked, he reminded himself it didn't have to be tonight. Maybe the right moment would come and maybe it wouldn't. If not, he'd wait because he wanted it to be special.

When she opened the door and her eyes widened, his three-little-words nerves gave way to a self-consciousness. Other than his Class A uniform, he only owned one real suit and he was pretty sure the only time he'd worn it in the last ten years had been to funerals. It was a little dated and wearing it made him uncomfortable, though he couldn't say if it was that he hated suits or the fact it was usually associated with somebody dying.

He'd settled for khakis, a dress shirt and a sport coat he'd bought for family court during the divorce. It wasn't up to par with the suits walking around this part of the city, but she could see he'd made an effort for her. And if she wanted to go to one of those snobby restaurants, it counted. He also had a tie in his pocket he'd like to avoid putting on. But he had it.

"You dressed up," she said, her welcoming smile broadening into a grin.

"I tried." And it had been worth the effort because she was wearing a gorgeous sundress with one of those short, open sweaters over it that framed her breasts perfectly. And she had on summery high heels that showed off her teal toenail polish. "You look beautiful. And I missed you."

She wrapped her arms around his neck and kissed him. "I missed you, too. Now that you're here, I'm almost sorry I made reservations."

"Trust me when I tell you I can be quick."

"If I hadn't put time into looking like this, I'd be tempted."

"So we'll go eat and after, I'll be able to take my time peeling you out of that dress. Should we take your car or mine?" he joked, because his car didn't really fit in here.

"It's a short walk. The weather's nice." She kissed him again before going to retrieve a small handbag from the counter. "We can hold hands."

The restaurant was the kind he'd seen in movies, with the snooty guy who made sure you knew you weren't worthy of his time before reluctantly showing you to your table. That kind of attitude made Derek want to act like an ass, but this was Olivia's neighborhood and he didn't want to embarrass her.

"Isn't it beautiful here?" She looked around, smiling. "The food's not quite as good as that place you've taken me, but the woodwork in here is stunning. And the art."

Things he generally looked for in a museum, not a

restaurant, but he agreed it was beautiful and opened his menu.

Holy shit. Did these people pay this much for dinner on a regular basis? He looked around, but nobody seemed to be celebrating anything in particular. Nothing that screamed special occasion. It was just a bunch of people eating food. Very expensive food.

He turned his attention to Olivia as she opened the menu, expecting her eyes to get wide. Maybe she'd lean across the table and whisper something funny or outraged about the ridiculous prices. But she didn't even blink.

Because she was one of these people, he reminded himself. She was one of the people who could eat in a place like this without calculating how many hours' worth of wages the meal would cost.

"What are you going to have?" she asked, looking up from the menu.

A glass of water and a package of oyster crackers? "I haven't decided yet. What do you recommend?"

The way she reeled off several dishes she correctly thought would tempt him confirmed it. This wasn't her first time in this restaurant. Or even her second or third. This place, with its meal prices that exceeded the weekly grocery budgets of some people he knew, was a part of Olivia's everyday life.

It didn't matter, he reminded himself. Trying to convince himself Olivia didn't care about the material things that surrounded her was becoming a habit, but he was going to keep doing it because the alternative meant he was screwed. He'd been with the department a long time. He made good money and got good benefits, but unless he won the lottery, this kind of lifestyle was out of his reach. And she sure as hell wasn't going to give all this up to move into his second-floor apartment.

"Derek?"

He looked across the table at her and didn't have to force the smile that erased the slight concern in her expression. Right now, all that mattered was that he was here with the most gorgeous woman in the room. He'd missed her and he'd pay their ridiculous prices if it meant making her happy.

"I'm trying to decide what to have," he lied. "Everything sounds good."

Once he decided to relax and enjoy Olivia's company, things improved. She told him about the people she met in Kansas City, and he teased her for never leaving the hotel to go in search of good Kansas City barbecue. She laughed a lot, looking beautiful in the fancy lighting setup the restaurant had.

But he couldn't help but notice how at ease she was here. And as they walked home after dessert—and after a long argument over who was paying, which he lost— hand in hand, he wondered if she felt as out of place in his neighborhood as he did in hers. They lived in different worlds.

She's out of your league.

He didn't want those words in his head anymore because they weren't true of Olivia. But if there *was* a league, she played in the pros and he was minor league.

Chapter Fourteen

Derek was quiet when they got back to her apartment, which wasn't really like him. He didn't seem upset, really. Just lost in thought, but she couldn't tell if they were good thoughts or bad thoughts. And she was a little afraid to ask and possibly spoil the night.

He hadn't been happy about her paying for dinner, and she wasn't sure what—if anything—to do about that. She not only didn't expect him to pay for everything just because he was the guy, but she thought that entire way of thinking was outdated and stupid. And she wouldn't be shy about telling him so if he tried it.

But the possibility had more to do with pride than being old-fashioned, and that was a far touchier subject. She wouldn't have chosen that particular restaurant if she hadn't assumed she'd be picking up the tab. It was overpriced, but it had good food and a really great atmosphere. She'd been there a few times with clients and she'd fallen in love with the place.

So she'd thought, maybe if Derek *had* been about to tell her he loved her on the phone last night, that restaurant would be the perfect location for a conversation about how they felt and where they saw things going between them.

She hoped things were going someplace good. There was no denying their relationship was serious. And she'd met his kids and they didn't hate her.

He walked to the living room windows, hands shoved in his pockets. "I still can't believe this view. You have an amazing place, here."

So it *was* the money, she thought. "Thank you."

She wasn't sure what else to say, since it wasn't really her issue. The apartment was expensive. The restaurant had been expensive. She could afford them. If he was having trouble with that concept, he was going to have to come to terms with it because she wasn't going to diminish herself or her accomplishments for the sake of his ego.

And she'd like to think it was more of an adjustment than a problem for him. While he obviously had his pride, she didn't think he was the kind of guy who'd feel emasculated by a woman earning more money.

Then he turned away from the view to face her and his expression softened. "I was surprised by how much I missed you. Knowing you were that far away was tough on me."

"I like knowing you missed me, because I missed you, too." She crossed the room to him, and he pulled her into his arms as he always did. Any trace of what might have been bothering him was gone, and she relaxed in his embrace.

Now, she thought. If he'd been about to tell her he loved her on the phone and stopped himself, now was when he'd say the words and she desperately wanted to hear them.

She loved him—was *in love* with him—and though she was fairly sure he felt the same way, until he said the words, she couldn't be certain. If they were in love with each other, all of the doubts and obstacles could be overcome. She had to believe that.

His gaze held hers so intensely, she shivered in his arms. But when his lips parted, it was to kiss her and not to speak. She sighed against his mouth, trying to shove her runaway thoughts to the back of her mind and lose herself in the kiss.

He took her to bed and made love to her so thoroughly, she barely noticed when he got out of bed to dispose of the condom and turn off the lights. But when the mattress dipped again, she rolled into his arms. Morning was going to come early and she was exhausted, but she didn't mind cuddling for a few minutes.

Derek kissed her forehead, squeezing her tight. "I know I should go because you've probably got a big Monday ahead of you, but I just want to hold you for a bit."

And she wanted to be held, so she snuggled closer. "You were right when you said the distance made the missing harder. I felt far away from you."

"Because you *were* far away from me. Having you in my arms is much better."

I love you, Derek. She could say it. She could be the one who stepped out on that cliff, hoping he'd catch her.

But she'd been so certain he was going to say it tonight and the fact he hadn't held her back. Maybe she'd been wrong about his feelings for her—although she didn't think so—or maybe he just wasn't quite ready. And if he wasn't ready, she didn't want to put that pressure on him.

Either way was scary, and she was still agonizing over whether or not to say the words when she drifted off to sleep.

The alarm going off startled her awake, but when she reached for it, she was stopped short by the fact her hair was trapped under Derek's arm. He stirred, releasing her, and she slapped her hand down on the off button.

They'd both fallen asleep, and it was Monday morning. Getting the day off to a good start set the tone for the week, and she usually got up and hit the ground running.

"Five more minutes," Derek muttered, and then he pulled her back into his arms. He was snoring again within seconds.

Olivia smiled and allowed herself to relax her head on his shoulder. This really wasn't a bad start to the day, either. Maybe not as productive as getting ready for work, but definitely more enjoyable.

"Hey, Olivia, are you sick?"

Kelsey's voice echoing through the apartment confused her for a few seconds, until she realized she must have gone back to sleep and Derek's five more minutes had become a lot more minutes.

"I'll be right out," she called, wishing they'd closed the bedroom door even though they'd had no reason to.

"You're usually in the—" Kelsey appeared in the doorway and then froze. "Oh. Sorry."

Since she'd sat up, Olivia scrambled to make sure she was covered. And Derek was awake, too, and he just lifted a hand in greeting. She took a calming breath because this might not be how McGovern Consulting usually opened for business on Monday mornings, but she had nothing to be embarrassed about, either.

"If you want to go in the office and get started, I'll be there in a few minutes," she said, making sure her voice was level and professional.

"No bacon?"

She looked at Derek, who was smiling innocently up at her from the pillow. "No bacon."

"There's yogurt in the fridge if you want one," Kelsey called as she walked away.

"So I assume that's Kelsey?" he said, once they heard the office door close. They usually left it open, but she probably wanted to give them some semblance of privacy.

"Yes. I'm usually ready for work by the time she gets here, so I'm already behind."

"I'm sorry. I fell asleep."

She ran her hand over his chest, unable to help herself. "So did I. And you're worth being a little late to work for."

That made him smile, and he lifted her hand from his chest to kiss the back of her knuckles. "I'm glad. I'm also glad I got to meet Kelsey, since I've heard so much about her. You've met my kids and the guys I work with. It's about time I get to meet somebody in your life."

"Other than my parents, she'd be the most important person for you to meet," she admitted. "She's become a good friend as well as being the best assistant ever. But I should warn you, she's young and maybe a little enthusiastic about me dating you. I think the whole *trapped in an elevator* thing really sparked her imagination."

"Oh, there were definitely sparks," he said, giving her a look that had her scrambling to slide off her side of the bed before she forgot the workday had technically started and they weren't alone.

Because of what he'd said, Olivia made sure to properly introduce him to Kelsey before he left. Despite her warnings, her assistant was on her best behavior and hit the perfect balance of friendly and professional.

Until Derek had kissed Olivia goodbye with a promise to call her later and they were alone.

"Holy crap, Olivia. He's hot."

"You're the one who creeped on his Facebook pictures."

"I didn't creep. And pictures don't do him justice. I hope you're planning to keep him."

Olivia laughed, though it sounded a little shaky. "It's a little soon to make that decision."

Judging by her expression, Kelsey didn't buy that for a second. "The fact you were still in bed when I got here tells me everything I need to know. There's only one thing that could throw you off your game plan like that."

She tried to tell herself Kelsey was talking about great sex, but Olivia knew she meant love. The thing she and Derek apparently weren't ready to talk about yet.

But just as she'd known it was time for her to meet Julia and Isaac if they were going to move forward, she knew it was going to be time to talk about the future. Not making concrete plans, of course. They hadn't been together long enough for that kind of commitment, but it didn't change one basic fact.

She did, in fact, want to keep him.

Dinner at the station on Tuesday was strangely quiet, which Derek knew shouldn't be a surprise after the day they'd been having. A stubborn electrical fire in the walls of a commercial building had been chaotic and did a lot of damage. And they'd followed that up with an MVA with a fatality.

He was almost done with his beef stew, mopping up the broth with a biscuit, when he put his finger on why the quiet seemed more oppressive than usual. Gavin and Grant were both talkers, seemingly incapable of not filling a silence. And once the thought was in his mind, he could see it. Gavin just looked quiet, but Grant looked…off. His face was set in hard lines and it was as though he'd put up a wall to keep everybody out.

Maybe because he was wrapped up in his own thoughts of the *I love you* he'd wanted so badly to say to Olivia, but hadn't been able to get out when the time should have been right, he hadn't given a lot of thought to it. But now that he'd noticed it, he realized Grant hadn't been himself all day.

It wasn't until the kitchen cleanup was almost done that the wall started to crack.

"I've got some ice time for tomorrow," Scott said. "Who's in?"

"I'm there," Danny and Aidan said almost at the same time.

"I'm in the mood for some hockey," Gavin said. "Grant? You in?"

Grant shook his head. "When I leave here, I'm heading straight home to New Hampshire for a couple days. I'll probably hang out with my dad for a while. Put some miles on my four-wheeler. And the guy who does my Jeep is up there, and I want to talk to him about some more customizations and some paint touch-ups. Maybe new rims."

Derek whistled, holding up his hands. "Sounds pricey. What happened to saving up for a ring?"

Grant's jaw clenched for a few seconds before he lifted one shoulder in a half-ass shrug. "Not gonna need one now. That's over."

"Oh, shit." Derek let that sink in for a few seconds. It looked like Gavin already knew, but it had to have been recent because he'd been talking about cool places to honeymoon just last week. "I'm sorry, man. I didn't know."

Seconds ticked by in awkward silence, but Derek wasn't sure what to say. He wanted to be there for the guy, but he couldn't tell if he wanted to talk about it or not. Derek hadn't wanted to talk about the divorce when he and Amber first split, and he'd hated how often people seemed to bring it up. He'd be having a decent day and then *bam*, some well-meaning person would ask him how his kids were taking the breakup.

"I don't even know what happened," Grant finally said. "I called her to say goodnight, like I usually do, and she said it wasn't working out for her and she didn't want to see me anymore."

"Just out of nowhere?"

"Yeah. We were fine and then she wanted out and wouldn't say why. She just kept saying it wasn't working for her, but I could tell she'd been crying. I kept asking her what was going on and she hung up on me."

"That sucks, kid," Chris said. "It surprises me she'd do that to you. She didn't seem like the type."

"I tried to call her back and it went to voicemail, so I went to her apartment and didn't get an answer." Grant shook his head. "It pissed me off that she wouldn't tell me what was going on, so I decided to give it a couple days so I could cool off and maybe she would be over whatever was making her cry. Then I'd try to talk her into changing her mind or at least telling me why."

"That was probably the right thing to do," Derek asked. "Cooling-off time, I mean."

"I thought so, until I tried to call her. A recording said her number was out of service, so I went back to her apartment. I got no answer when I knocked, and then a kid from down the hall told me the lady who lived there had moved out and they hadn't rented it yet, so nobody lived there." He looked up then, his expression so bleak Derek felt some real concern for the guy's state of mind. "She's just gone."

Derek shook his head. "That's a shitty thing to do, man. She could at least let you know what changed."

"I always knew she was holding back a little, but I took things slow until she started opening up and… fuck. I wanted to marry her and she didn't give a shit enough about me to tell me why she wanted out. She just fucking ghosted."

His face flush with anger, Grant started to walk away, but then stopped and turned around. "And you know what the worst fucking part is? I still love her. I'm worried about her. I'm worried that she held back so much because of something in her past and whatever that thing is maybe didn't *stay* in her past."

"Did you meet any of her family?" Rick asked. "Anybody you can reach out to?"

Grant shook his head. "She never said it outright and I can't really put my finger on specific things she said, but I always got the impression she's pretty much alone in the world."

"I didn't say anything because it didn't go anywhere," Gavin said, "but I looked around online and there's basically nothing. And Cait has a friend with PD who was willing to ask a couple of questions off the record. The landlord said she told him she was leaving and he inspected the apartment and took the key directly from her when she was done clearing it out. Which he said happened fast and without notice, but there didn't seem to be anything off other than that. And the only emergency contact listed on the paperwork he had was her boss, and she quit her job. And the emergency contact on her employment application was her landlord."

"How is that even possible?" Grant demanded to nobody in particular. "How the fuck can a person not have *somebody* who knows anything about them?"

"I don't know," Gavin said. "That was about as far as Cait's friend could or would go as a favor, but he said there's not really any sense in filing a missing person report because as far as he can tell, she just up and moved. And the landlord didn't ask where or why. It's the kind of place with a high turnover and he doesn't care."

"I care." Grant's face was still flushed, but his voice was quiet. "I care and it doesn't matter because she didn't."

"You don't know that," Rick said.

"I know that something happened in her life. I don't know if it was something bad. I don't know if it was something good. But I know that, either way, she didn't bother to come to me about it, and *that* is the bottom line."

There wasn't much any of them could say to that, Derek thought, because it *was* the bottom line. Grant was ready to spend the rest of his life with her, but Wren hadn't gone to him. Whether it was something from her past she was running from or some great opportunity she was running to, if she'd been on the same page as Grant, he should have been the first person she talked to about it.

"If she wanted my help or wanted me to chase after her, she would have told me what was going on or where she was going, so I don't want to talk about it again."

Grant was still for a moment, and then he shook his head slowly and headed for the door. "It's over."

They let him go, because there wasn't anything left to say and, even if there had been, he wasn't in the mood to hear it.

Derek felt for the kid. It was painful enough when a relationship ended, but to be on the verge of asking a woman to spend the rest of her life with him and then she ends it like that? That was plain shitty and there wasn't a damn thing any of them could say to help him feel better.

Suddenly, he had an urge to call Olivia. He just wanted to hear her voice. But he knew she had a very full schedule today and was still trying to catch up from traveling and spending the time she should have been catching up with him, instead.

He settled for telling himself they were okay. Sure, there was some stuff they were going to have to talk about soon, like the fact the distance between his place and hers became more of an issue the closer they got. He didn't want to move that far from his kids, but he was pretty sure she'd have no interest in living in his neighborhood. But that was a problem that could be solved. He hoped.

Because he didn't even want to consider the possibility of Olivia walking out of his life. He knew for damn sure he didn't want to feel the way Grant did right now. They were going to make it work.

Chapter Fifteen

"Admit it, that was a good movie." Olivia shivered as they stepped out of the theater into air that was a lot chillier than it had been when they went in. Now that they were heading into autumn, anything could happen when the sun went down.

"It was...not crowded." He laced his fingers through hers as they walked down the sidewalk. "I'm not sure if it's because it's a Wednesday night or if it's because you're one of only two dozen people who wanted to see it."

"You're a reverse movie snob, Derek. If there aren't any explosions, you think it's boring."

"Well, there was one bomb." He paused until she looked over at him. "That fake British accent."

She laughed and bumped his arm with her shoulder. "You're so bad. But thank you for seeing it with me, anyway, and you can pick the next movie."

"As long as I get to hold your hand and you share your popcorn with me, I'll watch anything with you," he said in a ridiculously bad British accent that made her laugh again. "You did promise me ice cream, though."

Even though it wasn't exactly ice cream weather, they walked to the ice cream shop and bought two cones—

black raspberry and strawberry for him, and orange sherbet for her. Then they found a bench where they could sit and watch the people go by.

"How are the kids doing?" she asked after a few minutes. "Is school going okay for them?"

"Yeah, they're good. Amber had to have a meeting with Isaac's teacher already because he reads fast and when they read together, he always reads ahead and doesn't know where they are if she calls on him. That's pretty typical for him. And Julia got seated next to a girl who keeps talking to her and getting them both in trouble."

"Oh, that happened to me once," she said, laughing. "You raise kids not to ignore people who speak to them because it's rude, and then you have a classmate talking to you when you're supposed to be quiet. I feel for her."

"Oh, you remember Wren? Grant's girlfriend?"

"His almost fiancée? Of course. I really liked her."

"I guess that's over. She broke it off with him and didn't even tell him why. And then she took off, with no forwarding information."

"No." While she didn't know Grant or Wren very well, she liked them both and she honestly thought they were a genuinely happy couple. "That's heartbreaking. Is he handling it okay?"

"I don't think so. He was kind of like an empty shell wrapped in anger last time I saw him. But he was going home to New Hampshire for a few days, so hopefully his family can help him get his head on straight. I heard him telling Gavin he might just pack up and go home for good. I hope he doesn't, not only because I'd hate to see him go, but he shouldn't be making decisions like that until the dust settles."

"They seemed so in love." She tried not to dwell too much on the *love* word, since it had become the elephant in the room whenever she thought about Derek or was with him.

"He was. He was definitely in love with her, and we all thought she loved him, too. But to not only break it off, but the way she did it? He's pretty messed up."

"I'm sorry to hear that." She licked around the bottom edge of her ice cream before it could drip onto her hand. "How's everybody else doing?"

He talked about work for a while, and then he told her a funny story about the time he had to help a rookie firefighter get out of a tree while the cat he'd been trying to rescue watched them from the ground. He was a good storyteller and she never got tired of listening to his voice when he told them. Luckily his job and the people he worked with offered plenty of tales for him to tell.

When they reached her building, he squeezed her hand. "I should go."

"It's not *that* late." She felt a twinge of guilt because, even though he didn't have to be at the fire station early tomorrow morning, it would take him a while to drive home. She'd known from the beginning that being in a relationship with somebody who lived on the other side of the city would be tough, but the deeper in they got the more difficult it became. And maybe it was time for just stay over, but not only was she getting up early, but Kelsey was showing up early, too. It wasn't a work night for him, but it was for her.

"You told me you have a meeting earlier than usual tomorrow because it's the only time the guy could fit you in," he said, echoing her thoughts. "If I go upstairs with you, you'll stay up late again and I know it's an important client you want to get."

Looking up into his face, with the streetlight shining behind him, it was so tempting to tell him she didn't care. So she'd be a little tired in the morning. He was worth it.

"Stop looking at me like that," he said, his voice low and rough. "I'm trying to be a gentleman and you're making it hard."

Her mouth curved into a smile as she raised an eyebrow. "Am I?"

"Oh, you know you are." He cleared his throat. "You're making it rough on me, trying to behave over here."

She sighed and moved in close, wrapping her arms around his waist. "I guess you're right."

He bowed his head, bringing his mouth close to her ear. "And you can make it up to me in the near future."

"Make it up to you? This isn't any easier for me than it is for you. And I really do think you have a thing for kissing on sidewalks."

"I told you, I have a thing for you."

I love you. It was right there, and she almost said the words. Not that she had a thing for him, but that she loved him.

But then his mouth was on hers, and she let him kiss her goodnight so thoroughly, she almost changed her mind about going upstairs alone.

He broke it off and took a step back. "Okay, you need to go in now and I'm going to walk away. But call me when you get a chance and tell me how your meeting went."

"I will. Goodnight."

She forced herself to walk because dragging out their goodnight would only make it harder for him to leave, and he wouldn't go until he saw that she was through the doors. As she pulled the heavy glass door open, she looked back and wasn't surprised he was in the same spot, watching her. He lifted his hand in a wave and then tucked his hands in his pockets and headed off in the direction of his car.

Olivia watched him until he was out of sight, wishing she'd changed her mind and called him back.

When the phone rang and Derek's name came up on her screen, Olivia almost sent it to voicemail. She was home, but they were doing a video-chat staff meeting in ten minutes and then she'd blocked off an hour for following up with contacts she'd made at the conference. Then she had a follow-up appointment with a smaller client who shouldn't have any problems, but it was still a tight schedule.

He knew she rarely answered phone calls during the workday. But she also knew that, other than in the evenings, he usually sent a text message, so it might be important. She answered it on the third ring.

"Hi, Derek."

"I'm sorry to bother you like this," he said, and she heard the stress in his voice. She could also hear sirens and a lot of noise in the background. "I hate to ask you this, but is there *any* way you could pick up Julia at school and hang with her at my place until Amber or I can get there? It would only be for a few hours. She has a key."

Only a few hours? She stared at the planner, which sat open on the counter next to her as always, and blinked. She didn't have ten minutes, never mind a few hours. "I...isn't there a babysitter or somebody?"

"Our regular sitter's in Pennsylvania with her family this week and we've called everybody else. Amber and Jason are on their way to an appointment with the orthopedic surgeon and if they cancel, it could be weeks before he can get another appointment." There was a pause. "I know it's a big ask, Olivia. I wouldn't ask if I had any other options. I'm on a scene. But she can wait for me in the nurse's office until we're cleared and I can get somebody to cover me if you can't get away."

"No." Leaving the poor child at school for hours wasn't an option. "I can work from your place. I'll leave in five minutes and be there as soon as I can. Will they dismiss her to me?"

"Yeah. Amber will call them and take care of that." She could hear the relief in his voice and felt guilty for having hesitated. "I'll make it up to you somehow."

Not unless he could manipulate time and get her some extra hours in the rest of the week. "Don't worry about it. Be safe."

As soon as the call ended, the panic hit. "Kelsey? Can you come in here?"

Kelsey appeared in the doorway two seconds later. "You okay?"

"I have to go."

"Go where? When?"

"Now. And I have to go pick up Derek's daughter at school because she's sick and then take her to his place and stay with her until he or his ex-wife can get there."

"Okay." Kelsey stared at her for a few seconds, obviously trying to wrap her head around this unexpected and unusual turn of events. "We'll still do the staff meeting and I'll do a transcript for you. We can follow up by email or with a second meeting. And I can do the follow-up appointment."

Olivia paused in the act of shoving her laptop into its bag. "On-site?"

"Yeah. I'm thoroughly versed in the system you implemented for them and we both know the visit's just a courtesy because it's in the contract. They're all set and if he has any questions, I'll answer them. And I'm wearing black leggings and boots. I'll grab a jacket out of your closet and rock that millennial office-casual look. It's no power suit, but I'll look professional."

"I don't know." Olivia shoved the power cord and mouse in the bag, zipped it and then set her planner on top.

"Your other option is to reschedule them, squeezing them into an already tight day in the future." Kelsey put her hand on Olivia's arm, making her stop and look at her. "You are amazing at taking a group of people, analyzing the various ways their brains are wired, and finding them the system that allows them to all work together efficiently. That's the magic you bring. But the actual tech? And troubleshooting the system you implemented? I can do that, Olivia."

"Okay." Decision made, she nodded sharply and grabbed her car keys. She'd drive herself because she wasn't sure how long it took to retrieve a child from a school building. And she wasn't sure just how sick Julia was. "Let me know how it went. If everything's quiet, maybe we can do a video chat. And good luck."

Kelsey laughed. "I think you'll need the luck more than I do."

"I don't actually believe in luck," Olivia said, picking up her bag. "It's just an expression."

But when she was standing in a school office, signing her name and waiting for Julia, she almost wished she *did* believe in luck because she could use a little right now. Maybe Julia just had a headache. Or she could even be faking to get out of a test she hadn't studied for. Olivia had tried that a few times before her parents decided she needed a better plan and taught her how to structure her study time.

But then a very pale, slightly sweaty Julia was walking down the hall toward her, a woman at her side, and Olivia's stomach sank. She wasn't faking.

"She was just sick again, so you have a short window to get her home," the woman said. She handed over Julia's backpack and an empty plastic shopping bag. "You're all signed out?"

"Yes, we are." She held the bag up. "What's this?"

"In case the window until she gets sick again is shorter than the drive home."

"Oh. Thank you." At least she had a leather interior. "You ready to go, Julia?"

The little girl nodded and they walked out to the Audi in silence. Olivia opened the door, but Julia just looked at her blankly for a few seconds.

"I'm not tall enough to sit in the front yet," she finally said. "The airbags."

"Sorry." Great. They weren't even in the car yet and she was failing at this.

Once Julia was buckled in, with the empty bag in her lap just in case, and her backpack next to her, Olivia punched Derek's address into the GPS. Luckily, it was a short drive and she caught mostly green lights, so she was able to get Julia out of her car and up the stairs to Derek's apartment without using the shopping bag.

The little girl was making a whimpering sound as she dug the key out of her backpack, though, and as soon as they were inside, Julia bolted for the bathroom. Olivia kicked the door closed and dumped everything on the kitchen table, anxiety clouding her brain.

She could list the pros and cons of every work and productivity program on the market for every business model, personality type and neurodiversity, but she knew absolutely nothing about taking care of small children.

Then she heard Julia retching and stilled for a moment. She'd never been responsible for a sick child before, but she'd been sick herself. All she had to do was offer what comfort she could until she could be with her mom.

The bathroom door was open and Julia was bent over, her little hands braced on the toilet seat. Olivia grabbed a clean washcloth from the shelf and wet it with cool water. After wringing it out, she put one hand on Julia's back and used the cloth to wipe her forehead. Then she unrolled some toilet paper and had the girl blow her nose.

"All done for now?" Julia nodded, so Olivia wiped her face again and then walked her to the couch. "I'll be right back."

She grabbed the pillows from Julia's bed, along with a small throw blanket that looked very well loved. On her way back, she opened cabinets until she found a large plastic bowl.

"When will Mommy be here?" Julia asked as Olivia set the bowl on the floor in front of the couch and then helped her sit up so she could put the pillows against the arm of the couch.

"I'm not sure, but I know she'll come as fast as she can."

Once Julia was snuggled against the pillows with her blanket, Olivia turned on the television and handed her the remote control. Then she went back into the girl's bedroom and looked around. There were a ton of ponytail elastics on her dresser, but she finally found a soft band that would hold all that dark, curly hair back without pulling on her scalp.

Derek didn't have any ginger ale in the fridge, but he did have some crackers, so she grabbed those, too. She took two out of the package and put a little bit of water in a cup. After setting them on the coffee table, she pulled it closer to the couch.

"If you want those, just little nibbles and sips, okay?"

"Okay." Julia kept her gaze on the TV screen, but her eyelids were heavy and it looked as if she might even sleep a little.

Olivia had no sooner unzipped her laptop bag than Julia jumped up and ran for the bathroom.

She almost made it.

About fifteen minutes after Olivia tucked a cleaned-up Julia back into her nest on the couch, her phone vibrated.

How's Julia? They're trying to find somebody to cover for me, but a lot of people took vacations this week, I guess. Amber might get there before I do.

There was nothing to be gained by frustration at the situation. She knew if Derek could be there, he would be. She's been sick several times, but she's resting right now.

Thank you again. I'm sorry.

We're fine.

Amber got there first, almost an hour later. She knocked this time, but was through the door before Olivia could cross the room to open it.

"Hi, Olivia. Thank you *so* much for picking her up. I swear, this almost never happens."

"I'm glad I was able to help," she said, but Amber had already turned her attention to her daughter.

"Oh, honey." She knelt next to the couch and put her hand on Julia's forehead.

"I went to the nurse and threw up there, so I didn't throw up in the trash can in class like Simon did last year."

"That's good, sweetie. How many times have you been sick?"

When Julia shrugged, Olivia stepped in and gave Amber a recap, wrapping it up with the single cracker and few sips of water that had stayed down for about twenty minutes now. "She's been drifting in and out, watching TV, but she looks a little less pale than she did when I picked her up."

"I can't thank you enough. Derek said you run your own business and you're super busy so I'm sorry he had to call you, but…Jason was nervous about this appointment and Julia seemed fine this morning. And it's hard with Derek, with the job and all. He's one of the most dependable people I've ever met, but you can't depend on him being available, if that makes any sense."

As if they'd summoned him, Derek walked through the door. He was still in his uniform pants and T-shirt, and his hair looked stiff and was sticking up. Probably from his helmet, Olivia thought. There were smudges on his face and he didn't smell great, but she was still glad to see him.

"How's she doing?" he asked, walking toward the couch without waiting for an answer. "Hey, pumpkin."

"I'm sick, Daddy."

"I heard. I'm sorry I couldn't pick you up, but I had to wait for somebody to come in to work for me."

"S'okay. Olivia got me and she took good care of me."

He ruffled her hair and then turned to give Olivia a smile that could warm a February day. "She did, huh?"

"Yeah. You should buy her a treat. Like a strawberry frosted doughnut with sprinkles."

"I'll do that."

Olivia gave Derek a firm look. "I'm going to hold you to that."

"Doughnuts are one of my big weaknesses," Amber said, "and I have no willpower around them, so the kids only get them as very special treats."

"Then I'm honored she thinks I deserve one."

They both laughed, and it felt as if a part of Olivia was watching from the outside. This was Derek's ex-wife and she was the new woman in Derek's life, and yet they were laughing together, talking about doughnuts. Amber was nothing like Deborah, and Olivia was no Marge, and she felt the weight of that concern fall from her shoulders. Hopefully forever.

After tucking Julia's blanket higher around her shoulders, Derek walked over to them so he could keep his voice low as he spoke to Amber. "Do you think she should stay here?"

"I don't know. We've all been exposed to whatever bug she's got, so if Isaac's going to get it, he's going to get it. And at least there's two of us there. It's a lot for one person."

After a long moment and a glance at Olivia she couldn't decipher, he shrugged. "Whatever you think is best. I just want to make sure it's not too much for you, with the baby and all."

Amber smiled. "If I get sick, I get sick. It won't hurt the baby, and it won't be the first time I've been sick while pregnant."

"As long as you're sure. I don't mind if she stays, but you know if she wakes up sick in the dark, she wants Mommy."

It didn't take long for Amber to gather Julia's things, and Derek pulled her SUV up to the curb before carrying his daughter out and buckling her in the back seat. Once they were gone, he closed the door and leaned against it with a sigh.

"I'm sorry, Olivia."

"You don't have to keep apologizing."

He looked past her and she knew he was looking at the kitchen table, where her laptop was still half in the case. She hadn't even opened it. "It's not easy to work with a sick kid."

She shrugged, faking a casual tone she didn't feel. "I'll make up the work later. And Kelsey took care of some things for me. Fortunately, I didn't have any high-priority meetings today."

"I'm glad it didn't mess up your day too much." He ran a hand over his hair and then winced. "I should take a shower. How about after I get cleaned up, I take you out. We can get something to eat and…whatever."

Olivia glanced over her shoulder at the pile representing the work she hadn't done today. What she should do was go home, lock herself in the office and not leave it until she was caught up. But she could tell Derek felt guilty and he'd feel worse if she didn't let him at least feed her a meal to make up for it.

"Sure. And maybe a glass of wine." She'd earned one.

When Derek got out of the shower, he could hear Olivia's voice and wondered for a moment who she was talking to. Then he heard a woman's voice he didn't recognize and realized it was probably the Kelsey he'd heard so much about because she was talking about work.

"I just hope you don't get sick," he heard Kelsey say.

"That would be a nightmare right now. Make sure you leave before I get back. By Monday I'll know how that went."

He winced, really hoping his daughter hadn't managed to infect Olivia with whatever bug she'd picked up. A lot of things tended to go around in the fall, when the kids were all closed up together in school again, so he was used to it. Olivia probably wasn't.

Fortunately, I didn't have any high-priority meetings today.

What if she had? He wondered how he'd feel right now if he'd called her and she'd said no.

After he took his time drying off and pulling on a pair of jeans—trying to give her time on the phone—

he took a moment to think about that possibility. Working it out in his head lessened the possibility something he'd regret might come out of his mouth.

He didn't totally understand Olivia's job. He had a grasp on the basic concept of it, but for a guy who needed his ex-wife to show him how to use his calendar app multiple times, it didn't all make sense. But what he did know was that big companies looking for organization and scheduling help wouldn't give money to somebody who couldn't keep to a schedule. He got that part.

And yet she hadn't said no. She'd packed up a mobile office—which she didn't even get to use—and driven across the city so his sick daughter wouldn't have to sit in the nurse's office, waiting for him or Amber to show up. That's what he needed to focus on. And if there *had* been a high-priority meeting scheduled, she probably still would have done it. She just wouldn't have smiled and assured him it was fine at the end of the day.

But when he walked out of the bathroom, she wasn't smiling. She actually had an expression that looked a lot like regret.

"I'm actually going to take a rain check on the dinner," she told him, and his stomach sank as he crossed to her. "Kelsey just got an email that a client I had to reschedule has some free time this evening, so I'm going to head back."

"They can't wait?" He trailed his fingers down her arm. "I feel like I should at least feed you. And you don't work at night, remember?"

"Not usually, but if I meet with this client and then spend a little time working tonight, that's less I have to carry over and I can start tomorrow fresh."

She said the words matter-of-factly, with no hint of

resentment or blame, but he still felt a pang of guilt. "Are you sure that's it?"

"What do you mean?"

"I just...nothing, really. I'm trying to get a hold on whether or not that's just a good excuse to leave because you're not happy with me."

"Your daughter was sick, Derek. It's nothing that can be controlled, so do you really think I'd hold that against you?"

Maybe not that she'd gotten sick, but that he'd asked her to drop everything and take care of her. "Of course not. Call me before you go to bed?"

She smiled, and he was comforted by the warmth in her eyes. "I will. I have a hard time sleeping if I don't talk to you first."

"Good." He cupped her cheek. "I want you to miss me when you're alone in bed."

"Oh, I do." She kissed him, a sweet kiss that felt almost like an apology. "I should go before I change my mind."

"Is that a possibility?" She zipped up her work bag and he lifted it off the table. The damn thing was heavier than it looked.

"With you, it's always a possibility, but it would be better for *me* to go back to work."

"Then I'll walk you down."

He felt her resolve wavering when he leaned her up against her car and kissed her goodbye, but he forced himself to step back and open her door. He'd already thrown off her schedule enough today. He wasn't going to compound it by talking her out of trying to catch up.

"Call me later."

"I will," she promised.

Once her car was out of sight, he sighed and walked back up the stairs. It felt weird to be alone after a tense day of scrambling, so he turned the television on and flipped through the channels until he found a game to watch. He'd give it a few more minutes and then send a text to Amber, asking for an update on Julia.

And then he'd wait for Olivia to call.

Chapter Sixteen

"Do you see her, Dad?"

Derek dutifully turned in a circle, looking for Olivia on Isaac's behalf, since his son was too short to see over the crowd in the arena's vestibule. "Not yet, but she's probably at the Village Hearts booth near the main door."

The charity hockey game—which Rick, Scott and Grant were playing in, along with other first responders from around the city—was raising money for a children's hospital, but they'd gotten permission to put a display for Village Hearts in the entrance, along with a few other booths. And while another couple had volunteered to man their booth, Derek had asked Olivia to join them to watch the game.

While they'd all gone to Aidan and Lydia's barbecue together, this would be their first outing as a *family*, so to speak, and Derek's stomach was in knots. And it didn't help that this would be the first time he'd seen her face since he'd asked her to pick up Julia at school a week ago.

They'd talked on the phone, of course. And sent text messages back and forth. But no matter how much she assured him everything was okay, he needed to see her.

And while he'd have to limit himself to a quick hug, he wanted her in his arms again.

"I don't know why I couldn't go with Mom," Julia muttered, and not for the first time.

Usually Derek let her get away with a little moodiness, but she enjoyed watching hockey and she'd never opted out of a charity game before. "What's the problem? Are you feeling okay?"

"I'm fine."

He'd thought he'd have a few more years before his little girl mastered the *I'm fine* that meant things were anything but fine. "Spill it, kid. Your brother and I want to have a fun night."

"And Olivia," she reminded him, and the attitude ratcheted up a notch. "Don't forget Olivia."

"Yes, Olivia's going to watch the game with us, too."

"And that's why Mom and Jason didn't come."

Derek sighed, and a little bit of frustrated growl seeped into the sound. He wanted to ask her why she'd waited until they were here to spit it out, but to be fair, she'd been hinting at being unhappy for several hours and he just hadn't wanted to deal with it. "Olivia's not the reason your mom isn't here."

"Mom always came, even after you got divorced. Now Olivia's here and Mom didn't want to come."

You take the kids to watch the game because Jason's going to take me out for a nice dinner and then we're going to take advantage of the alone time before this baby makes me feel like an unsexy beach ball.

He bent down so he could keep his voice low. "Jason wanted to take your mom on a date tonight since they know you like watching hockey with me. I know you have a lot of friends with divorced parents and you probably hear a lot of things, but you know your mom and I are friends. And your mom and Olivia will probably be friends, too, when they get to know each other better. They've already met and all six of us could be here together if we wanted to."

She gave the same head tilt and little eye roll her mother did to signify she'd lost, but didn't want to admit it. "Fine. We need to keep walking or we'll have bad seats."

But he put his hand on her shoulder to keep her from walking away from him. "Are we done with this? I don't want you to be snippy with Olivia."

"I won't." The premature pre-teen attitude melted away. "She's really nice."

"Come *on*," Isaac said, tugging at his hand. "I think she's over there."

Derek looked in the direction his son pointed and then he saw her and his heart stuttered in his chest.

Olivia's gaze locked with his and for a few seconds, he held his breath. Her face lit up and the smile that she sent in his direction let him exhale as the knots in his stomach loosened for the first time in a week. He smiled back as Isaac dragged him in Olivia's direction and, after saying something to the woman manning the Village Hearts booth, met them halfway.

Derek slid one arm around her waist and kissed her. He'd intended to go for a kiss on the cheek, but he couldn't help himself and pressed his mouth to hers for a moment.

But they were not only in the middle of a crowd, but it was a crowd of families—including his own—so he kept it short and sweet.

"We have to get good seats," Isaac said.

Olivia smiled at him. "Yes we do, because this is my very first hockey game."

"Ever?" Isaac looked confused. "But not on TV, right?"

"I have never seen a hockey game, even on television," she said, and both kids groaned in unison.

She laughed. "Don't worry, I have a plan. Instead of asking a bunch of questions, I'm going to cheer when you cheer and boo when you boo."

Derek chuckled and took her hand as they followed the kids into the rink. "That's a good plan."

She chuckled. "I'm sure I'll figure out what's happening along the way. Julia, are you feeling better?"

The girl turned and smiled at Olivia, all traces of her earlier bad mood gone. "I'm all better. And nobody else got sick, which is weird, so Mommy said I probably ate something bad. But I'm not sick anymore and I can have all the hockey food I want."

"There's official hockey food?"

Derek laughed. "Concession food is a hockey tradition. I should have warned you supper might not live up to your usual standards."

"There you go with that stupid standards crap again. I'll have you know that concession pizza and soft pretzels rate very high on my personal food pyramid, even if it does take days to wash the sodium out of my system." She gave him a smug look as the kids laughed at him. "So there."

They found good seats near some of the other E-59 and L-37 families. Olivia went in first and the seating habit was so ingrained that the kids followed, so Isaac went next and then Julia, so Derek found himself two kids away from her. But listening to Isaac trying to explain the rules to her—with help from Cait's younger brother, who was sitting with his mom, Cait and Gavin behind them—made up for being too far away to hold her hand.

Once the game started, there weren't many opportunities for talking. With the stands full of friends and family, and with friends and colleagues facing off on the ice, the cheering was deafening. But watching Olivia and the kids laughing together as she mimicked their reactions to the play, with only a few seconds of lag time, Derek was about as happy as he could remember being in a very long time.

Maybe he *could* have everything.

When Julia asked if it was time to eat yet, he saw his chance to get a few minutes with Olivia. Not private moments, of course, but away from the kids. After telling the kids to sit tight—under the watchful eye of Cait, who gave him a nod—he gestured for Olivia to go with him.

Holding her hand, he led her to the concession area. He waved and said a quick hello to countless people he knew, but he didn't stop until they were in the relatively quiet area where they sold the concessions. Because it was a charity game, they had a lot of donated food from local businesses to sell, so Olivia could get her pizza and soft pretzel. Derek asked for a couple of slices for himself, along with one for Julia and a hot dog for Isaac. They'd also have to balance a couple bags of popcorn.

"I hate to question your plan," Olivia said, "but how are we going to carry drinks?"

He laughed, shaking his head. "I hadn't gotten that far yet. Usually the kids carry their own stuff, but I wanted a minute alone with you."

"I'm not sneaking off into the locker rooms or whatever they have here." She gave him a stern look, but it only lasted a few seconds before it turned into a sheepish smile. "Not that I was thinking about the possibility of it, or anything. It's too bad you don't have a minivan."

"Why would I get a mini…oh." His cheeks got a little warm when she laughed at him. "I'm keeping the kids tonight, but what are the chances you can hang out for a while tonight?"

He knew it was a long shot, but he had to ask. He'd missed her and even if she couldn't stay, he needed for her to know he wanted her to.

When she leaned in close, a naughty smile playing with the corners of her mouth, his blood heated. "I wasn't sure how long hockey takes or if you'd have plans for after the game, so I don't have any appointments until mid-morning and Kelsey's going to do some admin stuff until I get there. If you're sure it's okay, with the kids and all."

"Until you get there? So you can stay the night?"

"Like I said, I wasn't sure if you'd have plans for after the game."

He had to forcibly remind himself they were at a family hockey game. "Oh, I have plans."

"What's happening?" Even though Olivia had promised not to ask questions, she was confused by what was happening on the ice.

And she wasn't getting any cues from the crowd. For the first time since the game started, it was quiet in the rink.

"Grant's in trouble," Isaac whispered.

She leaned her head close so she could whisper back. "In trouble for what? Did he break a rule?"

"That was a dirty hit."

Carter leaned forward from the row behind them so his head was between theirs. "It's a charity game, so they're supposed to have fun and keep it clean."

She nodded to show she got it now, and watched as Grant left the ice and disappeared through a set of doors. A few seconds later, Gavin left his seat, presumably to head to the locker room. Another player took Grant's place, but it took a few minutes for the crowd to resume full volume after the game resumed.

Olivia fell back into the pattern of mimicking Isaac and Julia's reactions, surprised to find herself enjoying the game far more than she'd expected to. Every few minutes, her gaze would meet Derek's over the tops of his kids' heads and he'd smile.

"We're gonna win!" Isaac was practically bouncing in his seat as the clock ticked down, and she wondered how long it would take for the soda Derek had gone back for to work through Isaac's system.

An hour and a half later, when she finally pulled her car in behind Derek's in his driveway, she had her answer. She watched him open the back door and, while he didn't carry Isaac, it was obvious the child had fallen asleep.

"They're going to be fun at school tomorrow," Derek said after sending the kids to brush their teeth and get ready for bed. "I should have thought about the fact I'm the one who has to get them up in the morning before I let them have soda."

Olivia laughed, even though she was already turning the morning's logistics over and over in her mind.

Since she'd be doing the drive-home-of-shame in tonight's clothes, she'd like to be up and out before it was time for Isaac and Julia to get up. She had no idea what time that was, but she was an early riser, so hopefully she could avoid any awkwardness.

After saying goodnight to the kids, she turned on the television and sat on the couch to wait while Derek went through the bedtime routine with them. And then she laughed when he flopped down beside her with an exaggerated air of exhaustion.

"No more soda for them," he said.

"How many times have you said that?"

He chuckled and took her hand in his as he turned his head to look at her. "Every time I take them out and buy them soda. Did you have a good time tonight?"

"I did. I'm not sure I'll ever really understand hockey, but it was fun. And Isaac and Julia obviously love it. He was so funny tonight."

"They enjoyed having you there." He tugged on her hand, pulling her closer. "I enjoyed having you there. And I'm enjoying having you here."

She moved closer, then yelped as he lifted her and turned her so she was straddling his lap. Then she covered her mouth. "Don't make me do that."

"They're probably already asleep." He kissed her, his hands at her hips.

She'd let him kiss her, she thought. They were both fully clothed and it was just kissing.

But as he deepened the kiss, his tongue parting her lips, she moaned. He gripped her hips harder with his fingertips and she couldn't stop herself from grinding against him.

His mouth left a hot trail of kisses down her throat

before he gently bit the side of her neck. "Do you know what watching hockey does to guys?"

"I'm starting to see the appeal of the sport," she said as his hands shifted to her breasts.

"I think it's bedtime for you, too."

She couldn't stop herself from glancing over her shoulder at the bedroom doors. "Are you sure they're asleep."

"I'd bet on it." He pinched her nipple through the fabric of her shirt and bra, and she pressed her lips together to keep from making a sound. "I changed the doorknob on my bedroom door so it has a lock because I'm an optimist, and we'll leave the TV on to make you feel better."

"You can't do anything that makes me loud," she whispered.

Derek laughed, and she put her finger over her lips to shush him. He took her wrist and brought her hand to his mouth. She sighed as he slowly drew that finger into his mouth, sucking gently.

She squirmed for a few seconds and then pushed off his lap. The options were to lock his door and try to behave or leave. And there was no way she was leaving right now.

They didn't waste any time getting naked, but Olivia put her hand on his chest to stop him as he joined her in his bed.

"I mean it. If I start getting loud, you have to put a pillow over my face or something."

"Suffocation's not really my thing," he said when he was done laughing at her again. "I think you need some distracting."

And he was damn good at distracting her. It didn't

take long before the only thing she could focus on was the feel of his hands on her body, and his tongue gliding over her skin.

And her last thought as she drifted off to sleep was that she hoped she hadn't actually left bite marks on the side of her hand. Or that they'd fade by morning.

Chapter Seventeen

Olivia's phone rang just as she and Kelsey finished their end-of-the-week review. Since it would take a few minutes for her to gather her stuff to leave, Olivia took the phone into the living room and answered it.

And it was Amber's voice on the other end of the line. "Olivia? It's Amber. Do you have a minute?"

Thoughts flew through her mind. Was everybody okay? The kids? It was Friday and Derek was working. Was he okay? "Yeah, I have a minute. What's up?"

"Actually, Julia wanted to talk to you about something, but you know she's a little shy and she didn't want to call you out of the blue. But I wasn't sure when you'd see each other again, so I told her I'd call and break the ice for her."

"Julia can call me anytime," she told Amber. "And I have time now."

"Great. Hold on a sec."

After a moment, Julia was on the line. "Hi, Olivia."

"Hi."

"I hope you're not busy, but thank you for talking to me."

"You're welcome. And I'm not too busy, so what's going on?"

She hesitated so long, Olivia thought for a few seconds they'd been disconnected. "We have a school project thing and we're supposed to bring somebody in to speak about the topic. It's like show-and-tell, but with people."

"That sounds fun. What's the topic?"

"Helping others."

"Well, your dad certainly helps others."

"Yeah, but he goes to my school, like, every year. But Daddy said you help others be successful. And they gave us homework planners this year so I thought you could talk about how you help people use things like that and maybe even show us?"

Olivia was speechless for a minute. Julia wanted to take her to school for show-and-tell. It was a big deal and her eyes actually welled up, though she managed to blink away the unshed tears and not sniffle. "I think that sounds really great. When would this be scheduled to happen?"

She got up and crossed to her planner as she asked the question. Hopefully it wouldn't be too soon because she had a busy couple of weeks ahead of her, but she'd figure it out. Not only was it another way to connect with Derek's daughter, but it had been hard for her to reach out, so Olivia wasn't about to tell her no.

"My teacher said the date, but I don't remember. It's in the middle of October, though."

She winced, because she couldn't work with that. Blocking off the entire middle of a month for one appointment wasn't going to happen. But flipping the page in her planner showed that she wasn't booked up yet and could surely make it happen.

"I'd love to be a part of your project," she said. "But

can you do me a favor and on Monday, ask your teacher for the exact date and write it down so you'll remember it for me?"

"Yes, I'll put a note in my homework folder to remind me and I'll write it on the note."

"Perfect. It's going to be fun."

"Thank you, Olivia."

"You're welcome."

When they'd hung up, Olivia took a sticky note from one of the leather pockets in her book and wrote a note about the project and the estimated mid-October date, which she stuck on the page.

"That sounded interesting," Kelsey said, her bag slung over her shoulder.

Olivia caught her up, amused when her assistant also cringed at the vague date. "If I don't hear from her Monday after school, I'll email Amber and ask her to touch base with the teacher."

"You have his ex-wife's email address?"

"She still volunteers with Village Hearts, so it's on the list they gave me."

"I think it's cool how you two get along."

"Me, too." Olivia closed her planner with a sigh. "It's definitely different than any of the divorces in my family. And I'm glad, since I'm not sure I can handle a relationship with an ex like my mother in it."

"You've seemed different since you started dating Derek. Happier, even when you're a little stressed out by how things have changed."

"I am happier. There are some issues, of course— there always are—and one of them is how my schedule sometimes feels like it was tossed in a blender without the lid on."

Kelsey laughed, but her amusement faded quickly into an uncharacteristic seriousness. "You know, since you've been seeing Derek, I've picked up some more responsibility and helped out with follow-up and stuff."

Olivia nodded, not surprised. It would have been about the time for the question of a raise even if nothing had changed in her personal life to put more weight on Kelsey's shoulders. "You have, and I appreciate it."

"I also know you're a little behind on your book, which you could technically write anywhere."

Olivia frowned, both because she didn't like being reminded she was behind schedule with the manuscript and because that didn't seem relevant to where she'd thought the conversation was heading.

"I'm not that far behind," she said, hating the defensive tone in her voice. "And I chip away at it."

"It wasn't an accusation." Kelsey blew out a breath and then gave her boss a nervous smile. "I'm just going to say it outright. I want to do more. I'm *ready* to do more, to the point you're wasting my skills on tasks any decent office manager can do. It's inefficient and fiscally irresponsible."

Olivia made sure her expression gave nothing away. "You're trying to push the buttons you know work on me."

"Just hear me out. I can do follow-ups. I can work with smaller clients on the basic systems. I can troubleshoot. There are a *lot* of things you're doing that I can take over without diluting or weakening your brand in any way. We could easily train an assistant to do most of my day-to-day things. Some of the work would still be mine and, combined with taking on some of your work, leaves me with a solid career path. And it leaves you more free hours to focus on the high-end and high-tech market. The big money. Or it leaves you more free hours to enjoy more time with Derek."

She wasn't wrong. Olivia knew Kelsey was capable of more than what she was given to do, and she trusted her knowledge and drive. Kelsey stepping up had always been part of the plan, but just not yet. "I'm not basing business decisions on my personal life."

"It's not that simple, though. You have to make room for him somewhere, and he can't come *after* everything else on your to-do list." She set her bag down and went to the fridge to grab a drink. "I've thought a lot about this lately."

"I have been, too," Olivia admitted. "I don't want him to come after everything else, but I also can't just let my responsibilities slide. I got here by making a solid plan and executing it. If I start wandering off the plan, it crumbles."

Kelsey put the cap back on her drink and picked up her bag. "I just know it's starting to weigh on you and I wanted to tell you that I'm ready to step up my role in your company so that when you're thinking about it, you have that information."

"Thank you."

Kelsey was almost to the door when she stopped and turned back. "And you might want to consider that fighting to stick to your plan isn't the right answer. It might be time to make a *new* plan."

Derek kissed his kids goodbye, feeling a pang of regret as they ran past their mom into the house. It was Saturday and they should be with him.

But Olivia was coming over around dinnertime and

there was no reason they couldn't all hang out at his place—and they probably *should* be—but he'd had the uneasy feeling he and Olivia were losing traction and it was time they talk about some things.

He wanted more.

And he didn't want to have that personal of a conversation in hushed voices with the kids asleep on the other side of their doors, so after spending the day with them, he'd asked them if they'd mind going home for the night. He'd pick them up again in the morning and do something fun. They didn't really care which place they physically slept in, so the *something fun* bribe worked.

"They're fine," Amber said, probably reading the second thoughts all over his face.

"This is their time with me. I don't get to see them as much when school starts, so I feel guilty about not taking every minute."

"You are a part of every single day for them, whether they're here or there. And what you're doing is in their best interests, not just yours. You've looked happy these last couple of months, which makes *me* happy, but you also look tired. If she's the one for you, it's time to start looking forward at how it's going to work before you burn yourself out trying to be there for everybody."

When he'd called to ask about bringing them home, not wanting to break up any plans she and Jason might have made, he'd told her why.

"Yeah, it's time for us to start looking forward." And it made him nervous as hell.

He wasn't any less nervous when Olivia showed up, looking delicious in leggings and a lightweight summer sweater that draped over her hips.

"Where are the kids?" she asked after he'd kissed her

until his options were to stop or strip her naked in his kitchen. Since he knew they needed to talk, he stopped.

"I brought them back to their mom's for the night."

"Everything okay?"

"Yeah. I just thought it would be nice for us to have some time. To talk."

She got very still. "Uh-oh."

"There's no uh-oh." He hoped. "I just…wow. Somehow I'd pictured us having a nice quiet meal and then cuddling on the couch for this conversation."

"We can try for that, but now I'll probably be distracted by worrying about what's on your mind."

He nodded, because he understood. He should have known she'd ask about the kids and had a plan for what to say. Instead he'd told her the truth and now they were standing awkwardly in his kitchen.

"I'm in love with you, Olivia," he said, ripping off the bandage. "I am in love with you and I need for us to talk about what our future looks like together."

She sucked in a breath and tears shimmered in her eyes. "I'm in love with you, too. I have been for a while."

Relief made his knees weak, and he laced his fingers through hers. If he loved her and she loved him, everything else could be figured out. Somehow.

"I want us to figure out how we're going to work toward a future together," he said, the words hard to force through the tightness in his throat. "You've become part of every aspect of my life. My kids like you. All of my friends like you. You're a part of everything."

"But being in the Back Bay also separates me."

He nodded. "It's hard. It's one thing when we're dating, but if we're bringing our lives together, it's going to get harder. The amount of time spent traveling cuts into work time and family time. I was surprised when Julia told me you're going to go to her school because from where you are, that wrecks the day."

"You were surprised I'm doing a favor for your daughter?"

Something in her tone set off warning bells in his head, but there was no backing out now. "A little, I guess. I know it was a hardship for you when she got sick, so... I don't know."

Her jaw tightened and her eyes narrowed. "A hardship? Derek, it wasn't a hardship. It affected my schedule and that had to be dealt with, but it wasn't a *hardship*. You're making it sound like I was really put out and that you don't think I'd be willing to do things for Isaac and Julia."

He took a deep breath, determined to salvage this conversation. It was too important to him. "I hear you saying that, but I worry that you don't really know how messy it can be and that it'll be too much for you."

"You still don't trust me. And you don't trust that I know what's too much for me and what's not."

"It's not just that. I'll probably have the kids more when Amber has her baby. Especially the first couple of weeks so she doesn't have to worry about getting them to and from school. My schedule makes that a little tough, but we'll make it work."

"It takes juggling, but with proper planning and scheduling, anything can be made to work."

"But I'm hesitant to factor you into that." He shook his head. "I shouldn't be wondering if the person I want to be my partner in life is willing or able to help me out with my kids."

"And I can't believe you *would* wonder if I'd help

you. There's a difference between not being willing or able to help, and making a set plan with Amber and the kids so work can be scheduled around it."

"Life isn't something you can schedule in a book, Olivia. Especially in ink."

"*My* life is. It's worked for me pretty damn well so far. I made a plan for my life—in ink—and I've achieved everything I set out to do to this point."

"Because you're alone in that plan." It sounded harsh, even to his own ears, but it was true.

Her lips tightened for a few seconds. "I'm not alone. Trust me, the people in my life factor very much into my plan."

"Because they work for you. You're still ultimately in control. And maybe there are things happening in *their* lives that can complicate things, but I know how you work. Your core plan allows for that and you make sure things never spin out of control."

"You make that sound like a bad thing."

He pinched the bridge of his nose, trying to find the words to explain what was in his head. "I spend every day trying to maintain the slightest illusion I can control my life and I can't. If I wrote down my plan for the next twenty-four hours, it would probably be such a mess of crossed-out things and notes and rescheduling, I wouldn't even be able to read it. Fires refuse to be knocked down. One kid's puking. The other one's waiting for a ride because her mother got stuck behind an accident on the highway. Science projects forgotten until the night before. Emergency dentist appointments. Some guy I barely know gets the flu and all of a sudden I'm covering his shifts at a house a half hour away on a good day. Shit happens. There are people in my life I can't let down and I can't control that."

"I have people I can't let down, too."

"I know you do. I'm not trying to diminish that, I swear." He blew out a breath, because he knew it sounded that way. "But if you let those people down, they'll find other jobs."

"Oh, good job at not diminishing my obligation to my team."

"I'm talking about *family,* Olivia. You dealt with a messy family situation by moving several states away and you use the phone to control the impact they're allowed to have on your life."

"That wasn't messy. It was toxic." She shook her head, but it was a quick shake, like she was trying to stay in control. "I told you why I came to Boston and why I stayed. And don't you dare compare my choice to put distance between my parents and I to you thinking I wouldn't be willing to help your daughter with a school project."

"Right now you have distance from us, too."

"My life is in the Back Bay. You've known that from the day we met."

"Your *work* is in the Back Bay."

The look she gave him, full of hurt and disappointment, broke his heart. "No. That's my *home.* You've tried to diminish that truth over time by making jokes about hotels and calling it my office, but that's my home."

"I can't live that far away from my kids." She took another step back, and he couldn't do anything to stop the growing distance between them. He couldn't see himself—or his kids—making a home there. "I just can't see myself doing that. My kids are here. My work. My friends. My life is here."

"I know. And the life I've built, which includes my work and my friends, is there."

"And you're not willing to give it up."

"I'm willing to talk about it," she snapped, her temper flaring. "I'm willing to find a compromise, but what about you? What are *you* willing to give up to make it work? Because from over here, it sounds like nothing."

"I have the kids to consider."

"I know you and Amber have a great relationship so your kids are used to having access to both of you all the time. I know better than anybody how wonderful that is." She paused for a second, and took a deep breath. "But what I hear you saying is that you don't care that plenty of parents deal with some distance when seeing their kids, even living in different states. You're not willing to drive across the city to see them if that's what it takes to be with me."

"And you're not willing to commute if that's what it takes to be with me." He heard a note of finality in his voice that he didn't want to be real.

"What if we buy a place in between somewhere?" She asked the question calmly, but her body was trembling. "I'm sure we can find a nice neighborhood that's still close to the kids, and splits the work commute between us."

"Jesus, Olivia, I can't afford anything deeper into the heart of the city." He ran his hand through his hair, blowing out a breath. "And before you say it, no, I'm not okay with you paying for the kind of place you're talking about. A man wants to be able to take care of his family."

"Okay." She said it so softly, he barely heard the word. Then swiped at her eyes with a hand that was visibly shaking.

He wanted to go to her, but he felt frozen to the spot. Their hearts were both breaking, but he didn't know how to stop it. He wanted to hold her and kiss away the pain on her face, but he didn't have the answers. He didn't know how to keep them from being in the exact same place when the tears dried.

"I'm going to go," she said as she moved toward the door. Then she paused with her hand on the doorknob and took a long, shuddering breath. "I'm not going to come back. Goodbye, Derek."

She didn't look back. He stared at the door without moving for what felt like days after she closed it behind her, but it didn't open again.

She wasn't coming back.

Olivia stared at her open closet, neither remembering nor caring why she'd opened it in the first place.

Nothing made sense to her right now. Nothing mattered. She'd never given a thought to what a broken heart felt like. If she had, she probably would have looked at the trail of broken hearts in her family tree and guess it felt like a bottomless pit of anger.

She felt empty. There was a void in her life where Derek had been—whether he was physically with her or not—and it was a big one.

When the phone she'd tossed on the bed rang, her heart jumped and for the few seconds it took her to cross the room to look at the screen, she allowed herself to hope it was Derek. That they'd talk and work it out and everything would be okay.

That hope died when she saw her mother's name. Since she didn't think it was possible to feel worse than she already did, she answered it.

"Hi, Mom."

"You sound weird. What's the matter?"

"I literally said two words."

"You're usually very brisk, and you just sound… tired or sad."

She was surprised her mom had even noticed, which probably wasn't fair. While both parents had blind spots when it came to how much their hostility hurt her, they both loved her. And she loved them.

"I'd been seeing somebody for a while and we…it ended."

"Oh honey, I'm sorry. I didn't know you were dating anybody. I thought you were focused on your company right now. And your book."

"I was. I still am. I just…"

"You just what?"

She wasn't capable of spilling the entire story right now. It was too raw. "I just wasn't ready for a committed relationship right now."

"I'm sorry it didn't work out for you, honey, but you have a plan and you know success lies in the execution."

"I know, Mom. You taught me well."

"I did, and look at you. You've made yourself a nice business and in a few years, you'll be able to relax and find yourself a nice, like-minded man, just as you planned." Her mom paused, and then made a smug sound. "You're a smart woman, like your mother."

Olivia froze, unable to summon the right words to stroke her mom's ego as pieces fell into place. Or maybe it was more like somebody strolling through her brain, flipping on light switches. Smart, like her mother. Successful, like her mother. Focused and driven, like her mother.

Alone and unhappy.

Like her mother.

"Olivia?"

"I'm here." She needed to get off the phone before she said something she couldn't take back. *I'm here, thinking about the fact I've lived my life the way you taught me and I've achieved professional and financial success, but I didn't leave any room for the people I love to actually* be *a part of my life, and I learned it from you.* "What did you call me for?"

"Oh, I just wanted to know if you were coming home for Thanksgiving this year."

"It's September."

"I know. Which means you should already know your schedule for the quarter."

"I'll let you know soon." She hadn't even thought about the holidays this year. If she had, she probably would have assumed she'd be celebrating her first Thanksgiving with Derek. Maybe she would have been meeting his parents and the rest of his family.

It didn't matter now. If she didn't go home, she'd do the same thing she'd done last year, which was politely decline Kelsey's invitation to join her family and then spend the day working.

"I have to go, Mom. I made a note to look at my schedule and I'll get back to you."

"Okay. Keep your chin up. If it didn't work out, he obviously wasn't the right man for you, so stay focused."

That was possibly the worst advice she could have given her daughter at that moment, but Olivia knew she meant well and it was the best she could do. "I will. I love you, Mom."

"I love you, too. I hope you know that. And I'll talk to you soon."

Once the call was over, Olivia let the phone drop back onto the bed. She should make a note about Thanksgiving. She should get some work done. She should do anything that took her mind off Derek.

"Hey, Olivia, I was looking for you. What are you doing?"

"I don't know." She sat on the edge of her bed, looking up at her assistant. "It's slipping away."

"What is?"

"Everything. Derek."

"Derek is a him, not an it. What's slipping away?"

"Control," she whispered, looking at her hands. "My plan. I don't know how to get back on track. He told me he loved me and I told him I love him, too. But then it just…blew up. I don't know what happened, but he wasn't willing to compromise on *anything*, so what was I supposed to do?"

"Maybe you need to let that plan go. Take a few days, then think about what you really want and make a new plan."

"I have a plan."

"Set it on fire."

Olivia's head jerked up. "What?"

"Take that book of yours outside and set it on fire."

"The thought of that makes me physically ill." She put her hand on her stomach because she wasn't lying.

"Okay, so that was a little radical. Let's start small. Since I see your task lists, I know you were looking for something to wear to the Village Hearts benefit. Did you find one?"

Olivia closed her eyes for a moment as a wave of fresh pain washed over her. "I have to go."

"Yup."

"Derek will be there."

"Also yup. Which is why the dress is important. Did you find one?" Olivia shook her head. "Let's go shopping. Right now."

"We can't just leave and go shopping. We have to go over the script for the next podcast."

"We don't have to do that right now. I know you're not going to set your planner on fire, but accept that your business will not come crashing down if we get out of here for an hour and clear your head a little."

It wasn't her head that was the problem. It was her heart. But finding something to wear for the benefit was technically a task for today. When she'd written it down, she'd meant to go through her closet and find something. But if she went into the office right now, she'd probably do more staring at the wall than working. She might as well get *something* checked off her list.

Kelsey claimed to know the perfect place and it was within easy walking distance. Olivia put herself in her assistant's hands and followed along. The weather was on the warm side, but the humidity wasn't bad, so she tried to focus on enjoying the present moment. Or at least not giving up, sitting on a bench and bawling her eyes out.

The dress shop was the small boutique kind that Olivia usually avoided because it was a lot more efficient to shop in larger stores so you could get everything you needed in one spot. But Kelsey dragged her over to a rack of dresses.

"You need to make a statement," she declared.

"Okay." Olivia sighed and lifted the sleeve of a dark green dress before dropping it. "Find me a dress that says I was living a perfectly planned life until a firefighter came and scribbled all over my plan with a Sharpie and broke my heart, and now I'm a mess."

Kelsey pulled a royal blue dress off the rack and held it up. "I was thinking the statement could be more along the lines of *that idiot had this and blew it.*"

Had he blown it? Or had she? Olivia wasn't even sure anymore. She just knew her heart had been blown apart. "That's not really my style. And it's a charity to raise money for children."

"But it's not a kids' party. And it's not even revealing."

Olivia knew the color would look amazing on her, but Kelsey was wrong about it not being revealing. Maybe it wouldn't show a lot of skin, but even on the hanger, Olivia could see that the fabric, the fitted waist and the deep V of the neckline would reveal plenty.

She tried it on and when she stepped out of the dressing room, Kelsey's eyebrows shot up and she gave a sharp nod.

"That's the one. Trust me."

Right now, it felt as if Kelsey was the *only* person she could trust with decision making, so she bought the dress. They walked back to the office and she forced herself to focus enough on the podcast script to check it off the list. She wasn't oblivious to the fact when they did the end-of-day review that Kelsey had shifted some things around and even pushed a few items back. She didn't argue.

Eventually there was nothing left for Kelsey to do,

so she left and Olivia was alone. She forced herself to eat because she had to. Then she took a long, hot bath scented with lavender and chamomile before putting on her favorite pajamas and crawling into bed with her phone.

Derek wasn't going to call. She knew it, but it didn't stop her from staring at the dark phone screen. She needed to hear his voice.

It wasn't until the sun had set and everything was dark that she finally let herself cry.

Chapter Eighteen

If there was one thing Derek wasn't in the mood to do tonight, it was smile and act like everything was okay.

But it was a big night for Village Hearts and he needed to be here. Not just because he'd put a lot of time and effort into the event, but because they'd been there for Julia when he and Amber had been wrapped up with her newborn baby brother. He could never repay them for that, but every dollar he could help them raise tonight counted.

He'd told himself Olivia probably wouldn't show up. She'd put time and money into it, but she didn't have the emotional connection. It would be easier for her to simply make a donation and not have to spend the evening with a fake smile on her face.

But she was there. Seeing her walk through the door had been such a blow, he'd actually taken a step backward. She looked stunning tonight. The blue dress hugging her curves was elegant and sophisticated, but for a man who knew every inch of that body intimately, it was a torturous reminder of what he used to have and let get away.

Watching her made him ache. His hands ached to touch her. He ached to hear her voice and see her smile.

But it was his heart that ached so much the pain made it hard to breathe.

But every time she moved or smiled, he could see that she was hurting, too. She looked brittle, as if she was so tense, she'd shatter if somebody touched her.

He knew the feeling.

"You okay?"

"Yeah." He jerked his attention away from Olivia to look at Scott, and then shrugged. "No. Not really."

"I've been there, man, and it sucks. Honestly, I can't believe you're both here tonight. I couldn't have come to a thing like this with Jamie here while we were broken up. It would have killed me."

"It is killing me," he admitted. "Just really slowly for maximum pain effect."

"If it hurts that much, you might want to consider fixing it."

"If it was that easy, I would."

Scott snorted. "Easy? Nothing about it's fucking easy. But it's worth it. I had to learn some hard lessons to get Jamie back and it was worth it because every time I open my eyes, I'm excited to see Jamie, even if she's right there lying in bed next to me."

"I know that feeling." He missed that feeling. Now when he opened his eyes, it was to dread facing a day without Olivia.

"It was a lot of work." Scott tilted his head for a second. "It's still work. We're both on the job. She outranks me. We worry about each other. We're going to have kids soon and that's a whole new bunch of challenges. But we do the work together because it's worth it."

There was a time Derek would have laughed out loud at the idea of Scott Kincaid giving him advice about his love life. And not just love, but the serious and forever kind of love. But Scott and Jamie were the real deal, and somehow the knowledge that they'd gone through a rough time and come out the other side together eased some of the tightness in his chest.

Scott clapped his hand on Derek's shoulder. "You'll work it out. In the meantime, some of us want to go in together on a bid for that deep-sea fishing package. You in?"

"That'd be a fun way to ring in the summer."

"It's for six but we're thinking a four-way split. Me, Aidan, Chris and you, and then we all pitch in for Isaac and Chris's boy."

Maybe it was because his emotional walls were beaten and battered as hell right now, but that actually choked him up a bit. Losing Jeff to retirement had been a big blow for these guys, but when Derek replaced him, they'd made it clear right from his first day of permanent duty with them that he was family. "Let's do it."

They wandered around the tables, checking out the different auction listings and bidding on a few things. He was pretty sure the deep-sea fishing trip was going to end up out of their price range, but they wrote down a bid anyway.

Then he sucked it up, plastered a smile on his face and went to work the room. He lost himself in small talk and schmoozing. George and Ella were in their element, sweet-talking the wealthier people in the room, while he circulated among the rest of the supporters and their families. It got him out of his own head for a while, until George took the microphone and asked everybody to find their names on the place cards and be seated for dinner.

There was a seating chart. And, after much moving around to get a good mix of Village Hearts supporters and potentially generous donors at each table, it had been nailed down before he and Olivia broke up.

This was going to hurt.

After the marathon strategic seating plan session, he didn't have to look for his name on the place cards. He was sitting at a round table for six, with Olivia seated on his right and a wealthy surgeon whose grandson was a firefighter on his left.

He was almost there when the crowd parted and Olivia was there. The careful, almost unconscious avoidance dance they'd been doing all evening had come to an end, and it seemed as if he had to make a deliberate effort to keep breathing.

"Olivia."

"Hello, Derek."

People moved around them in a blur of movement and sound, but for Derek, time had stopped and all he could do was look into Olivia's gorgeous eyes and see his own hurt reflected back at him. He wanted to make that pain go away. Pull her into his arms. Kiss her. Tell her he was sorry and that he loved her and whatever else he had to say to make her smile at him again.

"Jess made some last-minute changes to the seating arrangement," she said in a voice he had to strain to hear. "Amber's going to sit with you because you're not only a firefighter, but together you're a family who was helped by the organization and that's very powerful."

He didn't care. He didn't want to talk about the charity and trying to poke at a man's emotions until he opened his wallet. He wanted to talk about *them*.

"Did you ask her to do it?" He wasn't sure why he

asked, except wanting to gauge how much effort she was putting into avoiding him.

"No."

He nodded slowly. It had been obvious since he walked through the door that word had discreetly gone around. Not a single person, other than Scott, had mentioned Olivia to him, but nobody seemed surprised by the distance between them.

"You look amazing tonight," he said.

"Thank you." When her eyes started to shimmer, she sniffed and lifted her chin. "I'm going to find my seat. Enjoy your dinner."

There was not a snowball's chance in hell of that. "You, too."

Letting her walk away was one of the hardest things he'd ever done, but this wasn't the time or place. He wasn't sure there *was* a time or place, since nothing had changed in either of their lives since the last, awful time they spoke.

Nothing except not having her in it.

He sat in the chair next to his ex-wife, thankful the others hadn't found the table yet, and took a long drink from the fancy glass of ice water sitting next to his place setting. His mouth was dry and his throat felt so tight, it took everything he had not to loosen his tie and pop his top button.

"Derek, what did you do?" she leaned over to whisper. It hurt so much to even think about it, he wasn't sure he could say the words out loud. Fortunately, Amber knew him well enough to read his face, so he didn't have to. "Is it true that you guys aren't together anymore?"

He nodded slowly, staring at the condensation on his glass. "Yeah, it's true."

"Maybe you should go home. I'll tell them you had a headache. Or that you got called out or something. It's not like we haven't used that one before."

"It might be hard to explain why the other guys from the station who came don't leave with me." They would, if he asked them to back up his lie. But this night was too important to his family and to all the families Village Hearts helped. "I'm good."

"Okay, because I think that guy coming over here is who we're supposed to charm over dinner."

He inhaled slowly and held the breath for a few seconds before blowing it out. Then he drank some more water. "I've got this."

And he'd get through dinner because he'd made up his mind that he and Olivia were going to talk. Probably not tonight because it wasn't the place, but they were going to sit down and talk about their relationship when their emotions weren't heated and they could be calm.

He wasn't letting them end like this.

After dinner, the lights dimmed and the music started. They'd be interrupting over the course of the evening to auction off big-ticket items, but for the most part Olivia could linger in the shadows until she'd had enough and make her escape.

She should have left already. Seeing Derek was probably one of the most painful things she'd ever endured, and yet she couldn't bring herself to leave. It hurt like hell to see him across the room, but at least she was seeing him.

Jess found her and handed her a glass of wine. "You okay?"

"I will be." She always was. "Thank you for switching the seating chart. I don't know if I could have done it."

"It was no problem. What happened between you two, anyway? When I heard it was over, I couldn't believe it and I'm heartbroken for you."

She could hear the genuine concern in Jess's voice and she appreciated it, but Olivia didn't want to relive her breakup right now, so she just shook her head. "The dragons won this one. That's all."

"No." Jess gripped her arm. "No, that's not all. Slaying the dragons to get your happily-ever-after isn't one battle. You don't put down your sword the first time you get singed."

There was no amusement in her short bark of laughter. "I didn't get singed, Jess. I went down in flames."

"You're here. He's here. And I've seen the way you two keep looking at each other when the other's not looking, so dust yourself off and pick up your sword. It's not one-and-done, Olivia. There are always more dragons. Big dragons. Little dragons. Some breathe fire and some just hiccup little smoke rings at you, but you have to keep swinging that sword."

As improbable as it seemed, considering her current emotional state, Olivia smiled. "You're surprisingly romantic, in a fairy-tale kind of way."

"For a math brain, you mean?" Jess smiled and nodded her head in the direction of Rick. "I'm married to that guy. My life *is* a romantic fairy tale."

Then her eyes widened and she mumbled something about needing something before she practically fled in the opposite direction. And when she turned back to the crowd, she saw why.

Derek was coming toward her. Deliberately, his eyes locked on her. He was too close for her to pretend she hadn't seen him and she had too much pride to run.

"Please dance with me," he said and she knew she should say no. Being in his arms again might kill her. But the agony on his face seemed to tug at her soul and she held out her hand.

He didn't lead her out onto the makeshift dance floor. He pulled her into his arms and they swayed slowly to the music. Olivia didn't even know what the song was, the music drowned out by the pounding of her broken heart.

"I'm sorry," he said softly against her ear, and she shivered. "This hurts so much and I'm sorry."

"I'm sorry, too. I panicked." She was afraid she was only going to get this one chance to explain, but it wasn't easy to find the words. "When I hit middle school and started finding out there were a lot of things more fun than academics, my grades started slipping. I started getting in trouble and I was spiraling emotionally. My mother decided I needed to focus. She taught me how to set goals, break them down and make a plan. And from that time forward, I've accomplished everything I set out to do."

"It's obviously worked out well for you."

"It has, and that's why I panicked. Making a plan and sticking to it keeps me from failing to meet the goals I set for myself. For school. For my business. For my life." She took a deep breath before getting to the hard part. "I know it seems like I pushed you away because you were getting in the way of my plan, but I figured out that my plan is flawed. My goals changed—what I want in my life changed—and I got scared. I got rigid about needing to stick to my plan because it's saved me in the past."

"No, you were right about me not being willing to give anything up. I was afraid for so long that it would be too hard for us to compromise that I made it into some kind of self-fulfilling prophecy. I gave up. And I…I don't want to do this here, tonight. But please let me try again. We can talk somewhere. Your place. Anywhere."

"But what's changed, Derek?"

"Everything." She watched his Adam's apple work as he swallowed hard. "Now I know what life without you feels like and…I want to try."

She tried so hard not to let the hope in. There was a lot between them and he'd refused to give on anything. And she was afraid she might let him in again just because she hated his pain, but she couldn't give in.

It hurt and she still wanted him, but she wouldn't give up everything to make herself fit in his life. They both needed to compromise and make a new life together. She wouldn't settle for anything less.

"Please."

The hoarse whisper broke her and she looked up at him through a shimmer of tears. "Okay. But if you're not *really* willing to try, it's just going to make it harder and more painful."

"I fucked up, Olivia. Bad. And I know I hurt you. I hurt us both. I promise you I'm willing to try like hell. Tell me when and where, and I'll be there."

She nodded, blinking back tears. "A couple more

days, maybe. Tonight was a lot. Wednesday? After work at my place?"

"I'll be there."

Then silence hung between them for a second. Olivia thought he might kiss her. And she wanted that. She loved kissing him. But she wouldn't let it happen.

Then he smiled—a small smile that didn't reach his sad eyes—and squeezed her hand before letting her go. "Goodnight, Olivia."

"Goodnight."

She watched him go and it hurt almost as much as walking out of his apartment had, but now there was hope, whether she wanted to let it in or not. She had until Wednesday to look at her life and what she really wanted. What she was willing to do to get it. She'd been doing it for most of her life. Identify the goal. Identify the steps necessary to achieve the goal. Make a plan for accomplishing those steps.

For the first time in her life, she was afraid it wouldn't be enough because this time, her heart was involved and love wasn't always reasonable.

Chapter Nineteen

"Get your fucking head in the game, Gilman."

Derek snapped out an acknowledgment of the order and did as he was told. An active four-alarm fire wasn't the time to mentally relive the Village Hearts benefit.

But hours later, when the fire was finally knocked down and they were repacking the trucks, the memories crept back into his mind. The way that little flare of hope had lit up her sad eyes had haunted him every night since he said goodnight.

He had one shot. If he blew it, he'd never get another chance.

And that's how, when his shift ended, he wound up on his ex-wife's doorstep about twenty minutes after the kids left for school.

"Are you okay?" Amber asked when she opened the door to find him standing there. Then she took in the uniform he hadn't bothered to change out of after an early morning false alarm, and her eyes widened. "Are the kids okay?"

"They're fine. I'm okay. I just…can we talk for a minute?"

She looked into his face for a long moment and then

nodded, stepping back to let him in. "There's a pot of coffee."

She poured him one and then stood across the kitchen island from him. He took a few sips, letting the liquid warm him. He'd felt permanently chilled since leaving the benefit and he couldn't shake it.

"What's going on, Derek? Is this about you and Olivia?"

He nodded slowly, staring at the mug because it was easier than looking at her. "Was it easy for you guys?"

"For me and Jason?" She blew out a breath. "I don't think we had to overcome some of the obstacles you guys have. He didn't really have roots set down and I had this house. I don't really have a career to worry about, unless you call a part-time job at the market a career."

"So Jason was just all in on the family? There weren't really issues?"

"I didn't say that. Do you think Jason fell head over heels for Julia and Isaac when he first met them?" She gave him a *yeah, right* look. "He accepted them in his life because he fell in love with *me*. Then he got to know them and built a relationship with them, but it took time. Olivia will do the same, but it will also take time."

"He's a good stepfather."

"He is. He loves those kids, but he didn't magically appear in our lives that way. It took time and compromise, and trust on my part."

"Trust?" He nodded. "I get that. It wasn't easy to just trust some guy with my children."

"I know it wasn't. But in this case, I mean that I had to trust my gut. Or my heart, I guess. I had to trust that I wouldn't fall in love with a guy who wouldn't accept my kids. And you're not afraid of Olivia hurting the kids or you wouldn't be with her. You're afraid of feeling like you might have to choose."

"I would never choose anybody over my kids."

"*Why* do you feel like you have to? What is going on in your head right now, Derek?"

He shook his head, his throat feeling as if it was closed up. His eyes burned and he cleared his throat, trying to stop the emotion from bubbling to the surface, but he couldn't hold the words back. "If I move to Olivia's, will Isaac and Julia think I left them for her?"

"No." She covered his hand with hers and squeezed. "Jesus, Derek. No. They wouldn't think you left them because you would *never* leave them and they know that. That's not about how many minutes the car ride is. You are an amazing dad and that's not going to change if you live on the other side of the city. Hell, that wouldn't change if you lived on the other side of the country."

"It'll be harder for everybody."

"It'll be an adjustment. They'll adjust." She sighed. "I know I speak for everybody who cares about you when I say we'd all rather have you be happy over there than miserable and lonely up the street."

"And she makes a lot of money. Her apartment is... I can't even describe it."

She laughed. "Confession? Her building has a website and I looked at it."

"Can you picture the kids there?"

"Sure. The kids are going to be sprawled across the couch no matter what kind of couch it is. Isaac will be on his stomach on the floor, reading a book. Julia will sit in a chair to read and then slowly twist herself around so she's half hanging off of it. They'll spill things and leave fingerprints on the fridge."

"It's so…neat. She's not big on clutter."

"Enough," she snapped. "Stop using my kids as a shield against the risk of having your heart broken."

He opened his mouth to say something, then snapped it closed again because he wasn't sure what to say.

"You're hiding behind them," she continued. "You're using them as an excuse not to figure out some hard, maybe even scary changes in your life and that's bullshit. They're great kids who love you. They'll love you here. They'll love you there. They'll love you any… shit. I've got to stop reading Dr. Seuss to this baby bump."

He laughed, maybe for the first time in days, and she laughed with him. Then she topped off their coffees and leaned on the island again.

"I'm going to ask you one question, Derek, and you know I'll know if you lie to me. Do you love her? Yes or—"

"Yes." He didn't even have to think about it. He knew it without question.

"Then stop twisting yourself up. Remember when we sat down together and admitted to ourselves and to each other that the best way to take care of our kids was to take care of ourselves first? It's still true. Take care of you, be happy and the kids will be happy."

"Thank you, Amber."

"Hey, you know I'm always happy to give you a kick in the ass."

During the time between being notified Derek was on his way up and when he knocked on her door, Olivia stood in front of her windows and centered herself. She felt a little stronger than she had at the benefit, but with strength came hope.

The hope still scared her. But she wasn't ready to give up on them. And she believed the man she'd fallen in love with wouldn't put them through the wringer again for no reason. They'd already dumped all the issues in a tangled mess on the table. Now they were hopefully going to sift through them and find a solution.

She'd done nothing special for today. She was wearing her yoga pants and a long scoop-necked sweatshirt. Her hair was loose and she had no makeup on. Her feet were bare. And when she opened the door and saw him in worn jeans and a T-shirt, she was relieved he'd done the same. No fuss. No grand gestures. Just their two everyday selves.

"Come on in," she said, closing the door after him. "I have a glass of wine going, but you can help yourself to anything you want."

"I'm good, thanks." He looked around and then gave her a ghost of a teasing smile. "I thought you might have hung a big whiteboard up, with plans and arrows and stuff."

"I thought about it," she said, returning the smile. "But I didn't make a plan for tonight because then it would be *my* plan. The whole point is to come up with *our* plan, together."

"Together is the most important thing to me," he said. "I've done a lot of soul searching. I've gotten a verbal ass-kicking from Amber. Which probably sounds weird, but obviously nobody knows my kids like their mother."

"I get it." She gestured toward the couch because it felt too formal and strange standing in her living room.

"Sit down, for goodness' sake. This doesn't have to be weird."

"I want you to know I'm ready to do whatever you need me to do," he said, and her heart skipped a beat. "I'll move here. Whatever's going to make you happy."

"Derek." She reached across the space between them and took his hand. "I don't want you to do whatever it takes to make me happy. I want us to figure out what's best for *us* and for our family. And I don't think it's here. I don't think Isaac and Julia would feel at home in this building and I don't want them on company manners."

The relief in his face was obvious, but she also didn't doubt the sincerity of his offer. He was willing to make that sacrifice for her. But she didn't want sacrifice. She wanted compromise.

"I know my place doesn't work," he said. "And not because it's nothing like this place, but because it literally won't work. There's no room for you to have an office and even if you kept this place, you'd still need a space for that at home. And one bathroom's not fun."

"I do think a long-term plan includes a home office space and a master bath, yes."

"I'm sorry I said a man needs to be able to take care of his family. It was pride and it was stupid. The truth is *we* need to be able to take care of *our* family. Who writes the check doesn't matter as much as finding a place we both love."

Her heart was beating so fast, she was surprised she didn't pass out. This was what she almost hadn't dared hope for. "I'm promoting Kelsey. She's going to take on some of the workload that I've held on to simply because I thought I had to. Because we don't need a place open to the public, she was able to find an affordable office space, just big enough for the three of us to work out of, since we're going to hire an assistant for her. My career is still important to me, but I'll be able to be more flexible. And I can focus more on the writing and other things that don't require running around the city to keep appointments scheduled so tightly I can't stop for a slice of pizza."

He squeezed her hand. "Is that what you want to do?"

"I'm doing that no matter what. It's time and Kelsey's earned it." She took a deep breath. "And the rent on this apartment is ridiculous. I'd rather invest that money in a home that works for our entire family."

He struggled with that one for a few seconds, but she was quiet and let him work through it in his mind. Pride wasn't an easy thing to set aside, but then he nodded.

"That view, though," he said.

"You know what's an even better view?" She squeezed his hand. "You, in Aidan's backyard, chasing your kids with a water gun and laughing so hard you fell down. And you, when I wake up and you're the first thing I see."

"I want to wake up next to you for the rest of my life."

"I know Isaac and Julia are eight and ten and… I need to know if you want more kids."

"I do. When you're ready, we'll go for it."

"You're not worried about how much age difference there will be between them?"

"Nope. Julia and Isaac will be fine no matter what, and the baby or babies will love having a big brother and sister to do stuff with."

Olivia smiled and the crinkling of her eyes made a couple of tears spill over onto her cheeks. "I love you."

"That's the only thing that really matters. As long as you love me, we can do anything." He let go of her hand to wipe the tears away with his thumb. "And I love you. I love you so much and I'm sorry it scared the crap out of me."

"Well, it scared the crap out of me, too. Thank you for not giving up without a fight."

"Thank you for giving me another chance." He tugged on her hand until she slid across the couch and into his arms. "From now until forever, you and me are a team. If we're happy, everybody in our lives will be happy."

"You know what would make me happy right now?" she asked, almost giddy with relief and love for this man.

"Great sex followed by a pepperoni-and-sausage pizza?"

"Oh." She considered that for a few seconds. "I was going to say a kiss, but sex and pizza does sound good."

He was laughing when he flipped her around so she was straddling his lap. Then he buried his hands in her hair and kissed her until she forgot about pizza and everything else but the man she was going to spend the rest of her life with.

Epilogue

"Snow day!"

Olivia was pretty sure the bed slid a couple of inches across the floor as Isaac launched himself onto it. He landed next to his dad, catching him with a sharp knee or elbow, judging by the grunt.

"Snow day!"

"You've only been back to school from Christmas break for a week," Derek muttered. "It's mostly down-hill to school. Just get on your sled."

"There won't be anybody there, Dad," Julia said from the doorway. "He'd be alone."

"I was kidding, pumpkin."

Olivia peeked at the clock and groaned. "We had ten more minutes until the alarm went off. How come you don't get up like this when it's *not* a snow day?"

"I don't want to waste a snow day. And Dad, you said we wouldn't have a snow day today." Isaac jumped off the bed, but paused in the doorway to look back. "You were *wrong*."

When they were gone—probably heading to the kitchen to start getting their energy levels up for the unexpected day off—Derek rolled to face her. She loved the early mornings, when his face was still soft with sleep.

"I'm sorry," he mumbled after giving her a kiss good morning. "I really didn't think they'd cancel school for what was in the forecast. I can try to get somebody to cover my shift."

"If it's bad enough to cancel school, it'll probably be a busy day for you and it's late notice to call somebody in. We'll be fine."

"Maybe I can call Amber and see how she's feeling."

"No. Regardless of how she's feeling right now, having two kids with snow-day energy levels isn't going to help."

Amber still had a month or so before her due date, but she'd had some issues and they were worried about her blood pressure. While they hadn't directly confined her to bed, she was supposed to be taking it *very* easy. Sleep was an issue and she'd been struggling with mornings, so after the holiday vacation, they'd offered to take Isaac and Julia until she was back on her feet.

Derek and Olivia got them up and off to school in the morning. After school, they went to their mom's for a few hours, and then Derek would pick them up or Olivia would on her way back from the office or a meeting. Since Jason was home on the weekends, they'd probably stay with their mom, but they were all still feeling it out.

"What's your schedule today?" he asked. "We might be able to find a sitter."

She closed her eyes for a moment, visualizing the planner that was downstairs on the counter. "I can work from home today. I have a video conference with my team scheduled, so it doesn't matter where I am and if the kids interrupt a couple of times, it's no big deal. I do have one phone call with a client, so I'll bribe them with something."

He chuckled and snuggled closer to her. "You've really got this parenting thing down."

The alarm went off and they both groaned when he had to let her go to roll over and shut it off. "I want a snow day, too. You kept me up too late last night."

"Daddy?"

Julia was back, and Olivia was very thankful they'd adopted a wearing-pajamas policy when the kids were over since Derek had taken most of the covers with him when he rolled toward the bedside table.

"What's the matter, pumpkin?"

"When it's a snow day, how do you rescue people?"

"Our trucks are heavy, so we get around pretty well. If it's really slippery, we put chains on the tires. You've seen those before."

"Do the ambulances have them, too?"

Derek stood and started pulling out his clothes for the day. "Yeah, they do. They have a special system built in, actually, which is way cooler than ours. But don't tell Cait I said that, okay?"

When she didn't smile back at Derek, Olivia patted the bed beside her. When Julia climbed in, she pulled the covers up to their chins. "You should be running around the house yelling about snow days like your brother. Why so serious today?"

"I just wondered if ambulances can get to people's houses in the snow like fire trucks can. And what if the ambulances are busy?"

There was so much worry in her eyes, Olivia's heart clenched. "You know your mom is fine, right?"

"I know, but she's not *totally* fine, since that's why we're staying with you and Daddy on school nights."

The girl was an overthinker, which Olivia definitely understood. "She's tired and sometimes doesn't feel good. When you're carrying a baby, you get tired even faster, so it's best if she can sleep in. And if she did need help, an ambulance can get to her. And a fire truck can, too."

"And Mr. Keegan next door has that four-wheel drive," Derek reminded her. "You know they're looking out for her. And that guy across the street has a snowmobile in his garage. Can you imagine your mom with that belly riding on a snowmobile?"

Julia giggled, as he'd intended, and Olivia kissed her forehead. "Your dad has to get ready for work, so how about you and I go get his coffee ready?"

When they got downstairs to the kitchen, Olivia saw that Isaac had already poured himself a bowl of cereal, since the Gilman family rule was that there were no rules on snow days. Within reason, of course.

While Julia tried to decide what she wanted to eat, Olivia made two coffees—one in a regular mug and another in a massive travel mug Derek would take with him. Then she went to the large whiteboard hung on the wall. Each member of the family had a block, and the kids had decorated theirs with small stickers.

She picked up the eraser and wiped the kids' boxes for the day clean, which made them clap. Then she pointed to her name.

"Okay, kiddos. I can rearrange things, but I have one video chat with the people I work with that I have to do."

"With Kelsey and Jo?" Isaac asked. Kelsey and their new assistant had a lot of screen time with Olivia, and

Isaac had developed a habit of popping up over Olivia's shoulder to say hi. They'd had to set some boundaries, as far as when he could do that and when he couldn't—Kelsey and Jo were okay, but other people weren't—but he'd caught on quickly and charmed both women.

"Yes, and with Brynn and Wes, too. But I have one telephone call I have to make in my office that'll take about a half hour. What's the rule?"

"Don't interrupt or knock on the door unless it's a real emergency," Julia said.

"Like somebody being hurt or sick or a fire," Isaac added. "Because Julia not giving my turn on the video games is not a real emergency."

"And once my stuff is done, if the roads are okay, maybe we'll see if your mom's up to some company for board games. If the roads are still bad, maybe we can do the trivia game."

It was a silly game, but it was something Amber could do with them over FaceTime, so they'd started it when she was in the hospital for observation for a couple of days. Julia's face brightened at the reassurance nobody was going to forget to check on her mom, and Isaac started talking about board games.

While she waited for an English muffin to pop out of the toaster so she could smear it with peanut butter for Derek, Olivia watched the two kids at the table. Julia was nibbling on a banana, since she'd have eggs with Olivia after her dad left for work. They were trying to put the board games they owned into a list of most to least fun, but they didn't agree so she knew it would keep them busy for a while.

When Derek walked into the kitchen, he kissed each of the kids on top of the head and then gave her a long, minty kiss before taking his first sip of the coffee she'd made. Then he thanked her for the English muffin and went to sit with the kids. Usually he was leaving as they got up and she knew he'd be pushing it to make it to the station on time, but he didn't seem worried.

She poured herself a glass of juice, but she didn't walk to the table and join them quite yet. She just watched them, embracing the familiar sense of gratitude and wonder that warmed her heart.

This was her life.

The house. A pretty two-story, brick house in a nice neighborhood still close enough to Amber's to make running back and forth manageable, but closer to the office so her commute wasn't as bad as it could have been. Two funny, awesome kids who had managed to claim their own spaces in her heart and weren't simply *Derek's kids* anymore. Her business was still going strong and Kelsey was thriving in her new position and responsibilities.

And her husband.

They'd gotten married a few days before Christmas in a small civil ceremony. *Very* small. They went to City Hall, just the two of them, because that moment was theirs. No families or kids or friends. The ceremony belonged to them.

Then they'd spent the Christmas weekend in a series of mini-parties of celebration with everybody who mattered to them, and it had been an extra-special holiday for all of them.

A home, a husband, kids she loved, a business and next year—according to her new and improved life and *family* plan—hopefully a baby. She had it all and she hadn't even had to give up sleeping. Most of the time.

But now she understood why people were willing to make that sacrifice. This kind of happiness was worth it.

Derek stood, and then kissed Julia's cheek and ruffled Isaac's hair. "You guys be good for Olivia today. And when you're shoveling around the hydrant, stay out of the street and move away from the curb when a car goes by."

"We always do," Julia said. "And we give serious side-eye to the people down the street if they don't to shame them into shoveling theirs out."

"That's my girl."

Olivia laughed. Their mission to educate their new neighborhood about shoveling the hydrants out amused her, even though she knew it was serious business to Derek. "You guys know we're not even getting enough snow to shovel, right?"

"If you do it every time it snows, it becomes a habit. Firefighters like when people who *aren't* us are in the habit of clearing around the almost fourteen thousand hydrants in the city. You going to drink that juice or are you working on your juice-modeling pose today?" he teased, taking the glass from her and setting it on the counter behind her.

"That's my fallback career for when everybody decides to use the calendars and task apps that come with their phones."

He looped his arm around her and pulled her close, ignoring the *ew* sound from the peanut gallery at the table. "I love you, Ms. McGovern who's really Mrs. Gilman."

She laughed and wrapped her arms around his neck. She knew that other than agreeing they'd buy the house with the money she'd been paying as rent—because it was outside of his budget, but so perfect for their family—the name had been one of the harder compromises for Derek. But he was a smart man who loved her, so he'd accepted that everything she'd built in her life had her name on it and she didn't want to give it up.

"I love you, too, husband. And you're going to be late if you don't get going."

"You looked like you were a million miles away," he said in a low voice not meant for the kids to hear. "Everything okay?"

She looked into his eyes and smiled. "I was just thinking about how lucky I am."

"I thought you didn't believe in luck."

"I didn't until I got stuck in an elevator with you. That was definitely lucky."

He buried his face in her neck for a few seconds, and then gently nipped the soft skin under her ear. It always made her shiver. "I hope I'll get lucky when I get home tomorrow morning."

"You usually do," she whispered back. "Be safe and when you get home, you can crawl into bed with me and I'll warm you up."

He rewarded her with a soft groan. "There's nothing sexier than a woman with a plan."

* * * * *

To purchase and read more from Shannon Stacey, please visit her website at www.ShannonStacey.com.

Author's Note

The processes and organizational structures of large city fire departments and emergency services are incredibly complex, and I took minor creative liberties in order to maintain readability.

To first responders everywhere, thank you.

Acknowledgments

Writing books isn't easy, but having amazing support makes it a little easier. My gratitude for my editor, Angela James, as well as the entire Carina Press team for the work and enthusiasm they've brought to this series knows no bounds. Thank you.

Go back to the beginning of Boston Fire with this excerpt from Heat Exchange *by Shannon Stacey.*

Available now in ebook, mass market paperback and audio, wherever Carina Press books are sold.

Chapter One

Lydia Kincaid could pull a pint of Guinness so perfect her Irish ancestors would weep tears of appreciation, but fine dining? Forget about it.

"The customer is disappointed in the sear on these scallops," she told the sous-chef, setting the plate down.

"In what way?"

"Hell if I know. They look like all the other scallops." Lydia had a hairpin sticking into her scalp, and it took every bit of her willpower not to poke at it. Her dark hair was too long, thick and wavy to be confined into a chic little bun, but it was part of the dress code. And going home with a headache every night was just part of the job. "Ten bucks says if I wait three minutes, then pop that same plate in the microwave for fifteen seconds and take it out to her, she'll gush over how the sear is so perfect now."

"If I see you microwaving scallops, I'll make sure the only food you ever get to touch in this city again is fast food."

Lydia rolled her eyes, having heard that threat many times before, and accepted a fresh plate of scallops from the line cook. The sous-chef just sniffed loudly and dumped the unacceptable batch in the garbage, plate and all. She was pretty sure the guy spent all his off time watching reality television chefs throw tantrums.

Three hours later, Lydia was in her car and letting her hair down. She dropped the bobby pins and elastic bands into her cup holder to fish out before her next shift and then used both hands to shake her hair out and massage her scalp.

She hated her job. Maybe some of it stemmed from the disparity between the cold formality of this restaurant and the warm and loud world she'd come from, but she also flat-out wasn't very good at it. The foods perplexed her and, according to the kitchen manager, her tableside manner lacked polish. Two years hadn't yet managed to put a shine on her. The tips were usually good, though, and living in Concord, New Hampshire cost less than living in Boston, but it still wasn't cheap.

She'd just put her car in gear when she heard the siren in the distance. With her foot still on the brake, she watched as the fire engine came into view—red lights flashing through the dark night—and sped past.

With a sigh, she shifted her foot to the gas pedal. She didn't need to hold her breath anymore. Didn't need to find the closest scanner. Nobody she loved was on that truck so, while she said a quick prayer for their safety, they were faceless strangers and life wasn't temporarily suspended.

And that was why she'd keep trying to please people who wouldn't know a good scallop sear if it bit them on the ass and taking shit from the sous-chef. That job financed her new life here in New Hampshire, including a decent apartment she shared with a roommate, and it was a nice enough life that she wasn't tempted to go home.

Her life wasn't perfect. It had certainly been lacking in sex and friendship lately, but she wasn't going backward just because the road was longer or harder than she'd thought. She wanted something different and she was going to keep working toward it.

Thanks to the miracle of an apartment building with an off-street parking lot, Lydia had a dedicated parking spot waiting for her. It was another reason she put up with customers who nitpicked their entrées just because they were paying so much for them.

Her roommate worked at a sports bar and wouldn't be home for another couple of hours, so Lydia took a quick shower and put on her sweats. She'd just curled up on the sofa with the remote and a couple of the cookies her blessed-with-a-great-metabolism roommate had freshly baked when her cell phone rang.

She knew before looking at the caller ID it would be her sister. Not many people called her, and none late at night. "Hey, Ashley. What's up?"

"My marriage is over."

Lydia couldn't wrap her mind around the words at first. Had something happened to Danny? But she hadn't said that. She said it was over. "What do you mean it's over?"

"I told him I wasn't sure I wanted to be married to him anymore and that I needed some space. He didn't even say anything. He just packed up a couple of bags and left."

"Oh my God, Ashley. Where did this even come from?"

"I've been unhappy for a while. I just didn't tell anybody." Her sister sighed, the sound hollow and discouraged over the phone. "Like a moron, I thought I could talk to him about it. Instead, he left."

"Why have you been unhappy? Dammit, Ashley, what is going on? Did he cheat? I swear to God if he stepped out—"

"No. He didn't cheat. And it's too much for me talk about now."

"If you had been talking to me all along, it wouldn't be too much now. You can't call me and tell me your marriage is over and then tell me you don't want to talk about it."

"I know, but it's…it's too much. I called to talk to you about the bar."

Uh-oh. Alarm bells went off in Lydia's mind, but there was no way she could extricate herself from the conversation without being a shitty sister.

"I need you to come back and help Dad," Ashley said, and Lydia dropped her head back against the sofa cushion, stifling a groan. "I need some time off."

"I have a job, Ashley. And an apartment."

"You've told me a bunch of times that you hate your job."

She couldn't deny that since a conversation rarely passed between them without mention of that fact.

"And it's waiting tables," Ashley continued. "It's not like I'm asking you to take a hiatus from some fancy career path."

That was bitchy, even for Ashley, but Lydia decided to give her a pass. She didn't know what had gone wrong in their marriage, but she did know Ashley loved Danny Walsh with every fiber of her being, so she had to be a wreck.

"I can't leave Shelly high and dry," Lydia said in a

calm, reasonable tone. "This is a great apartment and I'm lucky to have it. It has off-street parking and my space has my apartment number in it. It's literally *only* mine."

"I can't be at the bar, Lydia. You know how it is there. Everybody's got a comment or some advice to give, and I have to hear every five minutes what a great guy Danny is and why can't I just give him another chance?"

Danny really *was* a great guy, but she could understand her sister not wanting to be reminded of it constantly while they were in the process of separating. But going back to Boston and working at Kincaid's was a step in the wrong direction for Lydia.

"I don't know, Ash."

"Please. You don't know—" To Lydia's dismay, her sister's voice was choked off by a sob. "I can't do it, Lydia. I really, really need you."

Shit. "I'll be home tomorrow."

"We got smoke showing on three and at least one possible on the floor," Rick Gullotti said. "Meet you at the top, boys."

Aidan Hunt threw a mock salute in the direction of the ladder company's lieutenant and tossed the ax to Grant Cutter before grabbing the Halligan tool for himself. With a fork at one end and a hook and adze head on the other end, it was essentially a long crowbar on steroids and they never went anywhere without it. After confirmation Scotty Kincaid had the line, and a thumbs-up from Danny Walsh at the truck, he and the other guys from Engine 59 headed for the front door of the three-decker.

Some bunch of geniuses, generations before, had

decided the best way to house a shitload of people in a small amount of space was to build three-story houses—each floor a separate unit—and cram them close together. It was great if you needed a place to live and didn't mind living in a goldfish bowl. It was less great if it was your job to make sure an out-of-control kitchen fire didn't burn down the entire block.

They made their way up the stairs, not finding trouble until they reached the top floor. The door to the apartment stood open, with smoke pouring out. Aidan listened to the crackle of the radio over the sound of his own breathing in the mask. The guys from Ladder 37 had gained access by way of the window and had a woman descending, but her kid was still inside.

"Shit." Aidan confirmed Walsh knew they were going into the apartment and was standing by to charge the line if they needed water, and then looked for nods from Kincaid and Cutter.

He went in, making his way through the smoke. It was bad enough so the child would be coughing—hopefully— but there was chaos in the front of the apartment as another company that had shown up tried to knock down the flames from the front.

Making his way to the kid's bedroom, he signaled for Cutter to look under the bed while he went to the closet. If the kid was scared and hiding from them, odds were he or she was in one of those two spots.

"Bingo," he heard Cutter say into his ear.

The updates were growing more urgent and he heard Kincaid call for water, which meant the fire was heading their way. "No time to be nice. Grab the kid and let's go."

It was a little girl and she screamed as Cutter pulled

her out from under the bed. She was fighting him and, because his hold was awkward, once she was free of the bed, Cutter almost lost her. Aidan swore under his breath. If she bolted, they could all be in trouble.

He leaned the Halligan against the wall and picked up the little girl. By holding her slightly slanted, he was able to hold her arms and legs still without running the risk of smacking her head on the way down.

"Grab the Halligan and let's go."

"More guys are coming up," Walsh radioed in. "Get out of there now."

The smoke was dense now and the little girl was doing more coughing and gasping than crying. "My dog!"

Aidan went past Kincaid, slapping him on the shoulder. Once Cutter went by, Kincaid could retreat—they all stayed together—and let another company deal with the flames.

"I see her dog," Aidan heard Cutter say, and he turned just in time to see the guy disappear back into the bedroom.

"Jesus Christ," Scotty yelled. "Cutter, get your ass down those stairs. Hunt, just go."

He didn't want to leave them, and he wouldn't have except the fight was going out of the child in his arms. Holding her tight, he started back down the stairs they'd come up. At the second floor he met another company coming up, but he kept going.

Once he cleared the building, he headed for the ambulance and passed the girl over to the waiting medics. It was less than two minutes before Cutter and Kincaid emerged from the building, but it felt like forever.

They yanked their masks off as Cutter walked over

to the little girl and—after getting a nod from EMS—put an obviously terrified little dog on the girl's lap. They all smiled as the girl wrapped her arms around her pet and then her mom put her arms around both. Aidan put his hand on Cutter's shoulder and the news cameras got their tired, happy smiles for the evening news.

Once they were back on the other side of the engine and out of view of the cameras, Kincaid grabbed the front of Cutter's coat and shoved him against the truck. "You want to save puppies, that's great. If there's time. Once you're told to get the fuck out, you don't go back for pets. And if you ever risk my life again, or any other guy's, for a goddamn dog, I'll make sure you can't even get a job emptying the garbage at Waste Reduction."

Once Cutter nodded, Kincaid released him and they looked to Danny for a status update. They had it pretty well knocked down and, though the third floor was a loss and the lower floors wouldn't be pretty, the people who lived in the neighboring houses weren't going to have a bad day.

Two hours later, Aidan sat on the bench in the shower room and tied his shoes. Danny was stowing his shower stuff, a towel wrapped around his waist. He'd been quiet since they got back, other than having a talk with Cutter, since he was the officer of the bunch. But he was always quiet, so it was hard to tell what was going on with him.

"Got any plans tonight?" Aidan finally asked, just to break the silence.

"Nope. Probably see if there's a game on."

Aidan wasn't sure what to say to that. He didn't have a lot of experience with a good friend going through a divorce. Breakups, sure, but not a marriage ending. "If you want to talk, just let me know. We can grab a beer or something."

"Talk about what?"

"Don't bullshit me, Walsh. We know what's going on and it's a tough situation. So if you want to talk, just let me know."

"She doesn't want to be married to me anymore, so we're getting a divorce." Danny closed his locker, not needing to slam it to get his point across. "There's nothing to talk about."

"Okay." Aidan tossed his towel in the laundry bin and went out the door.

A lot of guys had trouble expressing their emotions, but Danny took it to a whole new level. Aidan thought talking about it over a few beers might help, but he shouldn't have been surprised the offer was refused.

He'd really like to know what had gone wrong in the Walsh marriage, though. He liked Danny and Ashley and he'd always thought they were a great couple. If they couldn't make it work, Aidan wasn't sure he had a chance. And lately he'd been thinking a lot about how nice it would be to have somebody to share his life with.

A mental snapshot of the little girl cradling her dog filled his mind. He wouldn't mind having a dog. But his hours would be too hard on a dog, and he wasn't a fan of cats. They were a little creepy and not good for playing ball in the park. He could probably keep a fish alive, but they weren't exactly a warm hug at the end of the long tour.

With a sigh he went into the kitchen to rummage for a snack. If he couldn't keep a dog happy, he probably didn't have much chance of keeping a wife happy. And that was assuming he even met a woman he wanted to get to know well enough to consider a ring. So far, not so good.

"Cutter ate the last brownie," Scotty told him as soon as he walked into the kitchen area.

Aidan shook his head, glaring at the young guy sitting at the table with a very guilty flush on his face. "You really do want to get your ass kicked today, don't you?"

"Maybe I shouldn't have called you. I feel bad now."

Lydia dropped her bag inside the door and put her hand on her hip. "I just quit my job and burned a chunk of my savings to pay Shelly for two months' rent in advance so she won't give my room away. You're stuck with me now."

Tears filled Ashley's eyes and spilled over onto her cheeks as she stood up on her toes to throw her arms around Lydia's neck. "I'm so glad you're here."

Lydia squeezed her older sister, and she had to admit that coming back was about the last thing she'd wanted to do, but she was glad to be there, too. When push came to shove, her sister needed her and when family really needed you, nothing else mattered.

When Ashley released her, Lydia followed her into the living room and they dropped onto the couch. About six months after they got married, Danny and Ashley had scored the single-family home in a foreclosure auction. It had gone beyond *handyman's special* straight into the rehab hell of *handyman's wet dream*, but room by room they'd done the remodeling themselves. Now they had a lovely home they never could have afforded on their salaries.

But right now, it wasn't a happy home. Lydia sighed

and kicked off her flip-flops to tuck her feet under her. "What's going on?"

Ashley shrugged one shoulder, her mouth set in a line of misery. "You know how it is."

Maybe, in a general sense, Lydia knew how it was. She'd been married to a firefighter, too, and then she'd divorced one. But the one she'd been married to had struggled with the job, tried to cope with alcohol and taken advantage of Lydia's unquestioning acceptance of the demanding hours to screw around with every female who twitched her goods in his direction.

That wasn't Danny, so other than knowing how intense being a firefighter's wife could be, Lydia didn't see what Ashley was saying.

"He's just so closed off," her sister added. "I feel like he doesn't care about anything and I don't want to spend the rest of my life like that."

Lydia was sure there was more to it—probably a lot more—but Ashley didn't seem inclined to offer up anything else. And after the packing and driving, Lydia didn't mind putting off the heavy emotional stuff for a while.

"I should go see Dad," she said.

"He's working the bar tonight. And before you say anything, I know he's not supposed to be on his feet that much anymore. But you know he's sitting around talking to his buddies as much as being on his feet, and Rick Gullotti's girlfriend's supposed to be helping him out."

Rick was with Ladder 37 and Lydia had known him for years, but she struggled to remember his girlfriend's name. "Becky?"

Ashley snorted. "Becky was like eight girlfriends

ago. Karen. We like her and it's been like four months now, which might be a record for Rick."

Lydia looked down at the sundress she'd thrown on that morning because it was comfortable and the pale pink not only looked great with her dark coloring, but also cheered her up. It was a little wrinkled from travel, but not too bad. It wasn't as if Kincaid's was known for being a fashion hot spot. "And Karen couldn't keep on helping him out?"

"She's an ER nurse. Works crazy hours, I guess, so she helps out, but can't commit to a set schedule. And you know how Dad is about family."

"It's Kincaid's Pub so, by God, there should be a Kincaid in it," Lydia said in a low, gruff voice that made Ashley laugh.

Even as she smiled at her sister's amusement, Lydia had to tamp down on the old resentment. There had been no inspirational *you can be the President of the United States if you want to* speeches for Tommy's daughters. His two daughters working the bar at Kincaid's Pub while being wonderfully supportive firefighters' wives was a dream come true for their old man.

Lydia had been the first to disappoint him. Her unwillingness to give the alcoholic serial cheater *just one more chance* had been the first blow, and then her leaving Kincaid's and moving to New Hampshire had really pissed him off.

Sometimes she wondered how their lives would have turned out if their mom hadn't died of breast cancer when Lydia and Ashley were just thirteen and fourteen. Scotty had been only nine, but he was his father's pride and joy. Joyce Kincaid hadn't taken any shit from her gruff, old-school husband, and Lydia thought maybe she would have pushed hard for her daughters to dream big. And then she would have helped them fight to make those dreams come true.

Or maybe their lives wouldn't have turned out any different and it was just Lydia spinning what-ifs into pretty fairy tales.

After carrying her bag upstairs to the guest room, Lydia brushed her hair and exchanged her flip-flops for cute little tennis shoes that matched her dress and would be better for walking.

"Are you sure you want to walk?" Ashley asked. "It's a bit of a hike."

"It's not that far, and I won't have to find a place to park."

"I'd go with you, but…"

But her not wanting to be at Kincaid's was the entire reason Lydia had uprooted herself and come home. "I get it. And I won't be long. I'll be spending enough time there as it is, so I'm just going to pop in, say hi and get the hell out."

Ashley snorted. "Good luck with that."

It was a fifteen-minute walk from the Walsh house to Kincaid's Pub, but Lydia stretched it out a bit. The sights. The sounds. The smells. No matter how reluctant she was to come back here or how many years she was away, this would always be home.

A few people called to her, but she just waved and kept walking. Every once in a while she'd step up the pace to make it look like she was in a hurry. But the street was fairly quiet and in no time, she was standing in front of Kincaid's Pub.

It was housed in the lower floor of an unassuming brick building. Okay, ugly. It was ugly, with a glass door and two high, long windows. A small sign with the name in a plain type was screwed to the brick over the door, making it easy to overlook. It was open to anybody, of course, but the locals were their bread and butter, and they liked it just the way it was.

Her dad had invested in the place—becoming a partner to help out the guy who owned it—almost ten years before his heart attack hastened his retirement from fighting fires, and he'd bought the original owner out when he was back on his feet. Once it was solely Tommy's, he'd changed the name to Kincaid's Pub, and Ashley and Lydia had assumed their places behind the bar.

After taking a deep breath, she pulled open the heavy door and walked inside. All the old brick and wood seemed to absorb the light from the many antique-looking fixtures, and it took a moment for her eyes to adjust.

It looked just the same, with sports and firefighting memorabilia and photographs covering the brick walls. The bar was a massive U-shape with a hand-polished surface, and a dozen tables, each seating four, were scattered around the room. In an alcove to one side was a pool table, along with a few more seating groups.

Because there wasn't a game on, the two televisions—one over the bar and one hung to be seen from most of the tables—were on Mute, with closed-captioning running across the bottom. The music was turned down low because Kincaid's was loud enough without people shouting to be heard over the radio.

Lydia loved this place. And she hated it a little, too. But in some ways it seemed as though Kincaid's Pub was woven into the fabric of her being, and she wasn't sorry to be there again.

"Lydia!" Her father's voice boomed across the bar, and she made a beeline to him.

Tommy Kincaid was a big man starting to go soft around the middle, but he still had arms like tree trunks. They wrapped around her and she squealed a little when he lifted her off her feet. "I've missed you, girl."

She got a little choked up as he set her down and gave her a good looking over. Their relationship could be problematic at times—like most of the time—but Lydia never doubted for a second he loved her with all his heart. Once upon a time, he'd had the same thick, dark hair she shared with her siblings, but the gray had almost totally taken over.

He looked pretty good, though, and she smiled. "I'm glad you missed me, because it sounds like you'll be seeing a lot of me for a while."

A scowl drew his thick eyebrows and the corners of his mouth downward. "That sister of yours. I don't know what's going through her mind."

She gave him a bright smile. "Plenty of time for that later. Right now I just want to see everybody and have a beer."

A blonde woman who was probably a few years older than her smiled from behind the bar. "I'm Karen. Karen Shea."

Lydia reached across and shook her hand. "We really appreciate you being able to help out."

"Not a problem."

Lydia went to the very end of the back side of the bar and planted a kiss on the cheek of Fitz Fitzgibbon— her father's best friend and a retired member of Ladder 37—who was the only person who ever sat on that stool. She supposed once upon a time she might have known his real first name, but nobody ever called him anything but Fitz or, in her father's case, Fitzy.

There were a few other regulars she said hello to before getting a Sam Adams and standing at the bar. Unlike most, the big bar at Kincaid's didn't have stools all the way around. It had once upon a time, but now there were only stools on the back side and the end. Her dad had noticed a lot of guys didn't bother with the stools and just leaned against the polished oak. To make things easier, he'd just ripped them out.

About a half hour later, her brother, Scotty, walked in. Like the rest of the Kincaids, he had thick dark hair and dark eyes. He needed a shave, as usual, but he looked good. They'd talked and sent text messages quite a bit over the past two years, but neither of them was much for video chatting, so she hadn't actually seen him.

And right on Scotty's heels was Aidan Hunt. His brown hair was lighter than her brother's and it needed a trim. And she didn't need to see his eyes to remember they were blue, like a lake on a bright summer day. He looked slightly older, but no less deliciously handsome than ever. She wasn't surprised to see him. Wherever Scotty was, Aidan was usually close by.

What did surprise her was that the second his gaze met hers, her first thought was that she'd like to throw everybody out of the bar, lock the door and then shove him onto a chair. Since she was wearing the sundress, all she had to do was undo his fly, straddle his lap and hold on.

When the corner of his mouth quirked up, as if he somehow knew she'd just gone eight seconds with him in her mind, she gave him a nod of greeting and looked away.

For crap's sake, that was Aidan Hunt. Her annoying younger brother's equally annoying best friend.

He'd been seventeen when they met, to Lydia's twenty-one. He'd given her a grin that showed off perfect, Daddy's-got-money teeth and those sparkling blue eyes and said, "Hey, gorgeous. Want to buy me a drink?"

She'd rolled her eyes and told him to enjoy his playdate with Scotty. From that day on, he had seemed determined to annoy the hell out of her at every possible opportunity.

When her brother reached her, she shoved Aidan out of her mind and embraced Scotty. "How the hell are ya?"

"Missed having you around," he said. "Sucks you had to come back for a shitty reason, but it's still good to see you. I just found out about an hour ago Ashley had called you."

"She just called me last night, so it was spur-of-the-moment, I guess."

"It's good to have you back."

"Don't get too used to it. It's temporary."

She'd always thought if she and Scotty were closer in age than four years apart, they could have been twins, with the same shaped faces and their coloring. Ashley looked a lot like both of them, but her face was leaner, her eyes a lighter shade of brown and her hair wasn't quite as thick.

Scotty was more like Lydia in temperament, too. Ashley was steadier and liked to try logic first. Scott and Lydia were a little more volatile and tended to run on emotion. Her temper had a longer fuse than her brother's, but they both tended to pop off a little easy.

They caught up for a few minutes, mainly talking about his fellow firefighters, most of whom she knew well. And he gave her a quick update on their dad's doctor not being thrilled with his blood pressure. It didn't sound too bad, but it was probably good Ashley had called her rather than let him try to take up her slack.

Then Scotty shifted from one foot to the other and grimaced. "Sorry, but I've had to take a leak for like an hour."

She laughed and waved him off. "Go. I'll be here."

He left and Lydia looked up at the television, sipping her beer. She only ever had one, so she'd make it last, but part of her wanted to chug it and ask for a refill. It was a little overwhelming, being back.

"Hey, gorgeous. Want to buy me a drink?" What were the chances? She turned to face Aidan, smiling at the fact she'd been thinking about that day just a few minutes before. "What's so funny?"

She shook her head, not wanting to tell him she'd been thinking about the day they met, since that would be an admission she'd been thinking about him at all. "Nothing. How have you been?"

"Good. Same shit, different day. You come back for a visit?"

"I'll be here awhile. Maybe a couple of weeks, or a month." She shrugged. "Ashley wanted to take some time off, so I'm going to cover for her. You know how Dad is about having one of us here all the damn time."

His eyes squinted and he tilted his head a little. "You sound different."

"I worked on toning down the accent a little, to fit in more at work, I guess. Even though it's only the next state over, people were always asking me where I was from."

"You trying to forget who you are?" It came out *fuh-get who you ah*. "Forget where you came from?"

"Not possible," she muttered.

He gave her that grin again, with the perfect teeth and sparkling eyes. They crinkled at the corners now, the laugh lines just making him more attractive. "So what you're saying is that we're unforgettable."

She laughed, shaking her head. "You're something, all right."

Aidan looked as if he was going to say something else, but somebody shouted his name and was beckoning him over. He nodded and then turned back to Lydia. "I'll see you around. And welcome home."

She watched him walk away, trying to keep her eyes above his waist in case anybody was watching her watch him. Her annoying brother's annoying best friend had very nice shoulders stretching out that dark blue T-shirt.

Her gaze dipped, just for a second. And a very nice ass filling out those faded blue jeans.

Chapter Two

Aidan was just having a beer. Shooting the shit with the guys. Figuring out when they could get in some ice time at the rink. What he *wasn't* doing was checking out his best friend's sister.

That was Lydia over there, for chrissake. Scotty's sister. Tommy's daughter. She was bossy and sarcastic and pretty much the last woman on Earth he could mess around with. Except Ashley, who was all of those things *and* married to Danny, which put her one rung higher on the off-limits ladder. But he'd never been attracted to her the way he was to her sister.

Last he knew Lydia didn't even like him very much.

So why had she given him a look that said she might have mentally stripped him naked and was licking her way down his body?

He took a slug of his beer, trying to work it out in his head. She'd definitely been looking at him. The only other person in range had been Scotty, and she sure as hell hadn't been looking at *him* like that. And he hadn't imagined the heat, either. That woman had been thinking some seriously dirty thoughts. About him.

Yanking his T-shirt out of his jeans in the hope it would be long enough to cover the erection he was currently rocking seemed a little conspicuous, so he turned his body to the bar and rested his forearms on it. He seriously needed to get a grip.

He couldn't disrespect Tommy Kincaid by lusting after his daughter. The man was not only a mentor of sorts and a second father to him, being his best friend's dad, but he was the reason Aidan was a firefighter.

He'd been eleven years old when his family's minivan got caught up in a shit show involving a jackknifed 18-wheeler, two other cars and a box truck full of building supplies. His memories of the accident itself were hazy. Screeching tires. Shattering glass. His mother screaming his father's name.

But the aftermath imprinted on his memory so clearly it was like a movie he could hit Play on at will. A police officer had gotten them all out of the vehicle and Aidan had held his little brother's hand on one side and kept his other hand on his little sister's baby carrier.

A firefighter was working on his dad, whose head had a lot of blood on it. Aidan's mom was dazed and sat leaning against the guardrail, holding her arm. When his little brother called out to her, she didn't even look at him.

Then a woman started screaming and there were a lot of shouts. The firefighter who was holding some bandaging to his dad's head looked over his shoulder and then back to his dad. Aidan could tell he wanted to go help the woman who was screaming, so he stepped forward.

"I can hold that," he told the firefighter. "Just show me how hard to press."

The firefighter hadn't wanted to. But the screaming and the voices grew more urgent and he had Aidan kneel down next to him. After making sure Bryan put his hand on Sarah's carrier and wouldn't move, Aidan took over putting pressure on his dad's head wound.

"You're okay, Dad," he said, looking into his father's unfocused gaze. "Just keep looking at me and we'll wait for an ambulance together."

He'd been the one to give the paramedics their information and tell them his father took a medication for his blood pressure. Then he'd given them a description of his mom's demeanor since the accident. After asking them to retrieve Sarah's diaper bag from the van, he'd cared for his siblings until his aunt arrived.

The firefighter had shown up at the hospital and given him a Boston Fire T-shirt. "You did good, kid."

Aidan hadn't really known what praise and pride felt like until he looked into the man's warm eyes. "Thank you, sir."

"Some people are born to take charge in emergencies. It's a special thing and not everybody's got it. When you grow up, if you decide you want to save lives, son, you look me up. Tommy Kincaid. Engine Company 59."

Aidan rubbed the Engine 59 emblem on his T-shirt and smiled. He'd been only sixteen the first time he showed up at the old brick building that housed Engine 59 and Ladder 37, looking for Tommy. He met Scotty that day and together they'd never looked back. Friendship. A little bit of trouble here and there. Training. Testing. They'd been inseparable. Aidan didn't know if it was a favor to Tommy or if Fate played a hand, but when the station assignments went out, they'd even been assigned to the same engine company.

His extremely white-collar parents hadn't been able

to reconcile their hopes for their oldest son with his drive to serve the public, and things were still rough between them. And maybe his old man was embarrassed to only have one of his sons working with Hunt & Sons Investments—Sarah being destined for more feminine pursuits, like marriage and motherhood, according to their father—but Aidan wouldn't be swayed.

Tommy had become his father figure. Scotty and Danny and the rest of the guys were his brothers. This was his family, and he knew they had his back, anytime and anyplace.

Messing around with Lydia Kincaid was a bad idea. Like a *sticking a fork in a toaster while sitting in a bathtub cocked off your ass* kind of a bad idea.

"Earth to Hunt," Scotty said, and Aidan felt an ugly jolt of guilt for even considering messing around with Lydia while standing right next to her brother, for chrissake. "What the hell's wrong with you?"

"Nothing. Wicked tired is all."

"What's her name?"

Aidan snorted. "I wish."

"Piper's got a friend I could hook you up with. Her name's Bunny, and she's not bad."

"I'm too old for chicks named Bunny."

Scott shrugged. "I don't think that's her real name. At least I hope it's not. But whatever, man. Your loss."

Aidan didn't exactly wallow in regret. He was tired of it. He was tired of women who saw his face and didn't look any further. He was sick of women who got off on banging firefighters and the women who saw him outside the rink with his bag and wanted to spend a little time with a hockey player.

He didn't mind at all if a woman wanted to use him

for hot, dirty sex. But he also wanted her to laugh with him and enjoy a quiet evening on the couch. And he needed her to stroke his hair when the day was shitty and to hold him when the nightmares came.

Lydia's laughter rose above the noise of the bar, but Aidan didn't turn to look. He just knocked back the rest of his beer and kept his eyes on the television.

The overly chipper chime sound that indicated an incoming text made Lydia very reluctantly open her eyes the next morning. Ashley's guest room mattress had seen better days and it had taken her forever to fall asleep.

With a groan, she reached over to the nightstand and felt around until she found her phone. She had just enough charger cord to read the message without picking her head up off the pillow.

What the hell, girl?

She had no idea what the hell, since she wasn't even awake yet. But then she realized it was a group text, the group being her two best friends, Becca Shepard and Courtney Richmond. With Ashley as their fourth, they'd been inseparable growing up, and there was a group text going on more often than not.

This time it was Becca, and Lydia wondered which of them the message was aimed at. Probably her.

Before she could respond, another text from Becca came through.

Heard you were at KP last night. Ninja visit?

Lydia didn't have time to compose a reply before a response from her sister popped up.

I'm taking some time off. L's home to cover for me. How long?

Don't know.

Since Ashley was not only awake, but able to type coherently, Lydia dropped the phone onto the blanket and closed her eyes again. Kincaid's didn't open until eleven, so she didn't have to jump out of bed.

But when the phone chimed again she realized that, even if she didn't join in the conversation, the alerts would drive her crazy. After a big stretch, she picked up the phone again.

GNO!

That was Courtney, and Lydia rolled her eyes. While a girl's night out was appealing, she barely had her feet under her. She hadn't even worked a shift at the bar yet, so trying to get time off would be tough.

Soon. Stop at KP & say hi if you can.

That might hold them off for a while. Long enough to get coffee into her system, at least.

That turned out to be the end of the messages, but Lydia knew she'd tipped past the mostly awake point and wouldn't be able to go back to sleep now. After unplugging her phone, she made a quick stop in the bathroom and then headed downstairs.

Once she reached the top of the stairs, she could smell the coffee and followed the aroma to the kitchen. Ashley was sitting at the table, her phone in hand, and she looked up when Lydia walked in.

"Hey, how did you sleep?"

"Like a baby." It was a lie, but Ashley already felt bad about asking her to come home. No sense in piling on guilt about it. And even a crappy mattress was better than staying at her dad's.

Once she'd made her coffee, she sat down across from her sister and sipped it. If it wasn't so hot, she'd guzzle the stuff. Lydia was a better cook than Ashley, but her sister was definitely better at making coffee.

After a few minutes, Ashley put down her phone and looked at her. "It's been ten days."

"Ten days?" A week and half had gone by before her sister bothered telling her that her marriage was over?

"I thought he'd come back, you know? Like maybe he'd blow off some steam and then we'd talk about it. But he didn't come back. And when I called him, he just closed up and it was like talking to a machine." Ashley stared at her coffee, shaking her head. "More than usual, even. So the more I hope we can work it out, the more he does the thing I can't live with anymore."

Lydia took the time to consider her next words carefully. She had her sister's back, 100 percent, but sometimes having a person's back wasn't as cut-and-dried as blindly agreeing with everything they said. "He's always been quiet. I don't know how many times I've heard the other guys call him the ice man. It's not just with you."

"He can be however he wants with other people, especially the other guys. I'm his *wife*. If I'm upset and worried or pissed off, I need to feel like he at least cares."

"Have you thought about counseling?"

Ashley shrugged. "I mentioned it once and he changed the subject. I'm not sure what the point would be in talking to somebody when he doesn't talk."

"That *is* the point. A professional can help you guys communicate, including helping him break through whatever block he's got up and talk to you."

"I left a message on his voicemail, asking him if we

could set up a time to meet somewhere for coffee. If he shows up, I'll mention it."

"Just don't make it about him—that *he* needs help because he can't communicate. Make it about you feeling like it would be good for your marriage."

She nodded. "Assuming he even calls me back. He keeps texting me, but I want him to stop taking the easy way out and actually talk to me. I want to hear his voice."

"Where's he staying? With his parents?" Ashley's mouth tightened and Lydia leaned back in her chair. "No. Don't even tell me."

"He's staying with Scotty."

"Of course he is." Lydia's hand tightened around the coffee mug and it took supreme will not to chuck it at the wall. "Is Scott working today?"

Ashley looked at her, and then slowly shook her head. "Don't, Lydia. You'll only make it worse."

"It's not right. You're his sister."

"It's better than not knowing where Danny is or having him shack up with God knows who."

"There are plenty of other guys who could offer him a couch," Lydia argued. "He could crash with Aidan or Rick. Jeff. Chris. Any of them. It didn't have to be *your* brother. In our father's house."

When Ashley just gave a small shrug, Lydia wanted to shake her. As far as she was concerned, Scott had crossed a line and she wanted her sister to be pissed off about it. To demand the respect and loyalty the Kincaid men should be showing *her*, and not Danny.

But she knew Ashley wasn't wired the same way she was and it took a lot to make her angry. Just like their mother, once she'd had enough, she could give Lydia and Scott a run for their money, and that's what Lydia wanted to see.

"Did I really jam you up by asking you to come back?" Ashley asked. "I'm sorry about what I said about your job, by the way. I was so desperate to get out of being at the bar, but that was dirty."

"I forgive you because God knows I've vented at you often enough. That's what sisters are for. And you didn't jam me up at all. You were right about me hating that job and, when I go back, I'll find one I like more."

"You should go back to bartending. You're a natural."

Lydia shrugged. Bartending was something she was good at and she honestly enjoyed it, but she'd taken the waitressing job because she wanted something different. Tending a bar that wasn't Kincaid's Pub had seemed at the time like it might be too painful for her.

"I thought about going to school," she said. "But I spent weeks looking at brochures and stuff online and nothing jumped out at me. If I'm going to invest that time and money, I want it to be for something I *really* want to be, you know?"

"If I had the chance to go to college, I'd go for office or business stuff. I don't even know what it's called, but I think it would be awesome to work in a medical clinic, like for women's health."

"Have you thought about going to the community college?" They'd both been thrown into work young and college had never been a big deal in their family, but if Ashley wanted to go, she should.

"Danny and I talked about it a while back. He was supportive, but Dad made a big deal out of needing me at Kincaid's and you were getting a divorce. Plus working around Danny's hours would be a pain. It was easier to forget about it."

Lydia shoved back at the guilt that threatened to overwhelm her and make her say something stupid, like offering to stay in Boston so Ashley could go to college. Her dad had accused her of being selfish when she'd taken off, and maybe she was, but she couldn't be responsible for everybody's lives. She was still working on her own.

"I'm going to take a shower," Lydia said when it became clear Ashley had nothing else to say at the moment. "We should go out for breakfast."

"I already made pancake batter. I was just waiting for you to get up."

Her sister wasn't the best cook in the world, but she made amazing pancakes. "I hope you made a lot. I'm starving."

Ashley's face lit up with a real smile. "I know you and my pancakes. I practically had to mix it in a bucket."

Aidan held up a metal rod and looked over at Scotty. "What is this? Does this go somewhere?"

They both looked at the piece of playground equipment they'd spent the past hour assembling, and then Scotty shrugged. "It doesn't look like it goes anywhere."

"I don't think they said, 'Hey, let's throw a random metal rod in there just to mess with the idiots who have to put it together,' do you?"

"I don't know. If you set something on fire, I know what to do with it. Building things? Not my job."

Chris Eriksson joined them, scratching at a slowly graying beard. "I don't think you're supposed to have extra pieces. A bolt maybe. A few nuts. That looks important."

"Where did the instructions go?" Aidan asked, scanning the playground to see if they'd blown away.

"There were instructions?"

"Funny, Kincaid." Eriksson shook his head. "My kid's going to climb on this thing. If we can't figure it out, we're breaking it down and starting over."

Aidan stifled the curse words he wanted to mutter as he started circling the playground structure. They were surrounded by an increasingly bored pack of elementary students and a photographer waiting to snap a few pictures of the kids playing on the equipment the firehouse had donated and built. When Eriksson had come to them, looking for some help for his son's school, they'd been all-in.

And they still were. This was their community and they all did what they could. But it would have been nice if somebody had been in charge of the directions. After a few minutes, one of the teachers—a pretty brunette with a warm smile—moved closer and beckoned him over.

"We built one of these where I did my student teaching, and I think it's a support bar for under the slide," she whispered. "If you look up at it from underneath, you should see the braces where it bolts on."

"Thank you."

"No, thank you. We really appreciate you volunteering your time."

He gave her his best public relations smile, secure in doing so because of the ring on her finger and lack of *I'm hitting on a firefighter* vibe. "Just doing our part for the children, ma'am."

She nodded and went back to her students, leaving him relieved he'd judged the situation correctly. Having a teacher flirt with him in front of her students would be a level of awkward he didn't care to experience. He'd learned fairly quickly that, for whatever reason, there were women out there who really liked men in uniform, with police and fire uniforms ranking right up there. Fake kitchen fires were rare, but not unheard of, and it seemed like every firehouse had a story about busting through a front door to find the lady of the house wearing little to nothing.

For a few years, he'd been like a kid in a candy store, so to speak, but it had gotten old after a while. He'd grown to hate not being sure if a woman was attracted to him or his job, so one time he'd actually told a woman he was interested in that he was a plumber. It was a lie he kept going for several weeks, until she suffered a plumbing emergency and he was forced to admit he had no idea why disgusting water was backing up into her bathtub.

That had been his longest relationship, surviving his confession and lasting about a year and a half. He'd even been thinking about an engagement ring, but she struggled with his job and in the end, she opted out. Or rather, she opted for a guy who worked in a bank and was home by five and never worked weekends.

There had been a few almost-serious relationships since then, but they always fizzled out under the strain of his job. Flipping back and forth between day tours and night tours was something that came naturally to him at this point, but it was a lot harder on the people in his life.

He tried to stay hopeful, but sometimes it was hard to

be optimistic about finding a woman he'd spend the rest of his life with. Even Scotty's sisters—who'd grown up with Tommy Kincaid and surrounded by firefighters—hadn't been able to make their marriages to firefighters work. Sure, there were a lot of strong marriages if he looked around enough, but it got discouraging at times.

"Hey, Hunt, you gonna stand around yank—" Scotty bit off the words, no doubt remembering just in time they had a young audience. "Doing nothing, or are you gonna help?"

Once they'd gotten the metal rod bolted into the proper position, Chris Eriksson turned testing it out into a comedy skit that made the children laugh and then, finally, it was time for some press photos. The kids gave them a handmade thank-you card that the firefighters promised to hang on their bulletin board, and then it was time to get back to the station. Several guys had agreed to cover for them, but only for a few morning hours.

Once they were on their way back, in Eriksson's truck, Chris looked over at Scott. "Hey, I heard Lydia's back."

Aidan was glad he'd been too slow to call shotgun and was wedged into the truck's inadequate back seat because he felt the quick flash of heat across the back of his neck. He was going to end up in trouble if he didn't figure out how to stifle his reaction to hearing Lydia's name.

But the way she'd looked at him at Kincaid's last night...

"Yeah," Scotty said. "She's going to help out at the bar so Ashley can take a little time off while she and Danny figure out what the hell they're doing."

"I heard Walsh was staying with you. That's cozy."

Aidan wondered if Lydia knew that part yet, because he couldn't imagine she'd take it well. He'd known the Kincaid family almost a decade and a half, and he knew that Ashley was the older sister, but Lydia was the junk-yard dog. If you messed with the family, Ashley would try to talk it out with you, but Lydia would take your head off your shoulders.

"Lydia can worry about the beer and burgers and stay out of the rest of it," Scotty said.

Aidan laughed out loud. "I wouldn't recommend you tell *her* that."

"Hell, no. I'm not stupid."

As they got close, Eriksson sighed. "Fun time's over. Chief says we've gotta clean the engine bays today. And everything else that needs cleaning."

"That's bullshit," Scotty said. "I swear to God, the guys on night tour last week were all raised in barns. We should go drag their asses out of bed and make *them* clean up."

Aidan didn't mind the thought of filling the time around any runs with cleaning. It was mindless work that would keep him from having to look his best friend in the eye until he'd gotten a handle on thinking dirty thoughts about the guy's sister.

He didn't think the *she started it* excuse would cut it with Scott Kincaid.

Chapter Three

Lydia almost made it to Kincaid's Pub without getting sidetracked. She might have made it all the way if she hadn't heard sirens in the distance, which made her think of her brother. And thinking about her brother brought her back to the fact that—in her eyes—he'd chosen a fellow firefighter over his own sister.

She detoured down an alley and then over two blocks until she was standing in front of three stories of old, red brick. The bay doors were open so she could see the gleaming fronts of both trucks—Engine 59 written over the door on the left and Ladder 37 written over the right in big gold letters that gleamed against the chalky brick.

When she was a little girl, she'd thought it was a castle. She'd even drawn it into a picture for art class, the bricks towering behind a dark-haired princess in a long pink gown. The assignment had been fairy-tale illustrations, so the teacher had drawn a sad face on her picture. Lydia had been crushed. She'd also been the one who hid the unsealed bag of pastrami in the depths of the art teacher's desk supply cabinet, but nobody knew that but her.

Over the years, the tall and narrow brick building became less of a princess castle and more of a place that competed for her father's attention. More often than not, it had won. But there was no denying this place was woven into the fabric of her life.

There were a couple of webbed folding chairs in front of L-37, so she knew the guys had been sitting on the sidewalk, but there was nobody out there now. She stepped inside the open bay door, running her hand down E-59's glossy, red side as her eyes adjusted to the light.

She'd shown up in high temper, but the sights, sounds and smells of the house wrapped around her like a blanket that brought her familiar comfort, even if it chafed a little bit.

"Can I help you?"

Lydia looked at the guy standing in front of her, who looked as if he was about twelve years old. "I'm looking for Scott Kincaid."

He frowned, and then his expression morphed into a wide grin. "You must be his sister. You look just like him. I'm Grant Cutter. I was assigned here right after you moved away, I guess."

"Lydia," she said, shaking his hand. "Is Scotty around, do you know?"

"He was back in the cage with the air tanks. Let me—" There was a clang of metal and Grant broke off, peering around the end of the truck. "Here he comes. Hey, Scotty, your sister's here."

When her brother stepped around the back of the truck, a clipboard in his hand, Lydia nodded. "Hey, Scotty."

"Hey." He handed the clipboard to Grant. "Can you take this to Cobb?"

"Sure thing."

"Don't just put it on his desk or he'll claim he never saw it. Hand it to him directly." When Cutter nodded and headed for the stairs, Scotty turned his attention to Lydia. "Aren't you supposed to be at the bar?"

"I was on my way and took a little detour. I've got enough time and Don's cooking." Don had been with the bar since before the ownership and name change, and her dad trusted him with a key and the safe combination. If she ran late, he'd cover out front until she got there.

"So just a little detour for grins, or were you looking for me?"

She knew him well enough to hear the slight edge in his voice, which meant he was already feeling defensive. And that meant he knew he was doing something wrong. "I stopped by to talk about Danny, actually."

"Oh yeah?" Her brother put his hands on his hips, tilting his chin up slightly. "What about him?"

He knew very well what about him. "You don't think maybe it would have been more appropriate if he stayed with one of the other guys?"

"I have a spare bedroom and the other guys don't. Doesn't make sense for him to crash on a couch or burden a family when I have an extra bed. And when a guy's having a hard time, you try to be there for him. It's called loyalty, you know."

"How about your loyalty to our sister? Where's *that* loyalty?"

"Lower your damn voice. And I *am* being loyal to our sister. If Danny goes out and rents an apartment, and then starts making do for himself, it's just that much harder for them to get back together, and that's what we all want, right?"

"It doesn't matter what *we* all want. Do you want them back together because it's better for Ashley or because it's better for Danny?"

"I think it's better for both of them. If I didn't, I wouldn't *want* them back together. I love Ashley—and you're a liar if you claim you think otherwise—but I love Danny, too. He's like a brother to me."

"I get the whole brotherhood thing, trust me. I know all about it. But you're taking it too far in this case, Scott. You need to remember whose brother you *actually* are."

"You haven't even been around for two years. Who the hell are you talking to about remembering who you are? You left. You walked away."

"I left because of the same stupid bullshit Ashley is going through now, but at least when I left Todd, you had my back. It sucks that you don't have hers."

"You're out of line, Lydia."

"No, *you're* out of line."

The younger firefighter—Grant, she thought—walked back into the bay as she shouted at her brother and froze. After looking back and forth between the two of them, he turned and retraced his steps to make a hasty exit.

"Great. Nothing like a family spectacle to brighten everybody's day," Scotty said, his voice dripping with sarcasm.

"Ashley should be able to visit her own father without running into Danny," Lydia said, trying to dial back the temper. Not because she cared about being a spectacle, but because she wouldn't get anywhere butting heads with him. "You have to see that."

He shrugged. "Ashley goes in the front door. Danny

always uses the back stairs. She probably wouldn't even know he was there."

"Trust me, she'd know."

"It's not like she's in the habit of stopping by for regular visits, anyway."

"That's not the point. She should be able to if she wants to. The family home should be a safe place for her."

He rolled his eyes so hard she wondered if it hurt. "That's a little dramatic, even for you. They're just going through a rough patch."

"I'm going to show you dramatic in about thirty seconds if you don't get your head out of your ass. It doesn't matter if it's just a rough patch or if they end up divorced. Right now, they're separated and Danny shouldn't be living under Dad's roof."

"Look, Lydia, I'm working here, okay? And I'm not tossing Danny out. So why don't you go to work and leave Ashley and Danny's marriage to them." He turned and started walking away.

"I'm not done talking to you," she said, and he flipped her the bird without looking back.

Lydia inhaled deeply through her nose, trying to resist the urge to run after him and bring him to the ground in a full body tackle. That would be a family spectacle they wouldn't get over anytime soon.

When Scotty walked away, leaving Lydia alone in the bay, Aidan knew he needed to leave it well enough alone. Not only because he should mind his own damn business, but because Lydia in a temper could be a lot to handle.

But when her shoulders sagged and she looked up, as

if looking for some kind of divine guidance, he walked around the back of the truck. "Hey, Lydia. You okay?"

She jumped, and he wondered if the heat in her face was from being startled or if she was thinking about whatever it was she'd been thinking last night. "Oh, hey. I didn't know you were there."

When she tucked her hands in the back pockets of her jeans, it took every ounce of control Aidan had to keep his eyes on her face. But his peripheral vision happened to be excellent, so he couldn't miss the way the Kincaid's Pub T-shirt she was wearing stretched over her breasts when she put her arms behind her.

"Sorry. I wasn't trying to eavesdrop, but you guys aren't great at keeping things quiet."

She shrugged. "I don't care who knows. So I'm pissed my brother's letting Danny stay with him. It's not a secret."

Aidan didn't have a lot of experience with family dynamics outside of his own, and his own family was nothing like the Kincaids, but he suspected there was more to this than Danny crashing in Scott's spare room.

If things were heated and sides were being taken, he could see it. If Danny had gotten caught stepping out on Ashley or he'd put his hands on her or something, then Scotty would have to close the door in his face. But as far as he knew, Danny and Ashley were just going through a rough patch and needed a little space.

He held up his hands in a conciliatory gesture. "I'm Switzerland."

"Yeah, right." She shook her head, looking around the bay. "There's no Switzerland when firefighters are involved. Brotherhood first. Everybody else gets what's left."

And there was that *more to it* that he'd suspected might be an underlying problem. "That's not entirely true, you know."

She arched an eyebrow at him. "And you know what it's like to be on *this* side of it how exactly? Doesn't your family count money for a living?"

"It's a little more complicated than that, but I see what you're saying. But to us firefighters, that whole brotherhood thing kind of *includes* our families."

"In theory, maybe."

"Look, I love Tommy. You know that. He's been more of a father figure to me than my own father has been, but he's a hard-ass. Any…shortcomings he might have in the nurturing category might be his personality and not the job."

She stared at him for a few seconds, that dark gaze locked with his, and then she smiled. "Good effort, kid."

Kid? What the hell was that? She might have four years on him, but what was with the patronizing pat on the head? "It's my take on it. Whatever."

"This is exactly why I'm stuck back here again. Ashley can't even show her face at the damn corner market— never mind the bar—without somebody trying to convince her Danny's such a great guy and if she could just be more understanding and more supportive and give him another chance." She took her hands out of her pockets to point at him. "Not a single one of you—not even her own father or brother—has told her that maybe she did the right thing for *her* and that Danny needs to make an effort to resolve their problems, or that *he* needs to be more understanding and supportive."

Goddamn, but she was hot as hell when she got fired up. He tried to shove that awareness to the back of his mind, but it wasn't exactly a switch that could be flipped. "I admit that sucks."

"Yeah, it does." She stopped pointing at him, but he could still see the temper on her face and in the set of her shoulders. God help Scotty should he walk back in at that moment. "But I'm here now. And since you say you know my family so well, you know I'm not going to let anybody shit on Ashley. If Danny gets his head out of his ass, then good. If not, screw him."

She turned and walked away before he could say anything, not that he had any idea what to say to that. He actually was fairly neutral on the matter of the Walsh marriage, whether Lydia wanted to believe him or not. He liked them both a lot and he hoped they worked things out. And if they couldn't, he hoped the split was amicable and they both found happiness. That was about it for him.

Even though she left without giving him a chance to respond, he had to admit he liked watching her leave. She was a little taller than average, and nice and curvy. The long, angry strides did nice things for her ass, and Aidan was once again left with a Lydia-inspired hard-on.

And there wasn't a damn thing he could do about it.

The last thing he needed was to get caught jerking off in the bathroom. That had happened to a new kid once and they'd called him Palmer for so long they would have forgotten his real name if it wasn't written or sewn on his gear.

"Is my sister gone?"

Scotty's voice killed the hard-on as effectively as a cold shower. "Yeah. You're not exactly her favorite person at the moment."

"No shit." Scott walked to the bank of metal lockers

and yanked his open. "No wonder Todd drank so much and went looking for less bitchy company."

Anger rose in Aidan's chest and he turned away before it spilled out. Siblings fought and he was aware nobody knew your soft spots like family, but that was a cheap shot. It wasn't Lydia's fault her ex had turned out to be an asshole. And blaming her made Aidan want to plant his fist in his best friend's face.

"That guy was a dickhead," was all he said.

"Yeah, he was." Scott sighed and slammed his locker. "I didn't mean that. She just… God, she drives me crazy, you know?"

Aidan was starting to know a little something about being driven crazy by Lydia, yes. Just, in his case, for an entirely different reason.

Pick up Heat Exchange *by Shannon Stacey today from your favorite retailer.*

About the Author

New York Times and *USA TODAY* bestselling author Shannon Stacey lives with her husband and two sons in New England, where her two favorite activities are writing stories of happily-ever-after and driving her UTV through the mud. You can contact Shannon through her website, shannonstacey.com, where she maintains an almost daily blog, visit her on Twitter, Twitter.com/shannonstacey, and on Facebook, Facebook.com/shannonstacey.authorpage, or email her at shannon@shannonstacey.com.

To find out about other books by Shannon Stacey or to be alerted to new releases, sign up for her monthly newsletter at bit.ly/shannonstaceynewsletter.

We hope you enjoyed reading

UNDER CONTROL

by *New York Times* bestselling author

SHANNON STACEY

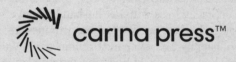

Connect with us for info on our new releases,
access to exclusive offers and much more!

Visit CarinaPress.com

Other ways to keep in touch:

Facebook.com/CarinaPress

Twitter.com/CarinaPress

CarinaPress.com/Newsletter

New books available every month.

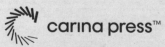

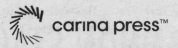

carina press™

If you enjoyed this story by *New York Times*
bestselling author

SHANNON STACEY

be sure to check out the next installment of her
fan-favorite Boston Fire miniseries

Nursing a broken heart while everybody around him seems
to be drowning in happiness has Grant Cutter wondering
whether staying with Engine 59—or even Boston Fire—is
in his future. It's tempting as hell to pack up what fits in his
Jeep and hit the road. But then a 911 call brings the woman
who shattered his heart back into his life, and he knows he
won't ever be able to fully leave her in his rearview mirror.

Available January 29, 2019, wherever books are sold!

**Don't miss the entire Boston Fire series
by Shannon Stacey!** *Heat Exchange, Controlled Burn,
Fully Ignited* and *Hot Response* are available now!

CarinaPress.com

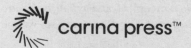

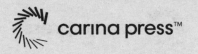

**Get the latest on Carina Press
by joining our eNewsletter!**

**Don't miss out, sign up today!
CarinaPress.com/Newsletter**

Sign up and get Carina Press offers and coupons
delivered straight to your inbox!

Plus, as an eNewsletter subscriber, you'll get the inside
scoop on everything Carina Press and be the first to
know about our newest releases!

Visit CarinaPress.com

Other ways to keep in touch:

Facebook.com/CarinaPress

Twitter.com/CarinaPress

CARENBPA0918

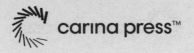
carina press™

Introducing the Carina Press Romance Promise!

The Carina Press team all have one thing in common: we are romance readers with a longtime love of the genre. And we know what readers are looking for in a romance: a guarantee of a happily-ever-after (HEA) or happy-for-now (HFN). With that in mind, we're initiating the **Carina Press Romance Promise**. When you see a book tagged with these words in our cover copy/book description, we're making you, the reader, a very important promise:

This book contains a romance central to the plot and ends in an HEA or HFN.

Simple, right? But so important, we know!

Look for the Carina Press Romance Promise and one-click with confidence that we understand what's at the heart of the romance genre!

Look for this line in Carina Press book descriptions:

*One-click with confidence. This title is part of the **Carina Press Romance Promise**: all the romance you're looking for with an HEA/HFN. It's a promise!*

Find out more at **CarinaPress.com/RomancePromise**.

CARRPBPA0918